THE MAN-EATER OF MALGUDI

R. K. Narayan was born in Madras, South India, and educated there and at Maharaja's College in Mysore. His first novel *Swami and Friends* (1935) and its successor *The Bachelor of Arts* (1937) are both set in the enchanting fictional territory of Malgudi. Other 'Malgudi' novels are *The Dark Room* (1938), *The English Teacher* (1945), *Mr Sampath* (1949), *The Financial Expert* (1952), *The Man-Eater of Malgudi* (1961), *The Vendor of Sweets* (1967) and *The Painter of Signs* (1977). His novel *The Guide* (1958) won him the National Prize of the Indian Literary Academy, his country's highest literary honour. As well as four collections of short stories, *A Horse and Two Goats, An Astrologer's Day and Other Stories, Lawley Road* and *Malgudi Days*, he has published two travel books, *My Dateless Diary* and *The Emerald Route*, two collections of essays, *Next Saturday* and *Reluctant Guru*, and a volume of memoirs, *My Days*. His latest novel is *A Tiger for Malgudi* (1983). In 1982 he was made an honorary member of the American Academy of Arts and Letters.

R. K. Narayan

THE MAN-EATER OF MALGUDI

A KING PENGUIN
PUBLISHED BY PENGUIN BOOKS

Penguin Books Ltd, Harmondsworth, Middlesex, England
Viking Penguin Inc., 40 West 23rd Street, New York, New York 10010, U.S.A.
Penguin Books Australia Ltd, Ringwood, Victoria, Australia
Penguin Books Canada Ltd, 2801 John Street, Markham, Ontario, Canada L3R 1B4
Penguin Books (N.Z.) Ltd, 182–190 Wairau Road, Auckland 10, New Zealand

First published in the U.S.A by The Viking Press 1961
First published in Great Britain by William Heinemann Ltd 1961
Published in Penguin Books 1983
Reprinted 1985

Filmset, printed and bound in Great Britain by
Hazell Watson & Viney Limited,
Member of the BPCC Group,
Aylesbury, Bucks
Set in VIP Baskerville

For
GRAHAM GREENE
to mark (more than) a quarter of a
century of friendship

Chapter One

I could have profitably rented out the little room in front of my press on Market Road, with a view of the fountain; it was coveted by every would-be shopkeeper in our town. I was considered a fool for not getting my money's worth out of it, since all the space I need for my press and its personnel was at the back, beyond the blue curtain. But I could not explain myself to sordid and calculating people. I hung up a framed picture of Goddess Laxmi poised on her lotus, holding aloft the bounties of earth in her four hands, and through her grace I did not do too badly. My son, little Babu, went to Albert Mission School, and he felt quite adequately supplied with toys, books, sweets, and any other odds and ends he fancied. My wife, every Deepavali, gave herself a new silk sari, glittering with lace, not to mention the ones she bought for no particular reason at other times. She kept the pantry well-stocked and our kitchen fire aglow, continuing the traditions of our ancient home in Kabir Street.

I had furnished my parlour with a high-backed chair made of teak-wood in the style of Queen Anne, or so the auctioneer claimed who had sold it to my grandfather, a roll-top desk supported on bow-legs with ivy-vines carved on them, and four other seats of varying heights and shapes, resurrected from our family lumber-room.

Anyone who found his feet aching as he passed down Market Road was welcome to rest in my parlour on any seat that happened to be vacant. While they rested there, people got ideas for bill forms, visiting cards, or wedding invitations which they asked me to print, but many others came whose visits did not mean a paisa to me. Among my constant companions was a poet who was writing the life of God Krishna in monosyllabic verse. His ambition was to compose a grand epic, and he came almost every day to recite to me his latest lines. My admiration for him was unbounded. I was thrilled to hear such clear lines as 'Girls with girls did dance in trance', and I felt equally excited when I had to infer the meaning of certain lines; that happened when he totally failed to find a monosyllable and achieved his end by ruthlessly carving up a polysyllable. On such occasions even the most familiar term took on the mysterious quality of a private code. Invariably, in deference to his literary attainments, I let him occupy the Queen Anne chair, while I sat perched on the edge of my roll-top desk. In the next best seat, a deep basket-chair in cane, you would find Sen, the journalist, who came to read the newspapers on my table, and who held forth on the mistakes Nehru was making. These two men and a few others remained sitting there till six in the evening when the press was silenced. I had no need to be present or attend to them in any way. They were also good enough to vacate their chairs without being told and to disappear when anyone came to discuss business with me.

Between my parlour and the press hung a blue curtain. No one tried to peer through it. When I shouted for the foreman, compositor, office-boy, binder or accountant, people imagined a lot of men working on the other side; if I had been challenged I should have gone in and played the ventriloquist. But my neighbour, the Star Press, had all the staff one could dream of, and if any customer of mine insisted on seeing machinery, I led him not through my curtain, but next door to the Star, where I displayed its original Heidelberg with pride as my own acquisition (although in my view the owner had made a mistake in buying it, as the groans of its double cylinder could be heard beyond the railway yard when formes were being printed). The owner of the Star was a nice man and a good friend, but he hardly got any customers. How could he when all the time they were crowding my parlour, although all I could offer them was an assortment of chairs and a word of welcome? But as few had ever stepped beyond the blue curtain, everyone imagined me equipped for big tasks, which I certainly attempted with the help of my well-wisher (I dare not call him staff) Sastri, the old man who set up type, printed the formes four pages at a time on the treadle, sewed the sheets, and carried them for ruling or binding to Kandan four streets off. I lent him a hand in all departments whenever he demanded my help and my visitors left me alone. On the whole I was a busy man, and such business as I could not take up I passed on next door to be done on the original Heidelberg. I was so free with the next-door establishment that no one knew whether I owned it or whether the Star owned me.

I lived in Kabir Street, which ran behind Market Road. My day started before four in the morning. The streets would be quite dark when I set out to the river for my ablutions, except for the municipal lamps which flickered (if they had not run out of oil) here and there in our street. I went down Kabir Street, cut through a flagged alley at the end of it, trespassed into the compound of the Taluk office through a gap in its bramble fencing, and there I was on the edge of the river. All along the way I had my well-defined encounters. The milkman, starting on his rounds, driving ahead of him a puny white cow, greeted me respectfully and asked, 'What is the time, master?' – a question I allowed to die without a reply as I carried no watch. I simpered and let him pass suppressing the question, 'Tell me the secret of your magic: how you manage to extract a milk-like product out of that miserable cow-like creature to supply thirty families as you do every morning. What exactly are you, conjuror or milk-vendor?' The old asthmatic at the end of our street sat up on the *pyol* of his house and gurgled through his choking throat, 'Didn't get a wink of sleep all 'night, and already it's morning and you are out! That's life, I suppose!' The watchman at the Taluk office called from beneath his rug, 'Is that you?' – the only question which deserved a reply. 'Yes, it's me,' I always said and passed on.

I had my own spot at the riverside, immediately behind the Taluk office. I shunned the long flight of steps farther down; they were always crowded, and if I went there I was racked with the feeling that I was dipping into other people's baths, but this point upstream seemed to me exclusive. A palmyra-tree loomed over the bank of the river, festooned with mud pots into which toddy dripped through a gash in the bark of the tree. When it fermented, it stank to the skies, and was gathered in barrels and sold to the patrons who congregated at the eighteen taverns scattered in the four corners of the city, where any evening one could see revellers fighting or rolling in the gutters. So much for the potency of the fluid dripping into the pot. I never looked up at the palmyra without a shudder. 'With his monopoly of taverns,' I thought, 'Sankunni builds his mansions in the New Extension and rides about in his four American cars driven by uniformed chauffeurs.'

All the same I was unable to get away from the palmyra. At the foot of the tree was a slab of stone on which I washed my dhoti and towel, and the dark hour resounded with the tremendous beating of wet cloth on granite. I stood waist-deep in water, and at the touch of cold water around my body I felt elated. The trees on the bank stood like shadows in the dusk. When the east glowed I sat for a moment on the sand reciting a prayer to the Sun to illumine my mind. The signal for me to break off from contemplation was the jingle of ox-bells as country carts forded Nallappa's grove, bringing loads of vegetables, corn and fuel from the near-by villages to the market. I rose and retraced my steps, rolling up my washing into a tight pack.

I had more encounters on my way back. My cousin from the fourth street gave me a cold look and passed. She hated me for staying in our ancestral home, my father having received it as his share after the division of property among his brothers. She never forgave us, although it had all happened in my father's time. Most of the citizens of this area were now moving sleepily towards the river, and everyone had a word for me. The lawyer, known as the adjournment lawyer for his ability to prolong a case beyond the wildest dream of a litigant, came by, a sparse hungry-looking man who shaved his chin once a fortnight. When I saw him in the distance I cried to myself, 'I am undone. Mr Adjournment will get me now.' The moment he saw me he cried, 'Where is your bed? Unless you have slept by the river how can you be *returning* from the river at this unearthly hour?'

There was one whom I did not really mind meeting, the septuagenarian living in a dilapidated outhouse in Adam's Lane, who owned a dozen houses in our locality, lived on rent, and sent off money-orders to distant corners of the Indian sub-continent, where his progeny was spread out. He always stopped to give me news of his relations. He looked like a new-born infant when he bared his gums in a smile. 'You are late today,' I always said, and waited for his explanation, 'I sat up late writing letters. You know how it is with one's children scattered far and wide.' I did not mind tarrying to listen to the old man, although my fingers felt cramped with encircling the wad of wet clothes I was carrying home to dry. The old man referred to four sons and their doings and five daughters, and countless grandchildren. He was always busy, on one side attending to the repairs of his dozen houses, about which one or the other of his tenants was always pursuing him; on the other, writing innumerable letters on postcards, guiding, blessing, admonishing, or spoiling with a remittance of cash one or the other of his wards.

I was content to live in our house as it had been left by my father. I was a youth, studying in Albert Mission, when the legal division of ancestral property occurred between my father and his brothers. I well remember the day when his four brothers marched out with their wives and children, trundling away their share of heirlooms, knick-knacks and household articles. Everything that could be divided into five was cut up into equal parts and given one to each. Such things as could not be split up were given to those who clamoured the loudest. A rattan easy chair on which my grandfather used to lie in the courtyard, watching the sky, was claimed by my second uncle whose wife had started all the furore over the property. She also claimed a pair of rosewood benches which shone with a natural polish, and a timber wooden chair that used to be known as the bug-proof chair. My father's third brother, as compensation for letting these items go, claimed a wooden almirah as his own and a 'leg' harmonium operated by a pedal. The harmonium was also claimed by another uncle whose daughter was supposed to possess musical talent. It had gathered dust in a corner for decades without anyone's noticing it. No one had even asked how it had come to find a place in our home, although a little family research would have yielded the information. Our grandfather had lent a hundred rupees to a local dramatic troupe and attached their harmonium as their only movable property after a court decree, lugged it home, and kept it in a corner of our hall. He died before he could sell and realize its value, and his successors took the presence of the harmonium in the corner of the hall for granted until this moment of partition.

All the four brothers of my father with their wives and children, numbering fifteen, had lived under the same roof for many years. It was my father's old mother who had kept them together, acting as a cohesive element among members of the family. Between my grandmother, who laid down the policy, and a person called Grand-Auntie, who actually executed it, the family administration ran smoothly. When my grandmother died the unity of the family was also gone. The trouble started with my father's second brother's wife, who complained loudly one day, standing in the passage of the house, that her children had been ill-treated and that she was hated by everyone; her cause was upheld by her husband. Soon various other differences appeared among the brothers and their wives, although all the children continued to play in the open courtyard, unmindful of the attitude of the elders to each other.

Before the year was out, on a festival day, they had their biggest open quarrel, provoked by a minor incident in which an eight-year-old boy knocked down another and snatched a biscuit from his mouth. A severe family crisis developed, as the mother of the injured child slapped the offender on his bare seat. My father and his brothers were sitting around, eating their midday meal. My father muttered mildly. 'If Mother were alive she would have handled everyone and prevented such scenes.'

Two of his brothers, incensed at the incident, got up without touching their food. My father commented, without looking at anyone in particular, 'You need not abandon your food. This is a sacred day. Such things should not be allowed to happen.' My mother, who was bending over him, serving ghee, whispered, 'Why don't you mind your business? They are not babies to be taught how to conduct themselves on a festive day.'

My father accepted her advice without a word and resolved at that moment to break up the joint family in the interests of peace. The next few days saw our family lawyers, assisted by the adjournment expert, walking in and out with papers to be signed, and within a few weeks the house had become empty. It had been a crowded house since the day it was built by my father's grandfather, numerous children, womenfolk, cousins, relations and guests milling in and out all the year round, and now it became suddenly bare and empty. The household now consisted of my parents, Grand-Auntie, me and my two sisters. My brother was away in Madras in a college hostel. As he grew older my father began to spend all his time sitting on the *pyol*, on a mat, reading *Ramayana* or just watching the street. Even at night he never went beyond the *pyol*. He placed a small pillow under his head and stretched himself there. He hardly ever visited the other parts of this immense house. Occasionally he wandered off to the back yard to pluck the withered leaves off a citrus tree, which had been his favourite plant. It had been growing there for years, and no one knew whether it was an orange- or lime-tree; it kept people guessing, never displaying on its branches anything more than a few white flowers now and then. This plant was my father's only concern. He hardly ever looked up at the six tall coconut-trees that waved in the sky. They were my mother's responsibility and Grand-Auntie's, who regularly had their tops cleared of beetles and withered shoots, sent up a climber once a month, and filled the granary with large, ripe coconuts. There were also pumpkins growing in the back yard, and large creepers covered the entire thatched roof of a cow-shed, which used to house four of Malgudi's best-bred cows, years before.

After my father's death my mother lived with me until Babu was a year old, and then she decided to go and live with my brother at Madras, taking away with her her life-companion Grand-Auntie. Thus I, with my wife and little Babu, became the sole occupant of the house in Kabir Street.

Chapter Two

Sastri had to go a little earlier than usual since he had to perform a *puja* at home. I hesitated to let him go. The three colour labels (I prided myself on the excellence of my colour-printing) for K.J.'s aerated drinks had to be got ready. It was a very serious piece of work for me. My personal view was that the coloured ink I used on the label was far safer to drink than the dye that K.J. put into his water-filled bottles. We had already printed the basic colour on the labels and the second was to be imposed today. This was a crucial stage of the work and I wanted Sastri to stay and finish the job.

He said, 'Perhaps I can stay up late tonight and finish it. Not now. Meanwhile will you . . .' He allotted me work until he should be back at two o'clock.

I had been engrossed in a talk with the usual company. On the agenda today was Nehru's third Five-Year Plan; my friend Sen saw nothing but ruin in it for the country. 'Three hundred crores – are we counting heads or money?' His audience consisted of myself and the poet, and a client who had come to ask for quotations for a business card. The discussion was warming up, as the client was a Congressman who had gone to prison fourteen times since the day Mahatma Gandhi arrived in India from South Africa. He ignored for the time being the business that had brought him and plunged into the debate, settling himself inexorably in a corner. 'What's wrong with people is they have got into the habit of blaming everything on the Government. You think democracy means that if there is no sugar in the shops, Government is responsible. What if there is no sugar? You won't die if you do not have sugar for your morning coffee some days.' Sen disputed every word of the patriot's speech.

I listened to the debate until I noticed Sastri's silhouette beyond the curtain. Sastri, when there was any emergency, treated me as a handy-boy, and I had no alternative but to accept the role. Now my duty would be to fix the block on the machine and put the second impression on all the labels and spread them out to dry, then he would come and give the third impression and put the labels out to dry again.

He explained some of the finer points to me, 'The blocks are rather worn. You'll have to let in more ink.'

'Yes, Mr Sastri.'

He looked at me through his small silver-rimmed glasses and said firmly, 'Unless the labels are second-printed and dry by three o'clock today, it's going to be impossible to deliver them tomorrow. You know what kind of a man K.J. is . . .'

What about my lunch? Sastri did not care whether I had time for food or not – he was a tyrant when it came to printing labels, but there was no way of protesting. He would brush everything aside. As if reading my mind he explained, 'I'd not trouble you but for the fact that this *satyanarayana puja* must be performed today in my house; my children and wife will be waiting for me at the door . . .' As it was he would have to trot all the way to Vinayak Street if his family were not to starve too long.

Wife, children. Absurd. Such encumbrances were not necessary for Sastri, I felt. They were for lesser men like me. His place was at the type-board and the treadle. He produced an incongruous, unconvincing picture as a family man. But I dared not express myself aloud. The relation of employer and employee was reversed at my press whenever there was an emergency.

I accepted the situation without any fuss. According to custom my friends would not step beyond the curtain, so I was safe to go ahead with the second impression. Sastri had fixed everything. I had only to press the pedal and push the paper on to the pad. On a pale orange ground I had now to impose a sort of violet. I grew hypnotized by the sound of the wheel and the dozen kinks that were set in motion by the pressure I put on the pedals. Whenever I paused I could hear Sen's voice, 'If Nehru is practical, let him disown the Congress . . . Why should you undertake projects which you can't afford? Anyway, in ten years what are we going to do with all the steel?' There was a sudden lull. I wondered if they had been suddenly struck dumb. I heard the shuffling of feet. I felt suddenly relieved that the third Five-Year Plan was done with.

Now an unusual thing happened. The curtain stirred, an edge of it lifted, and the monosyllabic poet's head peeped through. An extraordinary situation must have arisen to make him do that. His eyes bulged. 'Someone to see you,' he whispered.

'Who? What does he want?'

'I don't know.'

The whispered conversation was becoming a strain. I shook my head, winked and grimaced to indicate to the poet that I was not available. The poet, ever a dense fellow, did not understand but blinked on unintelligently. His head suddenly vanished, and a moment later a new head appeared in its place – a tanned face, large powerful eyes under thick eyebrows, a large forehead and a shock of unkempt hair, like a black halo.

My first impulse was to cry out, 'Whoever you may be, why don't you brush your hair?' The new visitor had evidently pulled aside the poet before showing himself to me. Before I could open my mouth, he asked, 'You Nataraj?' I nodded. He came forward, practically tearing aside the curtain, an act which violated the sacred traditions of my press. I said, 'Why don't you kindly take a seat in the next room? I'll be with you in a moment.' He paid no attention, but stepped forward, extending his hand. I hastily wiped my fingers on a rag, muttering, 'Sorry, discoloured, been working . . .' He gave me a hard grip. My entire hand disappeared into his fist – he was a huge man, about six feet tall. He looked quite slim, but his bull-neck and hammer-fist revealed his true stature. 'Shan't we move to the other room?' I asked again.

'Not necessary. It's all the same to me,' he said. 'You are doing something? Why don't you go on? It won't bother me.' He eyed my coloured labels. 'What are they?'

I didn't want any eyes to watch my special colour effects, and see how I achieved them. I moved to the curtain and parted it courteously for him. He followed me. I showed him to the Queen Anne chair, and sat down at my usual place, on the edge of my desk. I had now regained the feeling of being master of the situation. I adopted my best smile and asked, 'Well, what can I do for you, Mr . . .?'

'Vasu,' he said, and added, 'I knew you didn't catch my name. You were saying something at the same time as I mentioned my name.'

I felt abashed, and covered it, I suppose, with another of those silly smiles. Then I checked myself, suddenly feeling angry with him for making me so uneasy. I asked myself, 'Nataraj, are you afraid of this muscular fellow?' and said authoritatively, 'Yes?' as much as to indicate, 'You have wasted my time sufficiently; now say quickly whatever you may want to say.'

He took from his inner pocket a wad of paper, searched for a hand-written sheet and held it out to me. 'Five hundred sheets of note-paper, the finest quality, and five hundred visiting cards.'

I spread out the sheet without a word and read, 'H. Vasu, M.A., Taxidermist'. I grew interested. My irritation left me. This was the first time I had set eyes on a taxidermist. I said, assuming a friendly tone, 'Five hundred! Are you sure you need five hundred visiting cards? Could you not print them one hundred at a time? They'd be fresh then.'

'Why do you try to advise me?' he asked pugnaciously. 'I know how many I need. I'm not printing my visiting cards in order to preserve them in a glass case.'

'All right. I can print ten thousand if you want.'

He softened at my show of aggressiveness. 'Fine, fine, that's the right spirit.'

'If you'd like to have it done on the original Heidelberg . . .' I began.

'I don't care what you do it on. I don't even know what you are talking about.'

I understood the situation now; every other sentence was likely to prove provocative. I began to feel intrigued by the man. I didn't want to lose him. Even if I wanted to, I had no means of getting rid of him. He had sought me out and I'd have to have him until he decided to leave. I might just as well be friendly. 'Surely, whatever you like. It's my duty to ask, that's all. Some people prefer it.'

'What is it anyway?' he asked.

I explained the greatness of Heidelberg and where it was. He thought it over, and suddenly said, 'Nataraj, I trust you to do your best for me. I have come to you as a friend.' I was surprised and flattered. He explained, 'I'm new to this place, but I heard about you within an hour of coming.' He mentioned an obscure source of information. 'Well, I never give a second thought to these things,' he said. 'When I like a man, I like him, that's all.'

I wanted to ask about taxidermy, so I asked, looking at his card, 'Taxidermist? Must be an interesting job. Where is your er . . . office or . . .'

'I hope to make a start right here. I was in Junagadh – you know the place – and there I grew interested in the art. I came across a master there, one Suleiman. When he stuffed a lion (you know, Junagadh is a place where we have lions) he could make it look more terrifying than it would be in the jungle. His stuffings go all over the world. He was a master, and he taught me the art. After all we are civilized human beings, educated and cultured, and it is up to us to prove our superiority to nature. Science conquers nature in a new way each day; why not in creation also? That's my philosophy, sir. I challenge any man to contradict me.' He sighed at the thought of Suleiman, his master. 'He was a saint. He taught me his art sincerely.'

'Where did you get your M.A.?'

'At Madras, of course. You want to know about me?' he asked.

I wonder what he would have done if I had said, 'No, I prefer to go home and eat my food.' He would probably have held me down.

He said, 'I was educated in the Presidency College. I took my Master's degree in History, Economics and Literature.' That was in the year 1931. Then he had joined the civil disobedience movement against British rule, broken the laws, marched, demonstrated and ended up in jail. He went repeatedly to prison and once when he was released found himself in the streets of Nagpur. There he met a *phaelwan* at a show. 'That man could bear a half-ton stone slab on his cheek and have it split by hammer strokes; he could snap steel chains and he could hit a block of hard granite with his fist and pulverize it. I was young then, his strength appealed to me. I was prepared to become his disciple at any cost. I introduced myself to the *phaelwan*.' He remained thoughtful for a while and continued, 'I learnt everything from this master. The training was unsparing. He woke me up at three o'clock every morning and put me through exercises. And he provided me with the right diet. I had to eat a hundred almonds every morning and wash them down with half a *seer* of milk; two hours later six eggs with honey; at lunch chicken and rice; at night vegetables and fruit. Not everyone can hope to have this diet, but I was lucky in finding a man who enjoyed stuffing me like that. In six months I could understudy for him. On my first day, when I banged my fist on a century-old door of a house in Lucknow, the three-inch panel of seasoned teak splintered. My master patted me on the back with tears of joy in his eyes, "You are growing on the right lines, my boy." In a few months I could also snap chains, twist iron bars, and pulverize granite. We travelled all over the country, and gave our shows at every market fair in the villages and in the town halls in the cities, and he made a lot of money. Gradually he grew flabby and lazy, and let me do everything. They announced his name on the notices, but actually I did all the twisting and smashing of stone, iron, and what not. When I spoke to him about it he called me an ungrateful dog and other names, and tried to push me out. I resisted . . . and . . .' Vasu laughed at the recollection of this incident. 'I knew his weak spot. I hit him there with the edge of my palm with a chopping movement . . . and he fell down and squirmed on the floor. I knew he could perform no more. I left him there and walked out, and gave up the strong man's life once and for all.'

'You didn't stop to help him?' I asked.

'I helped him by leaving him there, instead of holding him upside down and rattling the teeth out of his head.'

'Oh, no,' I cried, horrified.

'Why not? I was a different man now, not the boy who went to him for charity. I was stronger than he.'

'After all he taught you to be strong – he was your guru,' I said, enjoying the thrill of provoking him.

'Damn it all!' he cried. 'He made money out of me, don't you see?'

'But he also gave you six eggs a day and – how much milk and almonds was it?'

He threw up his arms in vexation. 'Oh, you will never understand these things, Nataraj. You know nothing, you have not seen the world. You know only what happens in this miserable little place.'

'If you think this place miserable, why do you choose to come here?' I was nearest the inner door. I could dash away if he attempted to grab me. Familiarity was making me rash and headstrong. I enjoyed taunting him.

'You think I have come here out of admiration for this miserable city? Know this, I'm here because of Mempi Forest and the jungles in those hills. I'm a taxidermist. I have to be where wild animals live.'

'And die,' I added.

He appreciated my joke and laughed. 'You are a wise guy,' he said admiringly.

'You haven't told me yet why or how you became a taxidermist,' I reminded him.

'H'm!' he said. 'Don't get too curious. Let us do business first. When are you giving me the visiting cards? Tomorrow?' He might pulverize granite, smash his guru with a slicing stroke, but where printing work was concerned I was not going to be pushed. I got up and turned the sheets of a tear-off calendar on the wall. 'You can come tomorrow and ask me. I can discuss this matter only tomorrow. My staff are out today.'

At this moment my little son Babu came running in crying 'Appa!' and halted his steps abruptly on seeing a stranger. He bit his nails, grinned, and tried to turn and run. I shot out my hand and held him. 'What is it?' I asked. He was friendly with the usual crowd at my press, but the stranger's presence somehow embarrassed him. I could guess why he had come; it was either to ask for a favour – permission to go out with his friends, or cash for peppermints – or to bring a message from his mother.

'Mother says, aren't you coming home for food? She is hungry.'

'So am I,' I said, 'and if I were Mother I wouldn't wait for Father. Understand me? Here is a gentleman with whom I am engaged on some important business. Do you know what he can do?' My tone interested Babu and he looked up expectantly.

Vasu made a weary gesture, frowned and said, 'Oh, stop that, Mr Nataraj. Don't start it all again. I don't want to be introduced to anyone. Now, go away, boy,' he said authoritatively.

'He is my son . . .' I began.

'I see that,' Vasu said indifferently, and Babu wriggled himself free and ran off.

Vasu did not come next day, but appeared again fifteen days later. He arrived in a jeep. 'You have been away a long time,' I said.

'You thought you were rid of me?' he asked, and, thumping his chest, 'I never forget.'

'And I never remember,' I said. Somehow this man's presence roused in me a sort of pugnacity.

He stepped in, saw the Queen Anne chair occupied by the poet, and remarked, half-jokingly, 'That's my chair, I suppose.' The poet scrambled to his feet and moved to another seat. 'H'm, that's better,' Vasu said, sitting down. He smiled patronizingly at the poet and said, 'I haven't been told who you are.'

'I'm I'm . . . a teacher in the school.'

'What do you teach?' he asked relentlessly.

'Well, history, geography, science, English – anything the boys must know.'

'H'm, an all-rounder,' Vasu said. I could see the poet squirming. He was a mild, inoffensive man who was unused to such rough contacts. But Vasu seemed to enjoy bothering him. I rushed in to his rescue. I wanted to add to his stature by saying, 'He is a poet. He is nominally a teacher, but actually . . .'

'I never read poetry; no time,' said Vasu promptly, and dismissed the man from his thoughts. He turned to me and asked, 'Where are my cards?'

I had a seasoned answer for such a question. 'Where have you been this whole fortnight?'

'Away, busy.'

'So was I,' I said.

'You promised to give me the cards . . .'

'When?' I asked.

'Next day,' he said. I told him that there had been no such promise. He raised his voice, and I raised mine. He asked finally, 'Are we here on business or to fight? If it's a fight, tell me. I like a fight. Can't you see, man, why I am asking for my cards?'

'Don't *you* see that we have our own business practice?' I always adopted 'we' whenever I had to speak for the press.

'What do you mean?' he asked aggressively.

'We never choose the type and stationery for a customer. It must always be the customer's responsibility.'

'You never told me that,' he cried.

'You remember I asked you to come next day. That was my purpose. I never say anything without a purpose.'

'Why couldn't you have mentioned it the same day?'

'You have a right to ask,' I said, feeling it was time to concede him something. The poet looked scared by these exchanges. He was trying to get out, but I motioned him to stay. Why should the poor man be frightened away?

'You have not answered my question,' said Vasu. 'Why couldn't you have shown me samples of type on the first day?'

I said curtly, 'Because my staff were out.'

'Oh!' he said, opening his eyes, wide. 'I didn't know you had a staff.'

I ignored his remark and shouted, 'Sastri! Please bring those ivory card samples and also the ten-point copper-plate.' I told Vasu grandly, 'Now you can indicate your preferences, and we shall try to give you the utmost satisfaction.'

Sastri, with his silver-rimmed glasses on his nose, entered, bearing a couple of blank cards and a specimen type-book. He paused for a second, studying the visitor, placed them on the table, turned and disappeared through the curtain.

'How many are employed in your press?' Vasu asked.

The man's curiosity was limitless and recognized no proprieties. I felt enraged. Was he a labour commissioner or something of the kind? I replied, 'As many as I need. But, as you know, present-day labour conditions are not encouraging. However, Mr Sastri is very dependable; he has been with me for years . . .' I handed him the cards and said, 'You will have to choose. These are the best cards available.' I handed him the type-book. 'Tell me what type you like.'

That paralysed him. He turned the cards between his fingers, he turned the leaves of the type-book, and cried, 'I'm damned if I know what I want. They all look alike to me. What is the difference anyway?'

This was a triumph for me. 'Vasu, printing is an intricate business. That's why we won't take responsibility in these matters.'

'Oh, please do something and print me my cards,' he cried, exasperated.

'All right,' I said, 'I'll do it for you, if you trust me.'

'I trust you as a friend, otherwise I would not have come to you.'

'Actually,' I said, 'I welcome friends rather than customers. I'm not a fellow who cares for money. If anyone comes to me for pure business, I send them over to my neighbour and they are welcome to get their work done cheaper and on a better machine – original Heidelberg.'

'Oh, stop that original Heidel,' he cried impatiently. 'I want to hear no more of it. Give me my cards. My business arrangements are waiting on that, and remember also five hundred letter-heads.'

Chapter Three

An attic above my press was full of discarded papers, stacks of old newspapers, files of dead correspondence and accounts, and, bulkiest of all, a thousand copies of a school magazine which I used to print and display as my masterpiece and which I froze in the attic when the school could not pay the printing charges.

I called up a waste-paper buyer, who was crying for custom in the streets, and sent him up the rickety staircase to make a survey and tell me his offer. He was an old Moslem who carried a sack on his back and cried, 'Old paper, empty bottles,' tramping the streets all afternoon. 'Be careful,' I told him as I sent him up the stairs to estimate. 'There may be snakes and scorpions up there. No human being has set foot in the attic for years.' Later, when I heard his steps come down, I prepared myself for the haggling to follow by stiffening my countenance and assuming a grave voice. He parted the curtain, entered my parlour and stood respectfully pressing his back close to the wall and awaiting my question.

'Well, have you examined the lot?'

'Yes, sir. Most of the paper is too old and is completely brown.'

'Surely you didn't expect me to buy the latest editions for your benefit, or did you think I would buy white paper by the ream and sell it to you by weight?' I spoke with heavy cynicism, and he was softened enough to say, 'I didn't say so . . .' Then he made his offer. I ignored it completely as not being worth a man's notice.

At this point, if he had really found my attitude unacceptable, he should have gone away, but he stayed, and that was a good sign. I was looking through the proofs of a cinema programme and I suddenly left him in order to attend to some item of work inside the press. I came out nearly an hour later, and he was still there. He had set his gunny sack down and was sitting on the door-step. 'Still here!' I cried, feigning astonishment. 'By all means rest here if you like, but don't expect me to waste any more time talking to you. I don't have to sell that paper at all. I can keep it as I have kept it for years.'

He fidgeted uneasily and said, 'The paper is brown and cracks. Please have consideration for me, sir. I have to make one or two rupees every day in order to bring up my family of . . .' He went into the details of his domestic budget: how he had to find the money for his children's school-books, food, and medicine, by collecting junk from every house and selling it to the dealers for a small margin of profit, often borrowing a loan at the start of a day. After hearing him out, I relented enough to mention a figure, at which he picked up his sack and pretended to go. Then I mitigated my demand, he raised his offer, and this market fluctuation went on till three o'clock. Sastri came at three with a frown on his face, understood in a moment what was going on and muttered, 'Sometimes it's better to throw old paper into a boiler to save firewood than sell it to these fellows. They always try to cheat,' thus lending support to my own view.

Presently Vasu arrived in his jeep, and unpacked his valise, mumbling, 'Let me note something before I forget it.' He sat in the Queen Anne chair, took out a sheet of paper and wrote. Both of us, the parties to the waste-paper transaction, watched him silently. A lorry was passing down the road, raising a blanket of cloud; a couple of *jutkas* were rattling along on their wooden wheels; two vagrants had stretched themselves on the parapet of the fountain, enjoying a siesta; a little boy was watching his lamb graze on the lawn which the municipality was struggling to cultivate by the margin of the fountain; a crow sat on top of the fountain, hopefully looking for a drop of water. It was an ideal hour for a transaction in junk.

Vasu stopped writing and asked, 'What's going on?'

I turned to the waste-paper man and said, 'You know who he is? I'll have him to explain to if I give the paper away too cheap.'

Vasu raised his eyes from the paper, glared at the Moslem and asked, 'What are you supposed to be doing? Have a care!' The trader grew nervous and said, 'My final offer, sir. It's getting late; if I get nothing here I must at least find another place for my business today.'

'All right, go,' I said. 'I'm not stopping you.'

'Twenty-five rupees, sir.'

'If this gentleman approves,' I said. Vasu seemed pleased at being involved. He tapped the table and hummed and hawed. The ragman appealed to him, 'I'm a poor man. Don't squeeze me. If I invest it . . .'

Vasu suddenly got up, saying, 'Let's have a look at your loot anyway,' and, led by the Moslem, passed beyond the curtain and clambered upstairs. I was surprised to see Vasu enter the spirit of the game so completely.

Presently the Moslem came down with a pile of paper and took it to the front step. He came up to me, holding twenty-five rupees in currency, his face beaming, 'The master has agreed.' He made three more trips upstairs and barricaded my entrance with waste paper. He beckoned to a *jutka* passing down the street and loaded all the bundles into it. I asked, 'Where is that man?'

'He is up there.'

'What's he doing there?'

'I don't know,' said the old man. 'He was trying to open the windows.'

Presently Vasu called me from the attic, 'Nataraj, come up.'

'Why?' I cried. I was busy with the cinema programme. He repeated his command, and I went up. I had not gone upstairs for years. The wooden stairs creaked and groaned, unused to the passage of feet. There was a small landing and a green door, and you stepped in. Vasu was standing in the middle of the room like a giant. He had opened a little wooden window with a view of the fountain, over the market road; beyond it was a small door which led to a very narrow terrace that looked southwards on to the neighbouring roof-tiles. The floor was littered with pieces of waste paper; age-old dust covered everything.

Vasu was fanning around his ears with a cover of the school magazine. 'That fellow has done you a service in carrying away all that waste paper, but he has dehoused a thousand mosquitoes – one thing I can't stand.' He vigorously fanned them off as they tried to buzz about his ears. 'Night or day, I run when a mosquito is mentioned.'

'Let us go down,' I said, flourishing my arms to keep them away from my head.

'Wait a minute,' he said. 'What do you propose to do with this place?'

I ruminated for a moment; I had no plans for it, but before I could say so he said, 'I'll clean it up and stay here for a while. I want some place where I can throw my things and stay. The important thing will be to get a mosquito-net for sleeping in, a bed and one or two chairs. The roof comes down too low,' he added. He swung his arms up and down and said, 'Still a couple of feet above my arms, not too bad.'

I gave him no reply. I had never thought of the attic as habitable. He asked, 'Why are you silent?'

'Nothing, nothing,' I said. 'I shall have to . . .'

'What?' he asked mercilessly. 'Don't tell me you want to consult your seniors or partners, the usual dodge. I will stay here till a bungalow is vacated for me in the New Extension. I wouldn't dream of settling here. So don't be afraid. After all you would only put junk into it again.'

I said nothing and went down to my office. He followed me, drove away in his jeep and returned an hour later with four workmen carrying brooms and buckets. He led them past the curtain, up the stairs. I heard him shouting and bullying them and the mops and brooms at work. He discovered the water-closet below the staircase and made them carry up buckets of water and scrub the floor. Next day he brought in a builder's man and spent the whole day washing the walls of the attic with lime. He passed in and out, and hardly found time for a word with me. I watched him come and go. Two days later he brought a bedstead and a few pieces of furniture. Since I found it a nuisance to have Vasu and his minions pass up and down by the press I opened a side gate in the compound, which admitted his jeep into a little yard from Kabir Lane and gave him direct access to the wooden stairs. It took me another week to realize that without a word from me Vasu had established himself in the attic. 'After all,' I thought to myself, 'it's a junk-room, likely to get filled again with rubbish. Why not let him stay there until he finds a house?'

He disappeared for long periods and would then suddenly drop in. I had no idea where he went. Sometimes he just came and lounged in my parlour. My other visitors always tried to run away at the sight of him, for they found it difficult to cope with his bullying talk. The poet left if he saw him coming. Sen, the journalist, who was always loudly analysing Nehru's policies, could not stand him even for a minute. He had been unwittingly caught the very first day, while he was expatiating on the Five-Year Plan. Vasu, who had come in to collect some stationery, listened for a moment to the journalist's talk and, turning to me, asked, 'Who's he? You have not told me his name.'

'A good friend,' I said.

Vasu shook his head patronizingly and said, 'If he is so much wiser than Nehru, why doesn't he try to become the Prime Minister of India?'

The journalist drew himself up haughtily and cried, 'Who is this man? Why does he interfere with me when I am talking to someone? Is there no freedom of speech?'

Vasu said, 'If you feel superior to Nehru, why don't you go to

25

Delhi and take charge of the cabinet?' and laughed contemptuously. Words followed, Sen got up in anger, Vasu advanced threateningly. I came between them with a show of courage, dreading lest one of them should hit me. I cried, 'All are friends here. I won't allow a fight. Not here, not here.'

'Then where?' asked Vasu.

'Nowhere,' I replied.

'I don't want to be insulted, that's all,' the bully said.

'I am not going to be frightened by anyone's muscle or size. Do you threaten to hit me?' Sen cried. He pushed me out of the way and stepped up to Vasu. I was in a panic.

'No, sir,' said Vasu, recoiling. 'Not unless I'm hit first.' He raised his fist and flourished it. 'I could settle many problems with this, but I don't. If I hit you with it, it will be the end of you. But that doesn't mean I may not kick.'

Vasu sat in my parlour and expounded his philosophy of human conduct. 'Nataraj!' he would say. 'Life is too short to have a word with everyone in this land of three hundred odd millions. One has to ignore most people.' I knew it was just a fancy speech, because his nature would not let him leave anyone in peace. He'd wilt if he could not find some poor man to bully. If he found someone known to him, he taunted him. If he met a stranger or a new face, he bluntly demanded, 'Who is he? You have not told me his name!' No maharaja finding a ragged commoner wandering in the halls of his durbar would have adopted a more authoritative tone in asking, 'Who is this?'

Vasu's habit of using my front room as an extension of his attic was proving irksome, as I had my own visitors, not to speak of the permanent pair – the poet and the journalist. For a few days Sen and the poet left the moment they heard the jeep arrive, but gradually their views underwent a change. When Vasu came in, Sen would stick to his seat with an air of defiance as if saying, 'I'm not going to let that beefy fellow . . .' The poet would transfer himself without fuss from the high-backed Queen Anne chair to a poorer seat. He had developed the art of surviving Vasu's presence; he maintained a profound silence, but if he were forced to speak he would confine himself to monosyllables (at which in any case he was an adept), and I was glad to note that Vasu had too much on his mind to have the time for more than a couple of nasty, personal remarks, which the poet pretended not to hear. Sen suppressed the expression of his political opinions in Vasu's presence (which was a good thing again), but it did not save him, as Vasu, the moment he remembered his presence, said, 'What are the views of our wise friend on this?' To which Sen gave a fitting reply, such as 'If people are dense enough not to know what is happening, I'm not prepared to . . .', which would act as a starting point for a battle of words. But the battle never came, as on the first day, to near-blows – it always fizzled out.

I left everyone alone. If they wrangled and lost their heads and voices, it was their business and not mine. Even if heads had been broken, I don't think I'd have interfered. I had resigned myself to anything. If I had cared for a peaceful existence, I should have rejected Vasu on the first day. Now it was like having a middle-aged man-eater in your office and home, with the same uncertainties, possibilities, and potentialities.

This man-eater softened, snivelled and purred, and tried to be agreeable only in the presence of an official. He brought in a khaki-clad, cadaverous man one day, a forestry officer, seated him and introduced me, 'This is my best friend on earth, Mr Nataraj; he and I are more like brothers than printer and customer or landlord and tenant.'

'Actually, I am not a landlord and don't want to be one,' I said, remembering how much more at peace I used to be when my attic was tenanted by junk. Woe to the day I had conceived the idea of cleaning it up.

Vasu said, 'Even among brothers, business should be business.'

'True, true,' said the forester.

Now Vasu turned to the art of flattery. I would never have guessed his potentialities in this direction. He said, 'I have brought Mr . . . because I want you to know him. He is a very busy man, but came with me today.'

'Do you live in the forest?'

Before the forester could speak, Vasu answered, 'He *is* Mempi Forest. He is everything there. He knows and has numbered every beast, and he has no fear. If he were a coward he would never have joined this department.'

The forester felt it was time for him to put in a word about himself, 'I have put in thirty years in the department. They gave me a third extension of my service only two weeks ago.'

'See how he looks? Can you guess his age?' (I wanted to say that I could do so unerringly.) 'He is like a teak-tree – thousands of those trees in Mempi Range are in his charge, isn't it so, sir?'

'Yes, yes, that's a big responsibility,' he said.

'And you know, he looks wiry, but he must be like a teak log in strength. I am a strong man, as you know, but I'd hesitate to challenge him. Ha! Ha! Ha!' Vasu stopped laughing and said, 'Seriously, he is one of the best forestry officers in India. How many times has he been attacked by a rogue elephant?'

'Eighteen times,' said the man statistically.

'And you just gave it a four-nought-five charge at point-blank range?'

'Yes, what else could one do?' asked the hero.

'How many tigers has he tracked on foot?'

'An average of at least one every half-year,' he said.

'And in thirty years you may guess how much he must have done and seen,' Vasu said. He asked the hero, 'What did you do with all those skins?'

'Oh, presented them here and there,' said the man. 'I don't fancy keeping trophies.'

'Ah, you shouldn't say that. You must let me stuff at least one animal for you, and you will know the difference,' said Vasu. 'Nataraj,' he added suddenly, 'the main reason why I have brought him to you is he wants a small book printed.' My heart sank. It was terrible enough to have Vasu for a customer, and now to have to work for someone he was championing! The three-colour labels were still undelivered. 'Nataraj, you will have to clear your desk and do this.'

I held out my hand mechanically. The forester took out of his bag a roll of manuscript, saying, 'I have made a habit of collecting Golden Thoughts, and I have arranged them alphabetically. I wish to bring them out in book form and distribute them to school-children, free of cost. That is how I want to serve our country.'

I turned over the manuscript. Virtues were listed alphabetically. 'My Tamil types are not good,' I said. 'My neighbour has the best Tamil types available and his original Heidelberg . . .'

'Oh,' Vasu groaned, 'that original again!'

I looked at him compassionately. 'As a man of education, Vasu,' I began, 'you should not shut your mind to new ideas.'

'But why on earth should I know anything about the original what's-its-name?' he cried with mild irritation; it was evident that he was struggling to be on his best behaviour before the man in khaki.

'It's because,' I replied with the patience of a saint explaining moral duty to an erring soul, 'it's the machine on which fast printing has to be done. For instance work like our friend's here – Golden Thoughts – the right place for it would be the original Heidelberg – a lovely machine. What do you say, sir?' I said, turning to the man. I had spent a lifetime with would-be authors and knew their vanities from A to Z.

The forester said, 'Yes, I want the best service possible – the book must look nice. I want to send a specially bound copy to our Chief Conservator at Delhi through our chief at Madras.'

'So you want two special copies?' I asked.

'Yes, yes,' he agreed readily.

I looked through the pages of the manuscript. He had culled epigrammatic sentiments and moralizings from every source – *Bhagavad-Gita*, *Upanishads*, Shakespeare, Mahatma Gandhi, the Bible, Emerson, Lord Avebury and Confucius – and had translated them into Tamil. It was meant to elevate young minds no doubt, but I'd have resented being told every hour of the day what I should do, say, or think. It would be boring to be steadfastly good night and day. All the same the book contained most of the sentiments Vasu had missed in life and it would do him no harm to pick up a few for his own use. I told him, 'I'm sure you will enjoy going over the manuscript, in case our friend does not find the time to give it a final look-over.'

'Oh, yes, yes, of course,' Vasu said faintly.

I was confident now that I could dodge, at least for the time being, the responsibility of printing the golden book, but I couldn't judge for how long. If I took it on, with Vasu living overhead, he would storm the press night and day when the man in khaki was out of sight. There was going to be no money in it; I was positive about that. The whole transaction, it was patent, was going to be a sort of exchange between the two: Vasu wanted to win the other's favour through my help. I had already printed stationery for Vasu, and he had shown no signs of paying for the work.

I told the man, handing back the manuscript, 'Please go through it again and make all the final revisions and additions. Then if you are satisfied with the final form, we'll do something with it. I do not want you to incur any unnecessary expense later – corrections are rather expensive, you know. All the time you can give for revision in manuscript will be worthwhile.' Once again my experience of would-be authors saved me: authors liked to think that they took infinite pains to attain infinite perfection.

I could see Vasu's bewilderment: he could not make out whether it was a good thing or a bad thing that had happened: the manuscript had changed hands too swiftly. He looked at my face and then at the other's. I was a seasoned printer. I knew the importance of shuffling off a manuscript without loss of time. Once the manuscript got lodged with you, you lost your freedom, and authority passed to the writer. Vasu began to argue, 'How can you get him to come again? Do you know the distance he has to come – from Peak House, where he is camping.' Very encouraging! Sixty miles away. It would not be often that he would find the time, or the conveyance, to come downhill.

'He won't have to come here! You can fetch the manuscript,' I said, and Vasu agreed with alacrity. 'Yes, yes, that's a good idea. I'll always be round you, you know,' he said with servility.

A week later, a brown envelope from the Forest Department arrived for Vasu. His face lit up at the sight of it. 'Must be my game licence. It was embarrassing to go into the jungle without it. Now you will see what I shall do . . . The swine!' he cried when he had read the contents. 'They think I want to go sightseeing in the forests and permit me to shoot duck and deer – as if I cared!' He remained in thought for a while. 'Now they shall know what I can do.' He carelessly thrust the paper into his pocket.

Chapter Four

A month later Vasu stopped his jeep in front of my office and sounded the horn; he sat at the wheel, with the engine running. I looked up from a proof of a wedding invitation I was correcting. The adjournment lawyer was sitting in front of me – his daughter was to be married in two weeks and he was printing a thousand invitation cards. This was one piece of work I was obliged to deliver in time, and I didn't want to be interrupted. I shouted back to Vasu, 'Anything urgent?'

'Yeah,' he said. He seemed to have picked up his American style from crime books and films.

'I am busy,' I said.

'Come on,' he said aggressively. I placed a weight on the proof and went out. 'Jump in,' he said when I approached him.

'I really can't,' I said. 'That man is waiting for me.'

'Him! Don't be silly. Jump in.'

'Where are you going?'

'I'll bring you back in ten minutes,' he said. 'Can't you spare ten minutes for my sake?'

I said, 'No, I can't spare ten minutes.'

'All right, five minutes then.' I climbed into the jeep and he drove off. We crossed Nallappa's Grove and drove for ten miles on the trunk road; he drove recklessly. I asked him where he was going.

'I thought you might enjoy a visit to Mempi.'

'What . . . what's the meaning of this?' I asked angrily.

'So you don't like being with me! All right. Shall I stop? You may get down and go back.'

I knew it would be futile to exhibit temper. It'd only amuse him. I concealed my chagrin and said, 'I certainly should enjoy walking back ten miles, but I wish I had had the time to pick up my shirt buttons before leaving.' I had mislaid my buttons at home. My shirt was open at the chest.

He cast a look at me. 'No one will mind in the jungle,' he said and rocked with laughter. Now that I was at his mercy, I thought I might as well abandon myself to the situation. I only wished I had not left the adjournment lawyer sitting in my chair. How long was he going to be there and what was to happen to the marriage of his daughter without invitation cards? I said, assuming the most casual tone possible, 'It was a matter of an urgent marriage invitation.'

'How urgent is the marriage?' he asked.

'It's coming off in fifteen days, and they must have time to post the invitation cards. A printer has his responsibilities.'

'If the man is willing and the woman is willing – there is a marriage. What has a printer to do with it? It's none of a printer's business. Why should you worry?'

I gave up all attempts to explain; he was not prepared to pay any attention to my words. He was the lord of the universe, he had no use for other people's words. 'Why should you worry?' he asked again and again. It was so unreasonable and unseasonable that I didn't think fit to find an answer. I noticed that the speedometer needle was showing a steady sixty. 'Mind the road,' I said, as I saw villagers walking in a file, stepping aside as the jeep grazed them. Lorries and buses swerved away, the drivers muttering imprecations. Vasu enjoyed their discomfiture and laughed uproariously. Then he became suddenly serious and said, 'More people will have to die on the roads, if our nation is to develop any road sense at all!' A peasant woman was sitting on the roadside with a girl whose hair she was searching for lice. He saw them and set his course to run into them, swerving away at the last moment after seeing them tumble over each other in fright.

'Oh, poor creatures,' I said. 'I hope they aren't hurt.'

'Oh, no, they won't be hurt. These women are hardy and enjoy a bit of fun. Didn't you see how they were laughing?'

I felt it best to leave his words without comment. Even that seemed to annoy him. After we had gone a couple of miles, he said, 'Why are you silent? What are you thinking about? Still worrying about that invitation?'

'Yes,' I said to be on the safe side.

'Only fools marry, and they deserve all the trouble they get. I really do not know why people marry at all. If you like a woman, have her by all means. You don't have to own a coffee estate because you like a cup of coffee now and then,' and he smiled, more and more pleased with his own wit.

I had never known him so wild. He had seemed to practise few restraints when he visited me at my press, but now, in his jeep on the highway, his behaviour was breath-taking. I wondered for a moment whether he might be drunk. I asked testily, 'What do you think of prohibition, which they are talking about nowadays?'

'Why?' he asked. As I was wondering what to say, he said, 'Drink is like marriage. If people like it, it's their business and nobody else's. I tried to drink whisky once, but gave it up. It tastes bad.' He sat brooding at the wheel for a moment and said, 'I wonder why anyone should want to drink.'

My last hope that the man might be drunk was gone. A man who could conduct himself in this way dead sober! I shuddered at the thought. When we arrived at Mempi village I was glad to jump out. Riding in the jeep with one leg dangling out had made me sore in all my joints and my head reeled slightly with the speed of his driving.

Mempi village, at the foot of the hills, consisted of a single winding street, which half a mile away disappeared into the ranges of Mempi. A few cottages built of bamboo and coconut thatch lined the wayside; a tea-shop with bananas dangling in bunches from the ceiling was a rallying point for all buses and lorries plying on this road; a touring cinema stood in the open ground flanking the road, plastered over with the picture of a wide-eyed heroine watching the landscape. The jungle studded the sides of the hill. A small shrine stood at the confluence of the mountain road with the highway, and the goddess presiding was offered coconut and camphor flames by every driver on the mountain road.

Vasu pulled up his jeep and asked the man at the tea-shop, 'What's the news?'

The man said, 'Good news. There was a prowler last night, so they say. We saw pug-marks on the sand and sheep were bleating as if they had gone mad. Not where I live, but I heard Ranga talk of it today.'

'Did he see anything?' asked Vasu; and added eagerly, 'What did he see?'

The tea-shop had a customer waiting, and the owner mechanically handed him a bun and drew strong, red tea from a sizzling urn and poured it into a glass tumbler. I had been starving. I cast longing looks at the brown buns arranged on a shelf, although normally I would not have dared to eat anything out of a shop like this, where flies swarmed over the sugar and nothing was ever washed or covered; road dust flew up whenever a car passed and settled down on the bread, the buns, the fruit, sugar, and milk. The shop had a constant crowd of visitors. Buses and lorries halting on their way up to the coffee estates, bullock carts in caravans, pedestrians – everyone stopped here for refreshment.

When I put my fingers in my pocket, I did not find a single coin, but only the stub of a pencil with which I'd been correcting the proof of the wedding invitation. I called pathetically like a child at a fair tugging at the sleeve of his elder, 'Vasu!' He was busy discussing the pug-marks and the circle round him was growing: a coconut-seller, the village idiot, the village wag, a tailor, and a man carrying a bundle of tobacco on his head. Each was adding his own to the symposium on the tiger's visit.

Vasu did not hear me call him. I had to cry out, 'Vasu, lend me some cash; I want to try the tea here.'

He paused. 'Tea! Why?'

I felt silly with my shirt open at the chest and the dhoti around my waist. 'I'm hungry. I had no time for breakfast this morning.'

He looked at me for a minute and resumed his discussion about the pug-marks. I felt slighted. Hunger had given an edge to my temper. I felt indignant that I should have been dragged out so unceremoniously and treated in this way. I called out, 'Have you or have you not any loose coin on you? I'll return it to you as soon as I am back home.'

'So you think we are going back home, eh?' he said irresponsibly. I was struck with a sudden fear that this man was perhaps abducting me and was going to demand a ransom for releasing me from some tiger cave. What would my wife and little son do if they were suddenly asked to produce fifty thousand rupees for my release? She might have to sell the house and all her jewellery. I had not yet paid the final instalment on that gold necklace of hers that she fancied only because someone she knew had a similar one. Good girl, this had been her most stubborn demand in all the years of our wedded life and how could I deny her? Luckily I had printed the Co-operative Bank Annual Report and with those earnings paid off half the price of the necklace. But, but, that necklace cost in all only seven hundred rupees – how would she make up fifty thousand? We might have to sell off the treadle; it was rickety and might fetch just thirteen thousand, and then what should I do after my release, without my printing machinery? What was to happen to Sastri? He'd be unemployed, or would he go over to operate the Heidelberg? If my wife appealed to him would he have the sense to go to the police and lead them to the tiger cave guarded by this frightful man with the dark halo over his head? Suppose he mounted guard over me and the tiger returned to the cave and found him, would the beast have the guts to devour him first and leave me alone, retching at the sight of any further food?

All this flashed through my mind. It made me swallow my temper and smile ingratiatingly at Vasu, which had a better effect than any challenge. He relented enough to say, 'You see, when I'm out on business I rarely think of food.' ('Because you'll not hesitate to make a meal of any fool who has the ill-luck to go with you,' I remarked mentally.) Suddenly he left me, got into his jeep and said, 'Come on,' to someone in the group, and was off. I felt relieved at his exit, but cried like a lost child, 'When . . .? When . . .?' He waved to me saying, 'Stay here, I'll be back,' and his jeep raced up the mountain road and disappeared round a bend. I could hear the whining of its gears for a while.

I looked down at my chest, still unbuttoned. I felt ridiculous, standing there. This was no doubt a very beautiful place – the hills and the curving village road, and the highway vanishing into the hills. The hills looked blue, no doubt, and the ranges beyond were shimmering, but that could hardly serve as an excuse for the liberties Vasu had taken with me. I sat down on a wooden plank stretched over two empty tins, which served for a bench, and addressed myself to the tea-shop man, 'Is there a bus for Malgudi from here?'

'Yes, at two o'clock coming from Top Slip.'

It would be a good idea to catch it and get back to town, but how was I to pay for the ticket? I didn't have even a button to my shirt. I cursed myself for entertaining and encouraging Vasu, but I also felt relief that he had gone away without a word about the ransom. I explained my situation to the tea-shop man. He was very happy when he heard that I was a printer. 'Ah, I'm so happy, sir, to know you. Can you print some notices for me, sir?'

'With pleasure,' I said, and added, 'I'm here to serve the public. I can print anything you want. If you prefer to have your work done on a German machine, I can arrange that too. My neighbour has an original Heidelberg, and we are like brothers.' I became loquacious at the unexpected opening offered for a friendly approach.

The man explained, 'I have no time to leave this place and attend to any other business in the town, and so I have long been worrying how to get some printing work done.'

'Oh, you don't have to worry as long as I'm here. Your printing will be delivered to you at your door, that's how I serve my customers. I print for a wide clientele and deliver the goods by bus or train, whichever goes earlier.'

'Ah, that's precisely how I would like to be served,' he said. Then he launched on his autobiography. He was a self-made man. Leaving his home in Tirunelveli when he was twelve years of age, he had come to Mempi in search of work. He knew no one, and he drifted on to the tea plantations in the hills and worked as an estate-labourer, picking tea-leaves, loading trucks, and in general acting as a handy-man. In the August of 1947, when India became independent, the estate, which had been owned by an English company, changed hands, and he came downhill to look for a new job. He established a small shop, selling betel nuts, peppermints and tobacco, and expanded it into a tea-shop. Business prospered when a new dam construction was started somewhere in a valley ten miles out; engineers, ministers, journalists, builders, and labourers moved up and down in jeeps, lorries and station-wagons, and the place buzzed with activity night and day. His tea-shop grew to its present stature. He built a house, and then another house, very near the shop in a back street. ('I can go home in five minutes for a nap or a snatch of food,' he boasted.) He began to take an interest in the shrine at the confluence of the mountain and the plains. 'Hundreds of vehicles go up to those summits and to this day we have never heard of an accident – although some of those roads are narrow and twisting, and if you are careless you'll dive over the ridge. But there has not been a single accident. You know why?' He pointed at the little turret of the shrine showing above the roadside trees. 'Because the Goddess protects us. I rebuilt the temple with my own funds. I have regular *pujas* performed there. You know we also have a temple elephant; it came years ago of its own accord from the hills, straying along with a herd of cattle returned from the hills after grazing. It was then about six months old, and was no bigger than a young buffalo. We adopted it for the temple. His name is Kumar and children and elders alike adore him and feed him with coconut and sugar cane and rice all day.'

After all this rambling talk he came to the point. He was about to celebrate the consecration of the temple on a grand scale, carrying the Goddess in a procession with pipes and music, led by the elephant. He wanted me to print a thousand notices so that a big crowd might turn up on the day.

I readily agreed to do it for him, and asked, 'When do you want it?'

He was flabbergasted. 'I don't know. We shall have to discuss it at a meeting of the temple committee.'

I was relieved to note that it was only a vague proposal so far and said, 'Write to me as soon as your plans are ready, and I will do my best for you. I will print anything you want. By the way, why don't you let me taste your tea and a couple of those buns? Who is your baker in the town? He has given them a wonderful tint!' He concocted a special brew of tea for me and handed me a couple of brown buns on a piece of old newspaper. I felt refreshed and could view my circumstances with less despair now. At the back of my mind was a worry as to whether the adjournment lawyer might still be sitting waiting for my return. Return home? Ah, there was no such prospect. I would have been wiser if I had written my will before venturing out with Vasu. 'I'll pay your bill next time I visit you,' I said, 'maybe with the printed notices. You see, I had to come away suddenly and didn't know I'd come so far.' And then I made another request, 'Do you know these bus people? What sort are they?'

'Every bus must stop here for tea,' he said boastfully.

'I knew it'd be so. Can you do me a favour? Could you ask one of the conductors to take me back to town and collect the fare at the other end? The bus has to pass in front of my press, and I could just dash in . . .'

'Why do you want to go away? Aren't you going to wait for Vasu?'

I felt desperate. Was this man in league with Vasu? Probably they had plans to carry me to the cave at night – all kidnappers operated at night. They were saving me up for their nocturnal activities. I said desperately, 'I must get back to the press today; the lawyer will be waiting for me. A wedding invitation. You know how important it is.'

'But Vasu may ask why I didn't keep you here. I know him, and he is sometimes strict, as you may know.'

'Oh,' I said casually, 'he is a good fellow, though his speech is blunt sometimes. We are very close, and he knows all about this marriage invitation. He'll understand and . . . he is a good friend of mine. The trouble is I came away without picking up my buttons or cash.' I laughed, trying to import into the whole situation a touch of humour. 'I wonder when Vasu will be back!'

'Oh, that nobody can say. When he hears about a tiger, he forgets everything else. Now he'll be right in the jungle following the pug-marks, and . . .'

'A fearless man,' I cried in order to please the tea-seller. 'What is your name?' I asked.

'Muthu,' he said. 'I have four children, and a daughter to marry . . .'

'Then you will understand better than anyone else how anxious that lawyer will be.'

'Which lawyer?' he asked.

'Our adjournment lawyer, whom I left sitting in my office.'

'I'm sure you will help me to find a good bridegroom for my daughter.' He lowered his voice to say, 'My wife is scheming to marry her off to her own brother's son, but I have other ideas. I want the girl to marry a boy who is educated.'

'She must marry someone who is at least a B.A.,' I said.

He was so pleased with this that he gave me a third bun and another glass of tea. 'This is my treat. You don't have to pay for this cup,' he said.

Presently his customers began to arrive – mostly coolies carrying pick-axes, crow-bars and spades on their way to that mysterious project beyond the hills. Caravans of bullock carts carrying firewood and timber stopped by. Loudspeaker music blared forth from the tent-cinema, where they were testing their sound again and again – part of some horribly mutilated Elvis Presley tune, Indianized by the film producer. I sat there and no one noticed me: arms stretched right over my head for glasses of tea; sometimes brown tea trickled over the side of the glass tumbler and fell on my clothes. I did not mind, though at other times I'd have gone into a rage at any man who dared to spill tea over my clothes. Today I had resigned myself to anything – as long as I could hope for a bus-ride back to town on credit and good will. I glanced at the brown face of a very old timepiece kept on a wooden shelf inside the tea-shop. It was so brown that I could hardly make out the numerals on it.

Still an hour before the bus arrived and two hours since Vasu had gone. I only hoped that he would not return before the bus arrived. I prayed he would not: I reassured myself again by asking, over the babble of the tea-shop, if Muthu could tell when Vasu would be back, and he gave me the same reply as before. This was the only silver lining in the cloud that shrouded my horizon that day. Even so my heart palpitated with apprehension lest he should suddenly appear at the tea-shop and carry out his nefarious programme for the evening. He could pick me up between his thumb and first finger and put me down where he pleased. Considering his enormous strength, it was surprising that he did not do more damage to his surroundings. I sat in a trembling suspense as men came and went, buying tobacco, betel leaves, and cigarettes and tea and buns. I could hardly get a word with Muthu. I sat brooding over what I'd have to face from Sastri or my wife when I got back . . . Get back! The very phrase sounded remote and improbable! The town, the fountain, and my home in Kabir Street seemed a faraway dream, which I had deserted years ago . . .

The crowd at the tea-shop was gone. I sat on the bench and fell into a drowse. The hills and fields and the blindingly blue sky were lovely to watch, but I could not go on watching their beauty for ever. I was not a poet. If my monosyllabic friend had been here, perhaps he would have enjoyed sitting and staring; but I was a business man, a busy printer. I bowed my head and shut my eyes. I felt weak: I might eat all the buns in the world, but without a handful of rice and the sauce my wife made I could never feel convinced that I had taken any nourishment. The air far off trembled with the vibration of an engine. Muthu declared, 'The bus should be here in ten minutes.' Amazing man with ears so well attuned; I said so. I wanted to do and say anything I could to please this man, whom at normal times I'd have passed as just another man selling tea in unwashed tumblers.

The bus arrived, on its face a large imposing signboard announcing 'Mempi Bus Transport Corporation', although the bus itself was an old one picked off a war surplus dump, rigged up with canvas and painted yellow and red. It was impossible to guess how many were seated in the bus until it stopped at the tea-shop and the passengers wriggled and jumped out as if for an invasion. They swarmed around the tea-shop, outnumbering the flies. The conductor, a very thin man, in a peaked cap and khaki shirt over half-shorts, emerged with a cash-bag across his shoulder, and the driver jumped out of his seat. Men, women, and children clamoured for attention at the tea-shop. The driver and the conductor exchanged a few words, looked at the cash-bag, took out some coins for themselves. The conductor then addressed the gathering in a general manner, 'I am not stopping for more than five minutes; if anyone is left behind he will be left behind, that's all. I warn you all, don't blame me later,' and he looked around like a schoolmaster watching his erring pupils and passed into the tea-shop. He was given a seat of honour beside the owner. He called for a glass of tea and buns. He lit a cigarette. After he was well settled, I went to show myself to Muthu, who, I feared, might forget me in the midst of his booming business – a fear which was well-founded, for as soon as he saw me he said, 'Ah, I'd forgotten about our printing master.' Then he told the conductor, 'Brother, give him a seat to the town; he will pay at the other end.' The brother took time to grasp the meaning of the proposition. He looked at me with sour suspicion. 'Why should he not pay now?'

'Because he has left all his cash in town.'

'Then why did he come here? You know how many tell me that each day?' He moistened his upper lip with his tongue as smoke emerged from his nostrils. 'Another monster in league with Vasu,' I thought, and felt desperate. He demonstrated with his hands the act of wringing a neck. 'I'd like to do this to anyone who comes up with such a proposal. If our inspector checks mid-way, it'll end my career, and then I and my family will have to take a begging bowl and go from door to door.'

The man had a far-fetched imagination. Having always lived within the shelter of my press, I had probably grown up in complete ignorance of human nature, which seemed to be vicious, vile, vindictive and needlessly unfriendly everywhere. I went up to him with chest thrown out and said haughtily, 'I'll guarantee that you will not have to carry a begging bowl. Today I am stuck here, but generally I'm not a passenger in any bus, having a car – if not mine, my friend's which is as good as mine.'

'What car do you use?'

'Well . . .,' I said, reflecting, 'a Morris, of course,' mentioning the first make that came into my head.

'Model?' he asked, pursuing the subject.

'Fifty one, I think . . .'

'Four-door?'

'Yes.'

'Oh, you are lucky; it's worth its weight in gold, that particular model. I know several people who are searching for one desperately. Do you think you would care to quote a price for it?'

I shook my head. 'Oh, dozens of persons ask me that every day, but I want to keep it till it falls to bits, you know. I don't want to sell.'

He had now developed a wholesome respect for me as a member of the automobile fraternity. He was prepared to overlook my unbuttoned shirt and dishevelled appearance and ticketless condi- tion; I wished I had some more jargon to impress him further, but I had to manage as best I could with whatever rang in my memory as a result of the printing I had done for Ramu of Ramu's Service Station, who sometimes dropped in to talk of the state of the nation in the motoring world.

The bus-conductor said, 'Any time you want to dispose of your Morris, you must tell me.' He turned to Muthu and confided, 'Sooner or later I want to give up this endless ticket-punching and drive a baby taxi – I know a man who earns a net income of fifty rupees a day with just one baby vehicle. I have saved enough to buy a car now.'

Muthu nudged him in the midriff and muttered, 'Don't I know!' darkly, at which both of them simpered. I knew at once they meant that the conductor made money by pocketing a lot of the cash collected from passengers. I said, to add to the mood of the hour, 'One has to make money while one can. Otherwise, when one is old or down and out, who would give a paisa?'

When the conductor started nearly half an hour later, I walked along royally beside him and took my seat in the bus. I had taken leave of Muthu briefly but in touching terms; he assured me that he would write to me for any help he might need. I sat in the royal seat, that is, beside the driver. The conductor leaned over my shoulder from behind, to say, 'You will have to move and make space at the next stop. The Circle is expected.' The word 'Circle' in these circumstances indicated the inspector of police for this circle, whose seat at the front was always reserved. If another passenger occupied it, it was a matter of social courtesy to vacate it or at least move up closer to the driver and leave enough space at the end of the seat for the Circle. Once, long, long ago, a planter returning to his estate created a lot of unpleasantness by refusing to make way for the Circle, with the result that the Circle was obliged to travel in one of the ordinary seats inside the bus, with the rabble, and at the next stop he impounded the whole bus with the passengers for overcrowding.

The bus travelled for an hour. I felt happy that after all I'd slipped away from Vasu. I cast a look behind once or twice to see if his jeep was following us. Coming back from tracking the tiger, he might want to embark on the bigger expedition of tracking a printer who had escaped from a tea-shop.

The bus stopped under a tree on the road and the conductor issued a warning, 'We are not stopping for more than a minute. If anyone is impatient to get out, let him get out for ever. Don't blame me afterwards.' In spite of this threat a few of the passengers wriggled out and disappeared behind the bushes by the roadside. A constable in uniform was seen coming across a maize field, sweating in the sun and bearing under his arm a vast load of papers and files. He gesticulated from a distance to catch the eye of the driver. He arrived and placed the files on the seat next to me. I moved up to the inferior side of the seat close to the driver and cleared a space for the Circle. I couldn't, after all, be choosy as I was there on sufferance.

The constable said to the driver, 'The Circle is coming; you'll have to wait.'

'How long?' asked the conductor. The constable clung to the rail, rested his feet on the step, pushed his turban back on his head, and spurned answering. Instead he said, 'Give me a *beedi*,' and held out his hand. The driver produced from his pocket matches and a *beedi*. The constable smoked: the acrid smell of *beedi* leaf and tobacco overpowered the smell of petrol. The constable's face shone with perspiration. He said, 'I feared I might lose the bus; the Circle would have chopped off my head.' A couple of children started crying, a woman sang a soft but tuneless lullaby, someone was yawning noisily, someone else was swearing, a couple of peasants were discussing a litigation, someone asked wearily, 'Are we going to go on at all?' and someone else made a joke about it. I looked back furtively for Vasu's jeep coming in pursuit. I grew tired of the policeman's face, and the road ahead, and everything. I was beginning to feel hungry, the buns having been assimilated into my system long ago. All the passengers subsided into apathetic, dull waiting.

Finally the Circle turned up, a swarthy man in a khaki uniform, appearing suddenly beside the bus on a bicycle. As soon as he jumped off, work started: the constable held the handlebars; the conductor heaved the bicycle up to the roof; the Circle climbed into his seat and said, 'Start.' The driver squeezed the bulb of the rubber horn, and its short raucous bark resounded along the highway, past the hill, and brought a dozen passengers at the run who had strayed away from the suffocating bus into the surrounding country. For a brief while there was the disorder of people trying to clamber back to their original seats. One heard grumblings and counter-grumblings – 'I was sitting here,' 'No, this was my place,' until the conductor said, 'Keep quiet, everyone,' in deference to the presence of the Circle. The Circle, however, sat stiffly looking ahead; it was evident he did not want to embarrass the conductor by noticing the overcrowding.

I was overwhelmed by the proximity of this eminent person, who smelt of the sun, sweat and leather. I hoped he'd not take me for an ex-convict and order me out. He had a nice downward-directed short moustache. He wore dark glasses and his nose was hooked and sharp; his Adam's apple also jutted out. The driver drove with great caution; he who had been swerving away from collisions for over an hour (a pattern of driving which Vasu had already accustomed me to), now never exceeded twenty miles an hour, applied the brake when a piece of paper drifted across, and gently chided any villager who walked in the middle of the road. At this rate, he would not reach the town before midnight. His speed depended on where the Circle was getting out. I felt it imperative to know at once his destination. 'You are going to town, I suppose?' I said to him. Where was the harm in asking him that? There was no law against it.

He turned his sun-glasses on me and said, 'I'll be getting off at Talapur.'

'Is that where you stay?' I asked.

'No. I'm going there for an investigation,' he said, and I shuddered at the thought of the poor man who was going to be investigated. He talked to me about crime in his area. 'We've a lot of cattle-lifting cases in these parts, but the trouble is identification when the property is traced; they mutilate the animals, and then what happens is the case is dismissed and all the trouble one takes to frame a charge-sheet is simply wasted. We have a few murders too, and a certain amount of prohibition offences around the dry-belt areas.' I found that he was a friendly sort of man, in spite of all his grim looks. 'This is a difficult circle,' he said finally. 'Offenders often disappear into the jungles on Mempi, and sometimes one has to camp for days on end in the forests.'

At the Talapur bus-stand, which was under a tree, with a replica of Muthu's tea-stall, a constable was there to receive the Circle and haul down his bicycle from the roof. The Circle got on his cycle and pedalled away. Talapur was a slightly larger town than Mempi and was regarded as an important junction. It had more shops lining the street. The conductor uttered the usual warning to the passengers and vanished into the tea-shop. Most of the passengers followed suit and some dispersed to various corners of the city. I sat in the bus, nursing my hunger in silence, having no credit here.

When the bus started again, it was obvious that the Circle was no longer there to impede its freedom. It was driven recklessly and brought to a dead stop every ten minutes, to pick up a wayside passenger. The conductor never said 'no' to anyone. As he explained to me, 'These poor fellows will get stranded on the highway if we are not considerate. After all they are also human creatures.' He was a compassionate conductor, who filled his pockets with the wayside fare, never issuing a ticket. 'At this rate he could buy a Rolls-Royce rather than a Morris Minor,' I thought. The bus left the highway and darted across devious side-tracks through corn-fields in search of passengers. It would draw up at a most unexpected spot, and, sounding the horn, the driver would cry, 'Come on, come on, Malgudi, last bus for the town.' The bus penetrated into the remotest hamlet to ferret out a possible visitor to the town, and all the passengers had to go where the bus went and sit there patiently watching the antics of the driver and conductor, who seemed to have a fixed target of income for the day and to be determined to reach it. That was how a three-hour jeep ride in the morning was stretched out to eight on the return journey and it was eleven at night when the bus came to a halt in the public square beyond the market in Malgudi.

At eight o'clock next morning I sat correcting the proof of the adjournment lawyer's invitation. Sastri came in half an hour after I had opened the door of the press. He stood transfixed at the sight of me and said, 'We all waited till nine last night.'

'I've always told you that you should lock up the door at your usual time whether I am in or out,' I said grandly, and added, 'Sometimes I get so much else to do.'

'But that lawyer would not move. He kept saying you promised to be back in five minutes, in five minutes, and then there were the fruit-juice labels. He was very bitter and said . . .'

'Oh, stop that, Sastri,' I said impatiently. I did not like the aggrieved tone he was adopting. I'd had enough of nagging from my wife all night, after she had been forced to get up from sleep and feed me at midnight. 'If I disappeared abruptly it was my own business. Why should I be expected to give an explanation to everyone? If the fruit-juice man wants to print his labels elsewhere, let him clear out, that's all. I can't be dancing attendance on all and sundry. If he can find any other printer to bring out his magenta shade in the whole of South India . . .'

Sastri did not wait for me to finish my sentence but passed into the press, as it seemed to me, haughtily. I sat correcting the proof: the corrections were in the state I had left them on the previous day.

'Mr . . . requests the pleasure of your company . . .' Wrong fonts, and the bridegroom's name was misspelt. 'Company' came out as 'cumbahy'. I never cease to marvel at the extraordinary devils that dance their way into a first proof. The sight of 'cumbahy' provoked me to hysterical laughter. I was light-headed. I would not have to beg at a tea-shop and starve or go about without a button to my shirt. I had a feeling that I was in an extraordinarily fortunate and secure position, enough to be able to say 'fie' to Sastri or anyone. Life in Market Road went on normally. It was good to watch again the *jutkas* and cycles going round the fountain and the idlers of our town sitting on its parapet and spitting into it. It produced in me a great feeling of security and stability. But that lasted only for a few minutes. The adjournment lawyer, looking unshaven as ever, his shoulders draped in a spotted *khadi* shawl, a dhoti above his knee, and an umbrella dangling from his arm, stepped in, his face set in a frown.

'Do you think . . .,' he began.

One look at him and I knew what he was going to say, 'Won't you come in and take a seat, first?'

'Why should I?' he asked. 'I'm not here to waste my time.'

I was still motioning him to a chair, but he seemed afraid that once he sat there I'd abandon him and disappear again for the day.

He said, 'I'm printing my invitation elsewhere, so don't trouble yourself.'

'Oh, no trouble whatever. This is a free country, you are a free man. Our constitution gives us fundamental rights. How can I compel you or anyone to do what you may not want to do?' I knew he was lying; if he had wasted his time till nine last evening and was back so soon, when had he found the time to seek a printer? Anyway it was not my business; this was a free country, fundamental rights, every citizen was free to print his daughter's marriage card where he pleased, but if he had his wits about him he'd watch out where he got the best results.

'Sastri!' I called aggressively. 'Bring this gentleman's original draft – Lawyer so-and-so's daughter's wedding.' Sastri from his invisible world responded with his voice, but made no effort to bring the original. This gave everyone time to cool. The lawyer edged a step nearer the chair.

'Won't you take a seat, please? Mr Sastri should be with us in a minute.' He sat down, but remained in a state of hostile silence. I said, 'I suppose all your other arrangements are ready?'

He shook his head. 'How truly have our elders said . . .' He quoted a proverb to the effect that building a house and conducting a marriage were the two Herculean tasks that faced a man. I added a further sentiment that a man who marries off his daughter need perform no other meritorious acts in life as he is giving away his most precious treasure – which moved the lawyer so deeply that the tears came to his eyes. He said, blowing his nose, 'Susila is the gentlest of my children. I hope she will have no trouble from her mother-in-law!' He sighed deeply at the thought and I said consolingly, 'Mother-in-law! "Down with them," says the modern girl, college-educated and modern-minded.'

'I've given her the best possible education,' he said morosely. 'What more could I do? I pay her music master fifteen rupees a month, her school fees amount to fifteen rupees, and I pay ten rupees for her school bus . . .'

'And you have to manage all this,' I thought, 'by securing endless adjournments.' But I said aloud, 'Yes, life today is most expensive.'

After this agreeable *tête-à-tête*, I cried suddenly, 'Sastri, this gentleman is waiting to take away his invitation copy. After all we must give him time to print elsewhere.'

The lawyer behaved like one who has been stung. 'Oh no. Oh no,' he cried. 'Even if it means stopping the marriage, I will not go anywhere else for my printing.'

I said, 'I'm here to help humanity in my own humble way. I will never say no to anyone. Don't hesitate to command me for anything you may want me to do.' He took my offer promptly, and said, 'A thousand cards – or do you think we could do with less?'

Late that evening Vasu's jeep drew up before my press. It was past eight and the traffic in the street was thin. Vasu looked at me from his driving seat. His hair was covered with dust and stood up more like a halo than ever. He beckoned to me from his seat. I was overworking in order to finish the lawyer's invitations, and I had even undertaken to address and distribute them if he so ordered. He had acquired so much confidence in me that he did not feel the need to sit up with me, and had gone home. I shouted back to Vasu, 'Why don't you come in?' I was now on my own ground, and had no fear of anyone. He said, 'Hey, come on! I want you to see what I have here.' I went out, making up my mind not to step into the jeep, whatever might happen. I'd stand at a distance to see whatever it was that he was going to show me. There was dust and grime on his face, but also a triumphant smile exposing his teeth; his eyes had widened, showing the whites. I edged cautiously to the jeep. I only hoped that he would not thrust out his arm, grab me and drive off. He took a flashlight and threw the beam on to the back seat, where lay the enormous head of a tiger. 'How did you manage that?' I asked, there being no other way of talking to a man who had brought in the head of a tiger. A couple of curious passers-by slowed their pace. Vasu shouted to them, 'Get away and mind your own business.' He started his car to take it through the side gate and park it in the yard. I went back to my seat and continued my work. I could hear his steps go up the wooden stairs. When the breeze blew in from his direction, there was already a stench of flesh – it might have been my imagination.

The curtain parted; he came in and took a seat. He lit a cigarette and asked, 'Do you know what he measures? Ten and a half tip to tip; the head is almost eighteen inches wide! I got him finally in the block, you see; they will have a surprise when they next check the tiger population in their block.' He then described how he got information from various people, and had followed the foot-marks of the tiger from place to place. He had to wander nearly six miles within the jungle, and finally got it at a water-hole, at about two in the morning. He showed me the bleeding scratches on his feet from having to push his way through thickets; at any moment it might have sprung on him from some unsuspected quarter. 'I was prepared to knock him down with my hands and ram the butt of my rifle between his jaws if it came to that,' he said. It was evident that he was not going to wait for others to pay him compliments. He showered handfuls of them on himself.

'What about the permit? You didn't have one?'

'The tiger didn't mind the informality.' He laughed aloud at his own humour. 'That swine double-crossed me! Probably because you didn't print Golden Thoughts for him.' He never let slip an occasion to blame me or accuse me. I gave no reply, but I became curious to see his animal.

He took me to his room. This was my first visit there since he had occupied it. He had his bed draped over with a mosquito-net, a table in a corner, heaped with clothes and letters, and a trunk with its lid open with all his clothes thrown about. He had tied a string across the room and had more clothes hanging on it. On the little terrace he had put out some skins to dry; there was a tub in a corner in which the skin of the tiger was soaking. Skins of smaller animals lay scattered here and there, and jungle squirrels and feathered birds were heaped in corners. A lot of wooden planks and moulds and all kinds of oddments lay about. Ever since I had given him the attic, I had left him fairly alone, not wanting to seem an intrusive host, and all the while he had been surrounding himself with carcasses. The room smelt of decaying flesh and raw hide; he had evidently been very active with his gun, which now rested on his bed. ('I'm a man of business, and I cannot afford to waste my time. Each day that I spend without doing my work is a day completely wasted.') There was a resinous odour in the air which made me retch. I couldn't imagine any human being living in this atmosphere. Sastri now and then in the past weeks had complained of a rotting smell somewhere. We had searched our garbage cans and odd corners of the press to see if the paste we were using had gone bad. Once I had to speak severely to our binder; I called him names for possibly using some nasty slaughter-house material in binding. He was apologetic, although he had used no such material. Even after his promise to improve his material, the smell persisted. It was pervasive and insistent and Sastri found it impossible to stand at the type-board and compose. Then we thought a rat might be dead somewhere and turned up every nook and corner of the press, and finally we blamed the health department. 'Next time that fellow comes around for votes, I'll make him stand at the type-board and perform inhaling exercises,' I said bitterly. Sometimes my neighbour of the original Heidelberg came to ask if I noticed any smell around. I said emphatically that I did and asked his views on the municipal administration, little thinking that the fountainhead of all the stink was the attic over my own machine.

I sat down on an iron chair because the whole problem loomed enormously before me. If this man continued to stay here (I had really no idea how long he proposed to honour me with his presence), what was to happen to me and to my neighbourhood?

Vasu was stirring the broth in the tub with a long pole, at which the stench increased. I held my nostrils with my fingers and he ordered, 'Take your fingers away. Be a man.' When I hesitated, he came and wrenched my fingers apart. 'You are imagining things,' he said. 'What do you think that tub contains? Tiger blood? Ha! Ha! Pure alum solution.' He began to instruct me in the higher realms of carcass treatment. 'Actually the whole process of our work is much more hygienic and clean than paring the skin of vegetables in your kitchen.' I shuddered at the comparison. 'After all one takes a lot of care to bleed the animal, and only the skin is brought in. In order to make sure that there is no defect, I attend to everything myself. The paws and the head are particularly important.' He lifted the paw of the dead tiger and held it up. 'If there is the slightest flaw in the incision you will never be able to bring the ends together. That is what Suleiman taught me; he was an artist, as good as a sculptor or a surgeon, so delicate and precise! I killed the tiger last night. What do you think I was doing till tonight?'

'Hiding yourself and the carcass from the eyes of forest guards,' I thought.

'Bleeding, skinning, and cleaning it so that sentimentalists may not complain. To make still surer, we pack, or rather pickle, the skin in tins of salt immediately after flaying. So you will understand it is all done under the most hygienic conditions.' He swept his hand around, 'I do everything myself, not because I care for anyone's comments, but . . .'

'There are bits of flesh still there,' I said, pointing at the new tiger-skin.

'What if there are! Don't you have flesh under your own skin? Do you think you have velvet under yours? This was his idea of humour and I had no way of matching it. I looked around. On his work bench in a corner stood a stuffed crow, a golden eagle, and a cat. I could recognize the cat as the one that used to prowl in my press hunting for mice. 'Why did you shoot that cat? That was mine!' I cried shuddering. I fancied I could still hear its soft 'mew' as it brushed its back against my legs at the treadle.

'I didn't know,' he said, 'I only wanted it for study; after all, it's the same family as the tiger. I am trying to make a full mould of the tiger. There are some problems of anatomy peculiar to the *felis* family in this area and I needed a miniature for study and research. Without continuous application one cannot prosper in my line.'

'What did that crow do to you?' I asked.

'It's to serve as a warning to other crows to let Vasu's skins alone and not to peck at them when they are put out to dry.'

'And that golden eagle?'

'It was wheeling right over this roof four days ago; it's only five days old and do you notice any smell?' he asked victoriously. He had such a look of satisfaction and victory that I felt like pricking it a little.

'Yes, of course, there is a smell.'

'Oh, come on, don't be a fussy prude, don't imagine that you are endowed with more sensitive nostrils than others. Don't make yourself so superior to the rest of us. These are days of democracy, remember.' I was appalled at his notion of democracy as being a common acceptance of bad odours.

'What did that poor eagle do to you?' I asked. I could not bear to see the still, glazed look of the bird. 'See its stare!' I cried.

'Aha!' he said. He picked it up and brought it closer to me. 'So you think it's looking at you with its eyes!' Its dilated black pupils, set in a white circle, seemed to accuse us. He was convulsed with laughter and his voice split with mirth. 'So you are taken in! You poor fool! Those eyes were given it by me, not by God. That's why I call my work an art.' He opened a wooden chest and brought out a cardboard carton. 'See these.' He scooped out a handful of eyes – big round ones, small ones, red ones in black circles. The ferocious, striking, killing glare of a tiger, the surprise and superciliousness of an owl, the large, black-filled softness of a deer – every category of gaze was there. He said, 'All these are from Germany. We used to get them before the war. Now you cannot get them for love or money. Just lenses! Sometimes I paint an extra shade at the back for effect. The first thing one does after killing an animal is to take out its eyes, for that's the first part to rot, and then one gives it new eyes like an optician. I hope you appreciate now what an amount of labour goes into the making of these things. We have constantly to be rivalling Nature at her own game. Posture, look, the total personality, everything has to be created.' This man had set himself as a rival to Nature and was carrying on a relentless fight.

'You have no doubt excelled in giving it the right look, but, poor thing, it's dead. Don't you see that it is a *garuda*?'

'What if it is?'

'Don't you realize that it's sacred? That it's the messenger of God Vishnu?'

'I want to try and make Vishnu use his feet now and then.'

'You may be indifferent, but haven't you seen men stopping in the road to look up and salute this bird when it circles in the sky?' I wanted to sound deliberately archaic and poetic.

He ruminated for a second and added, 'I think there is a good business proposition here. I can supply them stuffed eagles at about fifty rupees each. Everyone can keep a sacred *garuda* in the *puja* and I'll guarantee that it won't fly off. Thus they can save their eyes from glare. I want to be of service to our religious folk in my own way.'

I shivered slightly at the thought and the way his mind worked.

Nothing seemed to touch him. No creature was safe, if it had the misfortune to catch his eye. I had made a mistake in entertaining him. I ought to send him away at the earliest possible moment. His presence defiled my precincts. My mind seethed with ideas as to how to throw him out, but he noticed nothing. He settled himself down on the easy chair, stretched his legs, and was preparing for a nice long chat. 'This is a minor job. I really don't care for it. My real work you will see only when the tiger is made up. You see it now only as a beast with a head and a lot of loose skin soaking in alum, but I'll show you what I can do with it.'

Chapter Five

He was a man of his word. He had said that he never wasted his time. I could see that he never wasted either his time or his bullets. Whenever I heard his jeep arrive, I would see some bloody object, small or big, brought in, if I cared to peep out. But nowadays, as far as possible, I tried to shut my eyes. I was having a surfeit. Not in my wildest dream had I ever thought that my press would one day be converted into a charnel house, but here it was happening, and I was watching helplessly. Sometimes it made me very angry. Why couldn't I ask him to get out? This was my own building, laboriously acquired through years of saving and scraping, and the place would not have come to me but for a good Moslem friend who migrated to Pakistan and gave me the first offer. If I opened the back door, I stepped into Kabir Street, and right across it to my own home. But all this had come about only to harbour the murderer of innocent creatures.

I had been brought up in a house where we were taught never to kill. When we swatted flies, we had to do it without the knowledge of our elders. I remember particularly one of my grand-uncles, who used the little room on the *pyol* and who gave me a coin every morning to buy sugar for the ants, and kept an eye on me to see that I delivered the sugar to the ants in various corners of our house. He used to declare, with approval from all the others, 'You must never scare away the crows and sparrows that come to share our food; they have as much right as we to the corn that grows in the fields.' And he watched with rapture squirrels, mice, and birds busily depleting the granary in our house. Our domestic granary was not built in the style of these days with cement, but with a bamboo matting stiffened with mud and rolled into cylinders, into whose wide mouth they poured in the harvest, which arrived loaded in bullock carts. That was in the days before my uncles quarrelled and decided to separate.

I was appalled at the thought that I was harbouring this destroyer, but I hadn't the courage to go up to him and say, 'Take yourself and your museum out of here!' He might do anything – bellow at me, or laugh scornfully, or rattle my bones. I felt dwarfed and tongue-tied before him. Moreover it was difficult now to meet him; he was always going out and returning late at night; sometimes he was away for three days at a stretch. He returned home late because he did not want his booty to be observed. When he was at home he worked upstairs with the broth and moulds; one heard the hammering, sawing, and all the other sounds belonging to his business, and sometimes during the day he hauled down packing cases and drove off to the railway station. I noted it all from my seat in the press and said to myself, 'From this humble town of Malgudi stuffed carcasses radiate to the four corners of the earth.'

He worked single-handed on all branches of his work. I admired him for it, until I suddenly realized that I too laboured single-handed at my job, with the slight difference that Sastri was with me; but Vasu had, I suppose, all those ruffians of Mempi lending him a hand in his nefarious trade. I do not know why I should ever have compared myself with him, but there it was. I was getting into an abnormal frame of mind. There was no person in whom I could confide, for I had always played that role myself. My visitors were, as usual, the journalist and the poet, both of them worthless as consultants. All the same I made an attempt to ascertain their views.

The journalist was frankly dumbfounded when he realized that there was no aspect of this particular problem which he could blame directly on the Government. He merely snapped, 'Why do you tolerate such things? As a nation, we are what we are today because of our lack of positive grip over our affairs. We don't know where we are going or why. It is part of the policy of drift, which is our curse.' I paid no attention to what he was saying; it was all too vague and round-about and irrelevant to the present case; the idea of Vasu provoked Sen into incoherent unpredictable statements. I left him alone. After all one should learn to bear one's burdens.

Still, two days later, the oppression on my mind was so great that I buttonholed the poet when he was struggling to start on the seventh canto of his opus and asked what he would do in my place. I feared that he might suggest reading poetry aloud as a possible step towards driving out the killer. He took time to comprehend my problem; even to myself, the more I attempted to speak of my problem, the more incomprehensible it seemed. I was left wondering if I were making too much of a very simple matter.

When he did understand, the poet asked, 'Why don't you try to raise the rent?'

I beat my brow, 'Oh, Kavi! Do I have to tell you that I am not a *rentier*? I let him in as a friend and not as a tenant. Do you want to heap on my head the reputation of being a man who takes rent for his attic space?'

The poet looked bewildered and said, 'Then you could surely tell him to go. Why not?'

It was impossible to explain. My wife also said the same thing. In my desperation I had turned to her, though I rarely discussed my problems with her. I had become abnormal. I was brooding too much on Vasu. His footsteps on the wooden stairs set my heart racing. I knew that it was involuntary anger which stirred my heart; the trouble was that it was both involuntary and suppressed! My wife said simply, sweetly, as she served my supper, 'Ask him to go, that's all. Babu is frightened of him, and refuses to go when I send him to you.'

All this worked on my mind. I waited for a chance to have a word with the man. It was like waiting for my father, in my childhood. I often had to spend days and days hoping to catch my father in a happy mood to ask him for a favour, such as cash for purchasing a bat or ball or permission to go out scouting. Most times he was preoccupied and busy, and I lost the taste for food until I was able to have a word with him. I would confide in my grand-uncle and he would help me by introducing the subject to my father at the appropriate moment, when he was chewing betel-leaves after a contented dinner. When my father turned to question me, I would squirm and find myself tongue-tied, unable to go on with my proposition. I was in a similar predicament now, with the added handicap of not having my grand-uncle around. I recollected that on the day I saw his dead body stretched out on the bier my first thought was, 'Oh Lord, who is going to speak for me hereafter?'

At last I stuck a note on Vasu's attic door when he was away, 'May I have a word with you when you have the time?' and waited for results. One morning, three days later, he parted the curtain and peeped in while I was at the treadle, printing the monosyllable forms. I had now barricaded the passage beyond, from the attic stairs to my treadle, with steel mesh, so that Vasu always had to come by the front door whenever he wanted to see me. The first thing he said was, 'You take a pleasure in making me go round, is that it?' My heart sank at the sight of him. There was a frown on his terrible brow. 'Perhaps he missed a target or his gun backfired!' I thought to myself. It was more dangerous than asking for a concession from my father. He flourished the note and asked, 'Is this for me?' He seemed to possess a sixth sense. He looked grim and unfriendly.

I wondered if someone had been talking to him. I looked up from my proof and just said, 'Nothing urgent. Perhaps we could meet later, if you are busy.'

'If *you* are busy it is a different matter, but don't concern yourself with my busyness. I am always busy.'

'Yes,' I added mentally, 'as long as the forests are full.'

He added, 'I cannot afford to lounge about, if you know what I mean. If I had the same luck as your other friends who congregate in your press, reading verse or criticizing the Government, I might . . .'

That settled it. He was in a challenging mood. I suppressed the qualms I had all along and said, 'Will you kindly take a seat? I will join you in a moment.' He was sitting in his chair when I came to him two minutes later, after taking enough time to put away the paper in hand. He said, 'You have made a fetish of asking people to sit in this room.' This was a surprise attack.

'I like to observe the ordinary courtesies,' I said.

'Do you mean to say that others don't?' he asked with his face puckering into the usual lines, and I knew he was getting back into his old mood of devilish banter. I felt relieved. I might have even gone to the length of inquiring about his dead or dying animals, but I checked myself, feeling an aversion to the subject. I said, 'Vasu, I don't want you to mistake me. Have you been able to secure a house?'

'Why?' he asked, suddenly freezing.

'I just thought I might ask you, that's all.'

'Not the sort of question a supposedly hospitable person should ask of his guest. It is an insult.'

I fought down my racing heart and my tongue which was ready to dart out like a snake's. I said very casually, 'I asked because I require the place for . . .'

'For?' he asked aggressively, cocking his ear, and waited for my answer.

'Someone is coming to stay with us, and he wants . . .'

'How many rooms in your own house are occupied?'

'Should one go into all that now?'

'Yes, the question is of interest to me,' he said, and added, 'Otherwise I would not mind if you had all your relatives in the world come and live with you.'

I suppressed the obvious repartees. Aggressive words only generate more aggressive words. Mahatma Gandhi had enjoined on us absolute non-violence in thought and speech, if for no better reason than to short-circuit violent speech and prevent it from propagating itself. I toned my repartee down to a cold business-like statement, 'My guest is a man who likes to stay by himself.'

'Then why should he seek solitude in this noisy press?'

I had no answer, and he said after some reflection, 'For years you did nothing more than house old decaying paper there; now I have made it slightly habitable you are getting ideas. Do you know how much it has cost me to make it livable in? The mosquitoes and other vermin would eat you up if you were slightly careless, the roof-tiles hit your head, there are cobwebs, smoke, and in summer it is a baking oven. No one but a fool like me would have agreed to live there!'

I remained silent. All I could say was obvious, such as, 'Is this the return I get for giving you shelter?' 'If you remember, you volunteered to stay,' and the most obvious one, 'After all you are living on my hospitality; get out if you do not like it.' 'You are not obliged to be here, you know,' etc. etc. I swallowed all such remarks. Instead I said sentimentally, 'I never expected you would be so upset.'

'Who says I am upset? You are fancying things. It takes a lot more to upset me. Well, anything else?' he asked, rising.

Not until his jeep moved did I realize that he had given me no answer to my question. He had treated it lightly, viciously, indifferently, but all to no purpose. He was gone; my problem remained unsolved, if anything made worse by my having irritated the man. Stag-heads, tiger-skins and petrified feathers were going to surround me for ever and ever. My house was becoming a Noah's Ark, about which I had read in our scripture classes at Albert Mission. There was going to be no help from anywhere. Nobody seemed to understand my predicament. Everyone ended up with the monotonous conclusion, 'After all, you invited him to stay with you!' I felt completely helpless. Sastri alone grasped the situation and now and then threw in a word of cheer such as 'These things cannot go on for ever like this, can they?' Or sometimes he was brazen enough to say, 'What can he do after all, if you really want him to clear out?' as he stuck alphabet to alphabet on his composing stick. He felt it necessary to cheer me up as nowadays I was involving him in a lot of worrying transactions with our customers. The co-operative society report and ledgers were overdue because I could not muster enough sharpness of mind to check the figures. The cash bill of Anand Bhavan Hotel remained half done for the same reason, and it was he who had to battle with the customers and send them back with a convincing reply. Anyway it was a slight comfort in a world where there seemed to be no comfort whatever. I was lulled into a state of resignation. Vasu saw me less and less. I could hear his steps treading the staircase more emphatically than ever. I detected in that stamping of feet a challenge and a sense of ownership. I raged within myself every time I heard those footsteps and I knew I had lost him as a friend. From now on our relationship was going to be of the coldest. I would be grateful if he left me alone and did not think of bringing that terrific fist of his against my chin.

That he had not been idle came to light very soon. Five days passed uneventfully, and then came a brown envelope brought by a court process-server. I received it mechanically, signing the delivery note. Opening it, I read, 'You are hereby asked to show cause why proceedings should not be instituted against you . . .' etc. It was from the House Rent Controller, the most dreaded personality in the town. The charges against me were: one, that I had given part of my press for rent without sanction to one Mr Vasu; and two, that I was trying to evict a tenant by unlawful means. It took me time to understand what it meant. Vasu had filed a complaint against me as a landlord. There were also other minor complaints, such as that I was not maintaining the house in a habitable condition, and was involving the said tenant in great loss, damage, and expense.

This involved me in a set of new activities. Up till now I had not known what it was to receive a court summons. I really did not know where to start and what to do next. Litigation was not in my nature. It was a thing I avoided. I had a shuddering fear of courts and lawyers, perhaps from the days when my uncles let them loose on my father and there was no other topic of discussion at home for months on end. I hid the summons away: they had given me three days' time to attend to it – a sort of reprieve. It gave me a feeling of being on parole. I did not confide even in Sastri. I realized that it would be futile to speak about it to anyone: no one was going to understand. Everyone would treat me as if I had done some unlawful act on the sly and was now caught, or trot out the old advice, 'After all it was *you* who agreed to take the man in. You have only yourself to blame.'

The situation seemed so dark that I surrendered myself to a mood of complete resignation. I even began to look relaxed. I attended to my work, listened to jokes and responded to them normally at my press. I counted the days – seventy-two hours more, sixty, twenty-four . . . 'Tomorrow, I shall probably be led off straight from the court to the jail.' Everyone was going to have a surprise. Vasu would chase out Sastri and my customers and utilize my front room and all the rest of the space for arranging his 'art' pieces. People would get used to it in due course, cease to refer to the place as a press, and rather call it a museum. My wife and child would fend for themselves and visit me in prison on permissible days. A strange sense of relief came over me when my mind had been made up on all these issues and I knew where I was going to end. People would no doubt sympathize with me, but always conclude with, 'Who asked him to encourage the man anyway? He brought it all on his own head. Let him not blame others.'

On the last day of my freedom, at dawn, I had gone as usual to the river for a bath and was returning to my house at five-thirty. As usual the adjournment lawyer was on his way to the river. An idea came to me: it had never occurred to me until now that he could be of use. I had only viewed him as a printing customer. Since I had printed his thousand cards, he had been avoiding me – because of the unpaid bill. The marriage was over, and the bill had become stale: after all I didn't charge him more than ninety rupees for the entire lot. These days I never saw him even on my morning walk back from the river. Perhaps he detoured and took a parallel road. But today, as my luck would have it, I came face to face with him.

A great feeling of relief came over me at the sight. 'Ah, my friend,' I cried. 'Just the person I was hoping to meet.'

He looked panic-stricken. Luckily I cornered him at the bend of Kabir Street where the house of the barber abuts the street, and with the storm drain on the other side a man cannot easily slip out if his path is blocked. He said awkwardly, 'Just today I was planning to see you at the press. You know, with one thing and another, after my daughter's marriage . . .'

I felt overjoyed at meeting him, and asked him, 'How is your daughter? Has she joined her husband? How is your son-in-law? How do you fare in the role of a father-in-law?'

He said, 'Most people think that with the wedding all one's troubles are over. It's only half the battle! Ha! Ha!' I laughed in order to please him. I didn't want him to think that I had accosted him so early in the day for my unpaid bill. He said, 'It's only after a marriage that one discovers how vicious one's new relatives can be. How many things they demand and keep demanding! Oh, God.'

'That's true,' I said. 'Taking your daughter up and down to visit her mother-in-law.'

'That I wouldn't mind,' he said. 'After all she is our child; it's my duty to help her travel in comfort.'

'Yes, yes,' I said, wondering what it was that he really minded.

His answer was not long in coming. 'All sorts of things, all sorts of things.' The first rays of the sun touched up the walls of the barber's house with the morning glory. Sparrows and crows were flying already in search of grain and worms. As I watched them a part of my mind reflected how lucky they were to be away from Vasu's attic windows. The lawyer was talking, habituated to rambling on until the court rose for lunch. 'The presents demanded are enough to sink one,' he was saying. 'The new son-in-law must be propitiated all the year round, I suppose,' he went on with grim humour. 'He must be given a present because it's the sixth month after the wedding, because it's the month of Adi, because it is Deepavali, because it is this and that; every time you think of the great man, you must part with a hundred rupees in cash or clothes! It's all an old, silly custom; our women are responsible. I would not blame the young man; what can he do? It's his mother who demands these things and the bride's mother at once responds by nagging her husband. These women know that if a man is sufficiently nagged, he will somehow find the cash.'

'So,' I thought, 'can the good lady be made to take an interest in the payment of my bill?'

The lawyer, as if reading my thought, said, 'Now you know why I could not really come over to see you. In spite of one's best efforts, small payments get left out. In all I had to find about ten thousand rupees for the marriage – savings, borrowings, loans, all kinds of things. Anyway it is all over. I will not have to face a similar bother for at least a decade more. My second daughter is just six years old.'

'That gives you a lot of time,' I said, and I hoped he would now let me say a word about my own problem. But he added, 'I am sorry I kept your bill so long; it escaped my notice.'

'Oh, that's all right,' I said reassuringly. 'I knew you must have been busy. Some of my customers are like a safe-deposit for me; I can ask for my money whenever I want. Don't worry, sir, I would not mistake you. Don't trouble to come to my press. I can send Sastri to collect the amount from you.' This I added out of a sudden apprehension that he might think I was writing off the account. The sun had grown brighter now, and still I had not told him of my problem. I did not know how to make a beginning. He was on the point of moving off, having had his say, when I said quickly, 'I want to see you on a legal matter.'

He drew himself up proudly now. He was on his own ground. He asked brusquely, 'Any more problems coming out of your property matters? I thought they had all been settled once and for all.'

'No, no, it's not that,' I began.

'Or are you thinking of a partnership deed? A lot of business men are having them now, you know.'

'Oh, no, I am not such a big business man.'

'Or estate duty; have you any trouble on that account?'

I laughed. 'Fortunately I own nothing to bring the estate duty on my head.'

'Or Shop Assistants' Act or Sales Tax? You know, half the trouble with Sales Tax problems is due to a lack of definition in the phrasing of the Act. Today I could tweak the nose of any Sales Tax Official who dared to tamper with my client, with all their half-digested manuals!'

'I have a summons from the Rent Controller.'

'What for?' he asked. 'Do you know how many people . . .' he began, but I wrested the initiative from him and cut in. 'It is some fancy summons as you'll see. Can I meet you at home?'

'No,' he said. 'Come to my office.' His office was above a cotton warehouse, or rather a bed-maker's shop, and cotton fluff was always flying about. Clients who went to him once never went there again, as they sneezed interminably and caught their death of cold; asthmatics went down for weeks after a legal consultation. His clients preferred to see him as he lounged about the premises of the district court in search of business, and he tackled their problems standing in the veranda of the court or under the shade of a tamarind tree in the compound. But he liked his inexperienced clients first to meet him at his office and catch a cold. I tried to dodge his proposal, but he was adamant that I should meet him in the narrow room above the cotton shop.

I went sneezing up the wooden stairs. The staircase was narrower than the one leading to my attic devoted to dead wild life, and creaked in a way which dimmed the sneezings of a visitor. Although I was born and bred in the district, this was the first time I had trod Abu Lane, which was only four blocks away from my press, conveniently tucked away from the views and turmoil of Market Road. There you saw his signboard, bleached by time and weather

– Mr . . ., Pleader – nailed to a pillar on which a more aggressive board announced Nandi Cotton Corporation. Inside you saw nothing at first except bales and bales of cotton, and then a heap in a corner with some women beating them into fluff for bed-making. It was this process which spread tuberculosis and asthma among would-be litigants. Our lawyer's chamber was right on the landing, which had been converted into a room, with one table, one chair, and one bureau full of law-books. His clients had to stand before him and talk. The table was covered with dusty paper bundles, old copies of law reports, a dry ink-well, an abandoned pen, and his black alpaca coat, going moss-green with age, hung by a nail on the wall. Down below, the cotton-fluffers kept up a rhythmic beating. He had a very tiny window with wooden bars behind him, and through it one saw the coconut tree by a neighbouring house, a kitchen chimney smoking, and a number of sloping roof-tiles, smoky and dusty, with pieces of tinsel thrown away by someone gleaming in the bright sun.

'Allergy?' he cried on seeing me. My sneezings had announced my arrival. I stepped in, blowing my nose and rubbing my eyes. There was a beatific smile on his face, and his single tooth was exposed. He sat at the table and commented, 'Some people suffer from allergy to dust and cotton. But I never notice such things.' He seemed to feel that his superior physique had come about through a special arrangement between himself and God, and he enjoyed the sight of allergy in others as if it gave him an assurance that God was especially good to him. 'Allergy, they say, is just mental, that's all,' he said. 'It is something you should overcome by your own resolution,' he added grandly. I stood in front of his table like a supplicant, and placed before him the brown document. He put on his spectacles, opened the paper, spread it out with the palm of his hand, put a weight on it (the inkless bottle), reared back his head in order to adjust his vision, and read. His unshaven jowl and chin sparkled as if dusted over with silver powder.

He sighed deeply. 'Of course, you have given him no sort of receipt?'

'Receipt? What for?' I asked.

'For the rent, I mean. I suppose you have been sensible enough not to take a cheque from him?'

I was appalled. He was falling into the same pattern of thought as a dozen others, including my wife. I declared, 'I have not rented him the house.'

'Have you taken a lump sum?' he asked.

'Look here, he is not my tenant.'

'Whose tenant is he then?' he asked, cross-examining me.

'I don't know. I can't say.' I was losing my equanimity. Why were people so pig-headed as not to know or want to understand my position? My legs felt heavy with climbing the ladder, and he would not give me a seat. He seemed to delight in punishing people who came to see him. I could hardly recognize my own voice, it sounded so thick with cotton dust.

The man was pursuing his inquiry. 'If he is not your tenant, what is he?'

'He is not a tenant, but a . . . friend,' I said, almost unable to substitute any other word.

He was quick to catch it. 'Friend! Oh! Oh! What sort of friend is he to file a complaint against you! This is a fairly serious offence according to the present Housing Act. Why could you not have straightaway gone through the usual formalities, that is . . .'

'Stop! Stop!' I cried. 'I swear that I gave him the attic free, absolutely free, because he asked for it.'

'If I were a judge, I would not believe you. Why should you let him live with you? Is he a relative?'

'No, thank God; it's the only thing that is good about the present situation.'

'Are you indebted to him in any way?'

'No. On the contrary, he should feel himself in debt to me, and yet he doesn't hesitate to have me hanged!' I cried. I explained to him at length how Vasu had come in search of me and how it had all come about. Feeling that perhaps the lawyer was too sympathetic to my enemy, I tried to win him over by saying, 'You remember that day when you came to have the wedding invitations printed, and how he pulled me out and left you – that's how he does everything. Now you understand what he is capable of.'

That prejudiced him. He reflected with bitterness. 'And I had to sit there and waste a whole day to no purpose.' He spoke to me on many legal technicalities, and took charge of my summons. He pulled out of a drawer a sheet of paper and took my signature. Then he put everything away with relief, 'I'll deal with it; don't worry yourself any more about it. How much money have you now?'

'Not an anna,' I said, and emptied my pockets to prove it. He looked gloomy at this bankruptcy.

'I would not charge more than a minimum, you know. Some routine charges have to be paid – stamp charges, affidavit charges, and coffee charges for the bench clerk. He is the man to help us, you know.'

'Oh, how?'

'Don't ask questions. Now I'm wondering how to pay these charges, absolutely nominal, you know. Even if you can spare about five rupees . . .'

'I thought since . . . since you have . . . you might adjust your accounts.'

He threw up his arms in horror, 'Oh, no, absolutely different situations. Don't mix up accounts, whatever else you may do. It always leads to trouble. Can't you send someone to your press to fetch your purse, if you have left it there?'

I felt like banging my fist on his table and demanding immediate settlement of my account, but I felt humbled by circumstances; the lawyer must save me from prison. So I said, 'If you will manage it somehow, I will send the amount to your house as soon as I'm back at the press.'

'I am not going home. There is no time today for me to go to court if I go home, and so, I don't want to seem to trouble you too much, but one oughtn't to start out on a business like this without cash of any kind.'

'I came only to consult you,' I said.

'I hope you have found it satisfactory,' he replied ceremoniously.

'Yes, of course,' I said. I felt like a pauper petitioning for help. How long would he keep me standing like this? I could not afford to be critical. So I asked breezily, 'Now what is to be done?'

'First things first.' He studied the sheet of paper intently. 'The summons is for 11 a.m. Tuesday the 24th; today is Monday the 23rd. It is 10.30 now. I must file your application for non-appearance almost at once. The ruling gives twenty-four hours if a summons is to be non-responded. It would have been a different matter if you had dodged the summons. Did you sign that little paper the fellow had?'

'Yes, of course.'

'Ah, inexperience, inexperience,' he cried. 'You should have consulted me before touching it or looking at it.'

'I had no idea it was coming,' I said, putting into my voice all the shock I had felt at Vasu's treachery.

'That's true, that's true,' he said. 'You must have thought it was some printing business from the district court, ha?'

'Now, is that all?' I asked.

'H'm, yes,' he said. 'I can always depend upon the bench clerk to help me. I'll do what I can. You must feel happy if you are not on the list tomorrow. I'll have to plead that you are away and need more time or notice.'

'But everybody can see me at my press,' I pleaded.

'Oh, yes, that's a point. But how can the court take cognizance if you are there? In any event, it'll be better if you don't make yourself too conspicuous during the hours of the court sitting.'

'Except when I am called out, I'm usually behind the blue curtain,' I said.

'That's good, it is always helpful,' he said.

'And what's the next step?'

'You will be free for at least four weeks. Rent court is rather overworked nowadays. They won't be able to re-issue the summons for at least four weeks.' I felt grateful to the man for saving my neck for four weeks; but now he added a doubt. 'Perhaps the complainant will file an objection.'

'He may also say that I've not gone anywhere, as he lives right over my head.'

'But the court is not bound to take cognizance of what he says. It's not that way that your *mala fides* can be established.'

I didn't understand what he meant.

'I have some work now,' I said apologetically. I did not want to hurt his feelings with the least hint that I didn't like to be kept standing there while he talked; as a matter of fact my legs were paining me.

'You may go,' he said grandly. 'I'll be back home at three o'clock. I will manage it all somehow. If you are sending anyone at all to my house, send an envelope with ten rupees in it. Anyway I'll give you a complete accounting when it is all over.'

The proof of the lawyer's handiwork: I was sitting unscathed at my press, printing three-colour labels, on the day following my D-day. I gladly sent him ten rupees through Sastri. He would account for it all at the end. I was not to mix up accounts. Great words of wisdom they seemed to me in my fevered state.

Chapter Six

Fifteen days passed uneventfully. We left each other alone. I heard Vasu come and go. His jeep would arrive at the yard, I could hear that mighty fist pulling at the brake, and feet stumping upstairs. Amidst all his impossible qualities, he had just one virtue: he never tried to come to my part of the house; he arrived and departed as he liked. Only the stench of drying leather was on the increase. It disturbed the neighbourhood. I had a visitor from the health department, one fine day – a man in khaki uniform. He was a sanitary inspector whose main business was to keep the city clean, a hard job for a man in a place like Malgudi, where the individual jealously guarded his right to independent action.

The sanitary inspector had the habit of occasionally dropping in at my press and sitting in a chair quietly when his limbs ached from too much supervision of the Market Road. He would take off his pith helmet (I think he was the only one in the whole town who had such headgear, having picked it up at an army disposal store), place it on the chair next to him, wipe his brow with a check-coloured handkerchief, sigh and pant and call for a glass of water. I could not say he was a friend, but a friendly man. Today, he leaned his bicycle on the front step of my press, and came in saying, 'There is a complaint against you.' He produced an envelope from his pocket and took out a sheet of paper, and held it to me.

I was beginning to dread the sight of brown envelopes nowadays. A joint petition from my neighbours, signed by half a dozen names, had been presented to the municipal authority. They complained that on my terrace they noticed strange activities – animal hides being tanned; the petitioners pointed out that the tanning and curing of skins should be prohibited in a residential area as it gave rise to bad odour and insanitary surroundings. They also complained of carrion birds hovering around my terrace. One part of my mind admired my neighbours for caring so much for sanitation; the rest of it was seized with cold despair.

I requested the inspector to take a seat and asked what he expected me to do. He said, 'Can I have a glass of water?' I called Sastri to fetch water. The sanitary inspector said, after gulping it down in one

65

mouthful (he was the most parched and dehydrated man I had ever seen in my life), 'By-law X definitely prohibits the tanning of leather indiscriminately in dwelling areas; By-law Y specifies exactly where you can conduct such a business. I did not know you were engaged in this activity. Why? Is your press not paying enough?'

I slapped my brow with my palm in sheer despair. 'I have not turned tanner!' I cried. 'I am still a printer. What makes you think I'm not?'

'Where is the harm?' asked the inspector. 'There is dignity in every profession. You don't have to be ashamed of it, only you must carry it on at the proper spot without violating the by-laws.'

'All right, I'll do so,' I said meekly.

'Oh, good, you will co-operate with us! That is the difference between educated people and uneducated ones. You can grasp our problems immediately. Of course people will do wrong things out of ignorance. How can we expect everyone to be versed in municipal by-laws? I never blame a man for not knowing the regulations, but I'm really upset if people don't mend their ways even after a notice has been issued. May I have another glass of water, please?'

'Oh, surely, as many as you want. Mr Sastri, another glass of water.' I could hear Sastri put away the urgent job he was doing and prepare to fetch the glass.

The inspector emptied the second supply at one gulp and rose to go. He said in parting, 'I'll send off an endorsement to the parties, something to silence them.'

'What will you say?' I asked, a sudden curiosity getting the upper hand.

'We have a printed form, which will go to them to say that the matter is receiving attention. That is enough to satisfy most parties. Otherwise they'll bombard us with reminders.'

I saw him off on the last step of my press. He clutched the handlebars of his bicycle, stood for a moment thinking and said, 'Take your time to shift, but don't be too long. If you get a notice, please send a reply to say that you are shifting your tanning business elsewhere and pray for time.'

'Yes, sir,' I said, 'I'll certainly do all that you say.' I was beginning to realize that it was futile to speak about any matter to anyone. People went about with fixed notions and seldom listened to anything I said. It was less strenuous to let them cherish their own silly ideas.

*

The septuagenarian came along, tapping his stick; he stood in the road, looked up through his glasses, shading his eyes with one hand, and asked in a querulous voice, 'Is Nataraj in?' The usual crowd was there. 'Now is the testing time for Nehru,' the journalist was saying. 'If the Chinese on our border are not rolled back –' The poet had brought the next canto of his poem and was waiting to give me a summary of it. The septuagenarian asked again, 'Is Nataraj here?' unable to see inside owing to the glare.

'Yes, yes, I'm here,' I cried, and went down to help him up the steps.

He seated himself and looked at the other two. 'Your friends? I may speak freely, I suppose?' I introduced them to him, whereupon he expatiated on the qualities of a poet, and his duties and social relationships, and then turned to me with the business on hand. 'Nataraj, you know my grandson had a pet – a dog that he had kept for two years. He was very much devoted to it, and used to play with it the moment he came back from school.' I almost foresaw what was coming. 'Someone killed it last night. It lay under the street-lamp shot through the heart; someone seems to have shot it with a gun. Who has a gun here in these parts? I thought no one but the police had guns.'

'Why did you let it out?'

'Why? I don't know. It generally jumps over the wall and goes around the neighbourhood. It was a harmless dog, only barking all night, sitting under that street-lamp. I don't know what makes these dogs bark all night. They say that ghosts are visible to the eyes of a dog. Is it true? Do you believe in ghosts?'

'I haven't been able to see any,' I began.

'Oh, that's all right. Most people don't see them. Why should they? What was I saying?' he asked pathetically, having lost track of his own sentence. I was loath to remind him. I hesitated and wavered, hoping that he'd forget the theme of the dead dog and concentrate on the ghosts. But the journalist said, 'You were speaking about the dog, sir.'

'Ah, yes, yes. I could not bear to see its corpse, and so I asked the scavenger to take it away. I don't know what you call that breed. We called it Tom and it was black and hairy, very handsome; someone brought it from Bombay and gave it to my son, who gave it to this little fellow – quite a smart dog, very watchful, would make such a row if anyone tried to enter our gate, would wait for me to get up from my morning prayer, because he knew he would get a piece of the bread I eat in the morning. For the last three years doctors have ordered me to eat only bread, one slice of it. Before that I used to take *idli* every day, but they think it's not good for me. My father lived to be a hundred and never missed *idli* even for a single day.' He remained silently thinking of those days.

I was glad he was not asking to be reminded of his main theme. I hoped he would get up and go away. Everyone maintained a respectful, gloomy silence. If it had continued another minute, he would have risen and I'd have helped him down the steps. But just at the crucial moment Sastri came in with a proof for my approval. As soon as he entered by the curtain, instead of handing me the proof and disappearing he stood arrested for a minute, staring at the old man. 'What was all that commotion at your gate this morning? I was coming to the press and had no time to stop and ask. But I saw your grandchild crying.'

'Oh, is that you, Sastri?' asked the old man, shrinking his eyes to slits in order to catch his features. 'How are you, Sastri? It's many months since I saw you. What are you doing? Yes, of course I know you are working with Nataraj. How do you find his work, Nataraj? Good? Must be good. His uncle was my class-mate, and he had married the third daughter of . . . He used to come and play with my nephew. Where do you live, Sastri? Not near us?' Sastri mentioned his present address. 'Oh, that is far off Vinayak Street; ah, how many centuries it seems to me since I went that way. Come and see me some time, I'll be pleased.'

Sastri seemed pleased to be thus invited. He said, 'I must, I must come some time.'

'How many children have you?' Sastri mentioned the number, at which the old man looked gratified and said, 'Bring them also along when you come. I'd like to see them.'

Instead of saying 'Yes' and shutting up, Sastri said, 'Even this morning I could have come for a moment, but there was too much of a crowd at your gate.'

'Oh, idiot Sastri! What on earth are you becoming so loquacious for?' I muttered to myself. 'Leave him alone to forget this morning's crowd.'

But he had stirred up mischief. 'Didn't you know why there was a crowd?'

'No, I only saw your grandchild crying. I was in a hurry.'

The reminder of his grandchild nearly brought the septuagenarian to the verge of a breakdown. The old man almost sobbed, 'That boy is refusing to cheer up. I can't bear to see the youngster in such misery.'

'Why? Why? What happened?' asked Sastri.

'Someone had shot his pet dog,' said the journalist.

'Shot! Shot!' cried Sastri as if he had been poked with the butt of a rifle. 'When? Was it shot dead? Oh, poor dog! I have often seen it at your gate, the black one!' Why was he bent upon adding fuel to the fire? 'Do you know who could have shot it?' he asked menacingly.

'For what purpose?' said the old man. 'It's not going to help us. Will it bring Tom back to life?'

But Sastri insisted on enlightening him. He gave the old man the killer's name, whereabouts, and situation, and added, 'He is just the man who could have done it.'

The old man tapped his staff on the floor and shouted at me, 'And yet you said nothing? Why? Why?'

'It didn't occur to me, that is all,' I said hollowly. The old man tapped the floor with his staff and cried, 'Show me where he is, I'll deal with him. I'll hand him over to the police for shooting at things. What's your connection with him? Is he related to you? Is he your friend?' I tried to pacify the old man, but he ignored my words. 'In all my eighty years, this is the first time I have heard of a shooting in our street. Who is this man? Why should you harbour him? Tomorrow he'll aim his gun at the children playing in the street!'

Knowing Vasu's style of speech with children, I could agree with the old man's views. The old man's hands and legs trembled, his face was flushed. I feared he might have a stroke and collapse in my press – anything seemed possible in my press these days. I said, 'Be calm, sir, it will not do to get excited. It's not good for you.'

'If it's not good for me, let me die. Why should anything be good for me? Death will be more welcome to me than the sight of my unhappy grandson.'

'I'll get him another dog, sir, please tell him that, a beautiful black one. I promise.'

'Can you?' asked the old man, suddenly calming down. 'Are you sure? You know where one is to be found?'

'Oh, yes,' I said, 'the easiest thing. I know many planters who have dogs, and I can always get a puppy for our little friend.'

'Will you accompany me now and say that to him?'

'Oh, surely,' I said, rising.

Sastri chose just this moment to thrust the proof before me and ask, 'Shall I put it on the machine?'

I didn't want anything to stop the old man from getting up and going, so I said, 'Wait a moment, I'll be back.' But Sastri would not allow me to go. 'If you pass this proof, we can print it off, everything is ready. They are shutting off power at eleven o'clock today. If we don't deliver . . .'

'Oh, Sastri, leave everything alone. I don't care what happens. I must see the child first and comfort him.' I was desperately anxious that the old man should be bundled off before someone or other should offer to point Vasu out to him.

As Vasu became more aloof, he became more indifferent, and everything that he did looked like a challenge to me. I was, I suppose, getting into a state of abnormal watchfulness myself; even the sound of his footstep seemed to me aggressively tenant-like, strengthened by the laws of the rent-control court. He pretended that I did not exist. He seemed to arrive and depart with a swagger as if to say, 'You may have got an adjournment now, but the noose is being made ready for you.'

He brought in more and more dead creatures; there was no space for him in his room or on the terrace. Every inch of space must have been cluttered with packing-boards and nails and skins and moulds. The narrow staircase, at which I could peep from my machine, was getting filled up with his merchandise, which had now reached the last step – he had left just enough margin for himself to move up and down. He had become very busy these days, arriving, departing, hauling up or hauling down packing-cases, doing everything single-handed. I had no idea where his market was. In other days I could have asked him, but now we were bitter enemies. I admired him for his capacity for work, for all the dreadful things he was able to accomplish single-handed. If I had been on speaking terms, I'd have congratulated him unreservedly on his success as a taxidermist – his master Suleiman must really have been as great as he described him. He had given his star pupil expert training in all branches of his work. Short of creating the animals, he did everything.

Vasu was a perfect enemy. When I caught a glimpse of him sometimes when I stood at the treadle, he averted his head and passed, perhaps stamping his feet and muttering a curse. He seemed to be flourishing. I wondered why he should not pay me the charges for printing his forms and letterheads. How to ask him? I did not want to do anything that might madden him further and worsen our relationship.

I was beginning to miss his rough company. I often speculated if there could be some way of telling him that all was well, that he should not give another thought to what had happened between us, that he could stay in my house as long as he pleased ('only don't bring too many carcasses or keep them too long, this is a fussy neighbourhood, you know'). I could never be a successful enemy to anyone. Any enmity worried me night and day. As a schoolboy I persistently shadowed around the one person with whom I was supposed to be on terms of hate and hostility. I felt acutely uneasy as long as our enmity lasted. I was never more than a few paces away from him as we started home from school. I sat on a bench immediately behind him and tried to attract his attention by coughing and clearing my throat or by brushing against his back while picking up a pencil deliberately dropped on the floor. I made myself abject in order to win a favourable look or word from my enemy and waited for a chance to tell him that I wanted to be friends with him. It bothered me like a toothache. I was becoming aware of the same mood developing in me now. I was longing for a word with Vasu. I stood like a child at the treadle, hoping he would look at me and nod and that all would be well again. He was a terrible specimen of human being no doubt, but I wanted to be on talking terms with him. This was a complex mood. I couldn't say that I liked him or approved of anything he said or did, but I didn't want to be repulsed by him. My mind seethed with plans as to how to re-establish cordiality. I was torn between my desire to make a grand gesture, such as writing off his print bill, and my inability to adopt it – as I didn't like the idea of writing off anything. I liked to delude myself that I collected my moneys strictly and never let anyone get away with it. So I decided not to rake up the question of the bill with Vasu until a smiling relationship could once again be established between us and I could refer to the question in a humorous way.

While I was in this state of mental confusion, Sastri came up with a new problem. There was a hyena at the foot of the stairs, the sight of which upset him while he was composing the admission cards of Albert Mission High School. I was sitting at my usual place when he parted the curtain and cried, 'How can I do any work with a wolf and a whatnot staring at me? And there's a python hanging down the handrail of the stairs.'

'Sastri, I saw it; it is not a wolf but a hyena. Don't you think it surprising and interesting that we should have all this life around us in Malgudi? They are all from Mempi hills!'

The educational value of it was lost on Sastri. He simply said, 'Maybe, but why should they be here? Can't you do something about it? It's repulsive and there is always a bad smell around – all my life I have tried to keep this press so clean!'

I could see that Sastri was greatly exercised. It was no use joking with him or trying to make him take a lighter view. I feared that he might take steps himself, if I showed indifference. He might call to Vasu through the grille that separated us and order him to be gone with the wolf. I didn't want Sastri to risk his life, so I said placatingly, 'Sastri, you know the old proverb, that when your cloth is caught in the thorns of a bush, you have to extricate yourself gently and little by little, otherwise you will never take the cloth whole?'

Sastri, being an orthodox-minded Sanskrit semi-scholar, appreciated this sentiment and the phrases in which it was couched; he set it off with another profounder one in Sanskrit which said that to deal with a *rakshasa* one must possess the marksmanship of a hunter, the wit of a pundit, and the guile of a harlot. He quoted a verse to prove it.

'But the trouble is that the marksmanship is with him, not with us. Anyway, he'll soon deplete the forest of all its creatures, and then he will have to turn to a tame life, and our staircase will be clear again.'

'He shows all the definitions of a *rakshasa*,' persisted Sastri, and went on to define the make-up of a *rakshasa*, or a demoniac creature who possessed enormous strength, strange powers, and genius, but recognized no sort of restraints of man or God. He said, 'Every *rakshasa* gets swollen with his ego. He thinks he is invincible, beyond every law. But sooner or later something or other will destroy him.' He stood expatiating on the lives of various demons in *puranas* to prove his point. He displayed great versatility and knowledge. I found his talk enlightening, but still felt he might continue with the printing of the school admission cards, which were due to be delivered seventy-two hours hence; however, I had not the heart to remind him of sordid things.

He went on; his information was encyclopaedic. He removed his silver-rimmed spectacles and put them away in his shirt pocket as being an impediment to his discourse. 'There was Ravana, the protagonist in Ramayana, who had ten heads and twenty arms, and enormous yogic and physical powers, and a boon from the gods that he could never be vanquished. The earth shook under his tyranny. Still he came to a sad end. Or take Mahisha, the *asura* who meditated and acquired a boon of immortality and invincibility, and who had secured an especial favour that every drop of blood shed from his body should give rise to another demon in his own image and strength, and who nevertheless was destroyed. The Goddess with six arms, each bearing a different weapon, came riding for the fight on a lion which sucked every drop of blood drawn from the demon. Then there was Bhasmasura, who acquired a special boon that everything he touched should be scorched, while nothing could ever destroy him. He made humanity suffer. God Vishnu was incarnated as a dancer of great beauty, named Mohini, with whom the *asura* became infatuated. She promised to yield to him only if he imitated all the gestures and movements of her own dancing. At one point in the dance Mahini placed her palms on her head, and the demon followed this gesture in complete forgetfulness and was reduced to ashes that very second, the blighting touch becoming active on his own head. Every man can think that he is great and will live for ever, but no one can guess from which quarter his doom will come.'

Vasu seemed to have induced in Sastri much philosophical thought. Before leaving, his parting anecdote was, 'Or think of Daksha, for whom an end was prophesied through the bite of a snake, and he had built himself an island fortress to evade this fate, and yet in the end . . .' and so on and so forth, which was very encouraging for me too, as I felt that everything would pass and that my attic would be free. I hoped we would part on speaking terms, but Sastri did not think it necessary. I was glad he left me suddenly without asking me to throw out the hyena, having found a solution to his problem through his own research and talk. He vanished behind the curtain as he suddenly remembered that he had left the machine idle and that the ink on the plate was drying.

My aim now was to save the situation from becoming worse and gradually to come back to a hallo-saying stage with Vasu. I was glad I had warded off the danger emanating from Sastri, but this gratification was short-lived. Sastri himself seemed to take a detached, synoptic view of the hyena and other creatures on the other side of the grille. He got quite busy with the admission cards and left me alone, and I thought I had given a rest to the problem of Vasu and might some time be able to greet him. But it was not destined to be. One fine morning, the forester came to my press to ask if Vasu was still with me. I thought he had come to get his book of morals printed, and said, 'I have not forgotten my promise, but just as soon as I am able to complete all the work . . .'

He didn't seem interested, but said, 'All right, I am in no hurry about anything, but I am here on official work. Is Vasu still here? If he is I'd like to speak to him.' A sudden doubt assailed me whether it would be safe to be involved in this. The forester might have come as a friend, or he might not. So I said dodgingly, 'I'm not seeing much of Vasu nowadays, although he lives upstairs. He seems to be very busy nowadays . . .'

'With what?'

I became cautious. 'I don't know, I see him coming and going. He has his own business.'

'Has he? That's what I want to find out. Would you answer some questions?'

'No,' I said point-blank. 'I wish to have nothing to do with anything that concerns him.'

'Rather strange!' he said. He had seemed such a timid moralistic man some months ago when he visited me. It was a surprise for me to find him adopting a tough tone. He continued, 'He is your tenant, as everybody knows, and he claims your friendship, and yet you disclaim all knowledge of him? Is it believable?'

'Yes. You should believe what I say. Won't you sit down and talk?'

'No, I'm spending Government hours now. I'm here on official duty, and they are certainly not paying me to lounge in your chair. I must get busy with what I came for.' This thin cadaverous man, whose neck shot straight out of his khaki like a thin cylindrical water-pipe, was tough. He said, 'Any man who violates the game laws is my enemy. I wouldn't hesitate to shoot him if I had a chance. A lot of game has been vanishing from our reserves and even tigers disappear from the blocks. Where do they go?'

'Perhaps to other forests for a change,' I said.

He laughed. It was a good joke in his view. I hoped that humour would establish a bond between us.

'That shows your ignorance of wild life.'

I felt relieved that he recognized my ignorance. That would certainly induce him to view me with greater toleration and absolve me from all responsibility for what Vasu was doing. He recovered his composure, as if he realized that he ought not to spoil me by smiling too much, and suddenly compressed his lips into a tight narrow line and became grim. He said, 'Joking apart, I shall lose my job if I don't track down this mischief going on in the forests of Mempi. Somebody is busy with his gun.'

'Can't you keep a watch?' I asked.

'Yes, but in a forest of hundreds of miles you can't watch every inch of ground, especially if the thief operates at night. Some of our guards are none too honest. We rely in some places on the jungle dwellers, and they are not wholly dependable. I must first have a talk with your tenant.'

'He is not my tenant. I take no rent from him.'

'Then he must be your friend.' I recognized the pincer-movement in which this man was trying to trap me as all the others had done.

I said, 'He is not even my friend. I never knew him before he came here.' This sounded even worse – much better remain his friend or landlord than his business associate. I could see the cadaverous face hardening with suspicion.

He thought over the situation for a moment, and asked, 'Why don't you help me?'

'In what way?'

'I want to get at this man who is destroying game. Can't you give me some clues?'

We had come around to the same starting point, and I said, 'I wish to have nothing whatever to do with this business of yours. Leave me out of it. What makes you think I should have anything to do with it?'

'Since you are not his friend, why don't you help me?'

'I am not your friend either,' I said.

It seemed silly to carry on a vague talk on friendship like this early in the day, while the Market Road traffic was flowing by and the treadle was rolling nicely on the admission cards. I said with an air of finality, 'If you like to rest, come in and take a chair.'

'Do I go through here to reach his room?'

'No, it's blocked this way. He has his own door . . .'

He stepped down without a word and went away. I could read his mind. He was now convinced that I was a joint owner of the poaching and stuffing factory. He went out with an expression that said when the time came he'd round up the gang.

I heard him go up the staircase and knock on the door. Vasu was unused to having visitors. He shouted from inside, 'Who is it?'

I heard the other reply,-'I wish to see you for a minute. Open the door, please.'

'I asked who you are; what is your name?'

'I am Ramaswami. I want to see you.'

'Ramaswami, whoever you may be, go down and wait near my jeep. I will be coming down in a short time.'

'Why don't you let me in now?'

Vasu shouted from inside, 'Don't stand there and argue. Get out and wait.'

I heard the forester go down the stairs, pausing for a moment to study the hyena. Half an hour later, steps once again came tumbling down the stairs, and voices sounded from the yard where the jeep was parked. 'So you are Ramaswami, are you? To what do I owe the honour of this visit?'

I had to follow all the conversation through the wall at my back and it filtered their exchanges into the lower octaves. I stood on a chair and opened a ventilator high up on the back wall in order to follow their conversation better. The cadaver was repeating his statement about the disappearance of game from Mempi Forest. All that Vasu said was, 'Why not?' The other merely remarked, 'Game in the sanctuaries is expected to be preserved.'

'Of course it will be preserved if you get help from a taxidermist who knows his job,' said Vasu jocularly.

The cadaver seemed a match for Vasu. 'Well, we may not get the taxidermist's services, but the taxidermist himself.'

By this time Vasu had climbed into his seat in the jeep, the forester standing beside it. What a contrast to the first day when he brought the forest official into my office and sat him down and flattered him as a noble writer!

'We will watch, and when we get at the man who is depleting the reserve, well, the law is pretty clear on that —'

'If your department needs my co-operation in any matter, don't hesitate to tell me,' said Vasu with that crude cynicism he was capable of. The forester ignored it, but said, 'How do you account for the hyena you have on the staircase?'

'The hyena came in search of me. I shot it right where you are standing now,' he said.

'What about . . .?'

'What about what? Nothing that's all. I am not bound to say anything.'

'From which forest did you get them?'

'Not from your jungle. Go and look again and see if there is any trade-mark on them proving that they are from Mempi. India is a big country with many jungles, and you can get everything everywhere. For your information, I've also some tiger-skins. Are they yours? Claim them if you can. I am hungry, and am going out for breakfast. No time to waste. Don't bother me unless you come with some more practical proposition.' He drove off unceremoniously. The forester stood where he was for a second and moved away.

Nothing happened for two days. I was in my usual chair one afternoon when Vasu's jeep pulled up at my door. My heart gave a thump. He sat in his jeep and said, 'Nataraj, come here.' I had an impulse to drop whatever I was doing, rush up to him and seize the chance to make friends with the monster again. But my pride was stronger. I suddenly resented all the trouble he had caused me. 'Come and speak if you have anything to say.' I was amazed at my own temerity.

He grinned, 'Ah, you are showing some spirit after all, that's good.'

I didn't like the paternal tone he adopted. I asked again, 'What is your business with me? I'm rather busy.'

'Yes, yes,' he said mockingly. 'I see it, and it's good to see a man do an honest job at his office instead of chatting away the time with friends who treat the place as a club lounge.' This was a reference to my two friends who had come to see me after a long time. He went on shouting from his jeep, 'I appreciate your guts, Nataraj. I had thought that you were rather spineless. I now know that you have a spine. I'd never have dreamt that you would set that ghost in khaki on me! You were smart to think it up. So that's your move; you want to know what I'll do next?'

'No, I'm not interested. I'm busy.'

'You showed him the way to my room. He sees all the things there. What of it? Ask your friends to put a rubber-stamp on the backs of all the beasts in Mempi, so that he may identify them later and not make a fool of himself, and not make a fool of you either.' He drove off.

Sen said, 'I don't envy your luck in getting a man like that to live with.'

I wondered what Vasu's menacing words might mean. Legally he had trapped me at the Rent Controller's court, and the adjournment lawyer was handling the case, every now and then tapping me for a five or ten, but I found that he was satisfied even if I gave him just a couple of rupees, and made no mention of the money he owed me for printing his daughter's wedding card. I thought Vasu had done his worst, but now what did he mean? I hoped he was not planning to abduct my son and hold him to ransom. He might be up to anything. That evening I told my wife, 'If you have any urgent business to call me, wait till I come home. Don't send the little fellow across.'

She grew nervous and asked, 'Why?'

I just said, 'I don't want him to come there and make a fuss, that's all.'

'You see so little of him,' she complained, and added, 'You leave before he wakes, and come home after he is asleep, and if he wants to see his father he mustn't even come to the press, I suppose?' Then I had to explain and she grew really frightened.

She was in a panic. She kept the front door shut. She was completely demoralized if the boy did not come home at six. She behaved as if the monster would be unleashed and come rushing in to swallow up the family if the back door of my press was opened. My son seemed to enjoy the thrill of the situation as long as there was daylight. He spoke to his friends about the dangers that surrounded his life, and I saw batches of schoolboys standing around in knots in front of my press, looking up at the attic window during the afternoon recess at school. I became curious and beckoned to a couple of children to come in. 'What are you all doing here?'

'Nothing,' said one of them. 'We are going home from school.'

'What are you looking for?' I asked.

'Babu said there was, was . . . some giant here . . .'

'You want to look at him?' They nodded. 'Better not. Go home, boys. There is no such creature here.' I was anxious they should not see Vasu, as they might shout and circle round him and infuriate him. Knowing his attitude to children, I did not want to risk a meeting between them. One of them asked, slyly, 'Is it true that he eats dogs?'

'Oh, no,' I said immediately. 'He eats rice and other stuff just as we do. That's all false.'

'Then why did he shoot Ramu's dog?'

'Oh, that! It was shot by mistake. He was expecting a black bear and had his gun ready, but at the same time this dog came . . .'

'It was called Lily,' said one boy. The other contradicted, 'No, it was Tom.'

'No, it's Lily,' persisted the first. 'Yes, what'll you give me if it is Lily? Shall we go and ask Ramu?'

'Yes, come on,' and both ran off as if they were a couple of birds

78

that had alighted at the window and were flying off. Two other children who were watching the scene also ran off happily shouting, 'Let us ask Ramu.'

My son came up with Ramu one afternoon two days later. Ramu said, 'My grandfather asked me to see you.' My son added, 'He has come to ask for his dog.' Several weeks had gone by since I had promised the septuagenarian that I'd replace his grandson's dog. Although at that time it had seemed a perfectly feasible thing to find another dog, as days passed it began to look more and more difficult. I had promised in a moment of emotional stress, and now in the cold light of day it appeared to me an unreal, impossible task. I did not know how to acquire a puppy or where one was to be had. I had no doubt mentioned some planter with a dog. I had had in mind Achappa, a coffee planter on Mempi, for whose estates I used to do printing work at one time. I remembered his saying that he had a Great Dane pair with nine puppies. Did I need one? That was years ago. Achappa was not to be seen nowadays; occasionally his manager was observed at my neighbour's press.

I walked across to the Star and said, 'If you see anyone from Consolidated Estates, please call me.' He replied that it was months since he had seen anyone from Consolidated Estates and suspected that Achappa was getting his printing done at Madras. So there it was. The dog-sources were drying up. I needed some expert help in the matter. My sincerity was unquestionable, but my resources were poor. I had no time either. Every day the boy came to my press and said, 'My grandfather asked me to see you.' And every day I gave him some reply and sent him off. It was becoming a mechanical action. And the boy went away satisfied with any answer I gave. My intentions were absolutely honest, but the press work was heavy nowadays and I did not have a moment to spare. In addition to other work Sen was giving me manifestoes to print and the poet was fetching his cantos with greater speed. With one thing and another my time flew swiftly each day. I had to work hard and make enough money at least to pay the lawyer whenever he held his hand out for cash! I had not given up hopes of recovering my dues from him, but I obeyed his advice not to mix up accounts.

I had no time actually to go out and seek a dog for the boy, but I had several plans in my head. I'd make a list of all my friends with dogs, tabulate each breed, note down their breeding time, make one of them promise to give one of the litter to me, make a round of visits every Sunday afternoon, and finally pick up a dog for the young fellow. My son asked me at nights while he nestled close to me (when night advanced the fear of the monster grew in him and he refused to sleep in a separate bed), as if he were a sharer of my dream, 'Get me a puppy too, Father, when you get one for Ramu.'

'Yes, yes,' I said. 'Why not?'

At the hyena's corner one day Sastri heard the jingling of bangles and turned to see a woman go down the steps and out of the building. He had been at the machine. I was in the front office, and presently the curtain parted and he peeped in. A look at his face and I knew something was wrong – some matter referring to Vasu. His face was slightly flushed and his spectacles wobbled as he raised and lowered his brow. There was no need for preambles and so I asked straightaway, 'What is the latest?'

He swallowed once or twice before saying, 'All sorts of low-class women are wandering around this press nowadays . . .'

'Where? Who are they?'

He flourished his arms upward, and I knew he was indicating not the heavens, but Vasu. I did not like to pursue the subject because I had a couple of visitors waiting to discuss a printing job. 'Sastri, I will be with you in a moment . . .'

He took my hint and vanished into the wings. After persuading my would-be customers to patronize the original Heidelberg, I went in to conduct the research with Sastri. He was printing the leaves of a bank ledger with a sullen face. I had never seen him so worried before. Even the first shock of finding a hyena beyond the grille had been nothing to what he seemed to face now. I stood beside him without a word except to sound bossy, 'There is too much ink. Watch the inking.'

He ignored my fussy advice and said, 'If this sort of thing goes on, our reputation in the town will be ruined. I saw Rangi going downstairs. Is she the sort of person we should encourage here? Is this a printing press or what?'

'Who is Rangi?'

He looked desperate, shy, and angry. I was enjoying his discomfiture immensely.

'Oh, you are asking as if you didn't know!'

'How should you expect me to know anything of Rangi, Sastri? I have so much to do!'

'As if I had nothing else to do.'

'I don't know anything about these people.'

'Best thing under the circumstances . . . We should not have this kind of person seen in a place like this, that's all.'

'I don't know what you are saying, Sastri. What is it all about?'

'That man has started bringing disreputable people here; where shall we be?'

I had no answer. Little by little I got it out of him. Rangi was a notorious character of the town. She lived in the shadows of Abu Lane. She was the daughter of Padma, an old dancer attached to the temple of God Krishna four streets off, our ancient temple. Padma herself had been an exemplary, traditional dedicated woman of the temple, who could sing and dance, and who also took one or two wealthy lovers; she was now old and retired. Her daughter was Rangi. Sastri darkly hinted that he knew who fathered her into this world, and I hoped it was not himself. His deep and comprehensive knowledge of the dancer's family was disconcerting. I had to ask him to explain how he managed to acquire so much information. He felt a little shy at first and then explained, 'You see my house is in Abu Lane, and so we know what goes on. To be frank, I live in a portion of the house, the other half is occupied by Damodar, who has a wholesale grain shop in the market. For many years he was keeping Padma, and after this daughter was born he suspected Padma's fidelity and gave her up, but she threatened to go to court to prove that he was the father, and finally he had to accept the situation and pay her a lot of money to get out of her clutches. He used to be a chum in our schooldays and he would never conceal his exploits from me.' Padma was now retired, being old, fat, and frightening like the harem guards of Ravana, and her daughter Rangi had succeeded her at the temple. Before that she had studied in a school for a while, joined a drama troupe which toured the villages, and come back to the town after seducing all the menfolk she had set eyes on. According to Sastri, she was the worst woman who had ever come back to Malgudi. She was a subject of constant reference in Abu Lane, and was responsible for a great deal of the politics there.

Next morning I was at the machine, after sending away Sastri to the binders to look to something. I heard the sound of bangles and there she was – Rangi, stepping between the hyena and the mongoose and making for the door. She was dark, squat, seductive, overloaded with jewellery; the flowers in her hair were crushed, and her clothes rumpled; she had big round arms and fat legs and wore a pink sari. She evidently didn't care how she looked now, this was her off-hour, and I could imagine no other woman who would be prepared to walk along the streets in this *déshabillé*. I felt curious to know what she would look like in the evenings – perhaps she would powder her face, the talcum floating uneasily over her ebonite skin. Anyway whatever might be the hour, every inch of her proclaimed her what she was – a perfect female animal. How did she get home? When did she come in? When did she go out? She went about her business with such assurance, walking in and out of a place like a postman. My mind seethed with speculations. Did Vasu bring her in his jeep at the darkest hour? Not likely. What a man he must be who could turn his mistress out in cold blood when morning came!

My further speculations on the theme of lust were cut short by the arrival of Sastri, who said, 'The binder says that one of his office boys is down with mumps, and that he cannot do the ruling until Friday.' He said this in a tone of utter fatalism.

'The sky is not going to fall because he holds it off till Friday,' I said.

'Unless the ruling is done, the bank ledger won't be ready and they'll come down on us.'

Why was Sastri always in a state of panic lest we should fail one or the other of our customers? He had no trust in my ability to manage things and no sort of confidence in me. I felt indignant. 'No need for panic! I have run this press for how many years? I've managed to survive and flourish, and so far not made a fool of myself. So why do you worry?' I could not conclude my sentence. There was no conclusion to it as there was no basis at all for beginning it. My mind was busy following the fleshy image of Rangi and perhaps I resented the intrusion.

I was mistaken in thinking that Rangi was the only woman. I had only to stand there between seven and eight in the morning, and it became a sort of game to speculate who would be descending the stairs next. Sometimes a slim girl went by, sometimes a fair one, sometimes an in-between type, sometimes a fuzzy-haired woman, some morning a fashionable one who had taken the trouble to tidy herself up before coming out. Most times Rangi came along also with one or the other of them, or by herself. Brisk traffic passed on the staircase. I guessed that after the challenge from the cadaver, Mempi Forest was being watched more carefully, and, his activities there neutralized, Vasu had turned his tracking instinct in another direction. I had had no notion that our town possessed such a varied supply of women.

Chapter Seven

It took me time to make him out. His face was familiar. I had seen those slightly fin-like ears and round eyes somewhere. He stood on my threshold and brought his palms together and cried, *'Namaskaram.'* On that voice, with its ring – I knew it. It was the afternoon hour. The Market Road was sleepy, a donkey was desultorily chewing an old newspaper at the fountain parapet, the black cow and its friend the free bull had curled up for a siesta right in the middle of the road, obstructing the traffic as was their wont. A couple of late school-children were dawdling along the edge of the road, gazing with fascination into the gutter; a bright scalding sun was beating down; the woman sitting under the acacia selling a ripped-up jack fruit was waving a stick over its golden entrails, trying to keep off a swarm of flies; a *jutka* was rattling along on the granite metalled road; a sultry, sleepy hour. I had returned to my seat after lunch; Sastri had not yet arrived. My brain was at its lowest efficiency as I had to battle within myself to wrench myself away from a siesta. I had arrears of work to clear. I sat on the Queen Anne chair and stretched my legs on the ancient table as a compensation for forgoing my siesta.

'Come in, come in,' I said as a general courtesy to whoever it might be that said *'Namaskaram'*. He came in hesitantly, with an umbrella tucked under his arm, and lowered himself gingerly into the first chair.

'I came by the morning bus, not the one that brought you but the earlier one.'

Oh, yes, now it came like a flash. 'Oh, Muthu!' I cried, almost jumping up and hugging him. 'Whom have you left to mind the tea-shop?'

'Oh, the boys are there, they can manage it. I am returning by tonight's bus.'

'How is your business?'

'Doing very well, sir.'

'How are your children? Have you found a bridegroom for your daughter?' His face fell at the mention of it. I would normally not really have troubled him with any reminder of his daughter's marriage, but in order to cover my initial lapse I now tried to show off my knowledge of his problems. I could not be blamed for my lapse. At his tea-shop he had been bare-headed; now he had donned a white khaddar cap, a long mull jibba and a dhoti, and had a lace upper cloth over his shoulder – he had dressed himself to come to town, I suppose. I was very happy to see him. He had rescued me from Vasu that day. I had always anticipated another meeting with him at least in order to pay off the tea bill. I opened the drawer of my table and took out a rupee and held it to him. I was suddenly inspired by the lesson taught by my adjournment lawyer not to mix accounts.

He looked at the rupee with some surprise and asked, 'What is this for?'

'I have long wanted to pay you that bill for the tea and buns . . .' Even as I was speaking, I realized how silly it sounded. The lawyer had taught me a rather coarse lesson. Muthu looked rather hurt as he said, 'I have paid a bus fare of fourteen annas for coming and will pay fourteen annas for going back; do you think I am spending all that in order to collect – how much was it?'

I was abashed, but said, 'My duty, you know. Can I get you coffee or tiffin or anything?'

He shook his head. 'I never eat anywhere outside, when I travel, and it keeps me fit. I like and enjoy a good meal when I go home.'

Now that all the awkwardness was gone, I asked, 'What's your command? Tell me what I can do for you.' A sudden fear assailed me lest he should ask me to go up to tell Vasu that his old friend was come. I said to test him, 'I saw Vasu go out in his jeep.'

'We see him at Mempi going up the hill now and then, but he doesn't stop to speak to us nowadays.'

I was pleased and relieved. 'What is the reason?' I asked.

'Why go into all that?' he said gently, tapping his umbrella on the floor. 'He is a man with a gun,' he said. 'Why speak of him? He doesn't care for us now.'

'He may have no more use for you,' I said, adding fuel to the fire.

'He has other people, who are more suitable to his temperament,' he said, hinting at a vast army of undesirable men, trailing behind Vasu, looking for mischief.

I didn't want to pursue the subject further. I merely said, 'He may drop them off when he finds someone more useful,' a sentiment on which we both immediately concurred. 'After all it may be for the best; it would be best to be forgotten by him and have nothing whatever to do with him,' I said, and then I tried to elaborate the statement with an account of all the happenings ever since he stepped over my threshold. I said in conclusion, 'He stood just where you stood; I welcomed him, he sat where you are sitting now. I make no distinction between men . . .'

Muthu sprang up as if he had occupied a wrong place, and said, 'I am not that kind.'

'I know, I know,' I said. 'Don't I know? You are a helpful man. You cannot see a man stranded. I know you.'

He was pleased and said, 'We helped that man so much. Now he thinks we have informed against him, and he came and created a scene at my shop and threatened us with his gun.' He laughed at the memory of it. 'As if we wouldn't know what to do, as if we would sit back and let him shoot us! We don't want to bother about him and so we leave him alone. He still passes up and down, but never stops for tea and doesn't seem to carry home much from the forests either – and he thinks we are responsible for it! Why, there are hundreds of people going up and down to the project on that road and anyone was bound to notice his activities.'

'It's all for the best if a *rakshasa* ceases to notice you,' I said and that put an end to our discussion of Vasu. I was very happy that he was no longer liked by Muthu. My enemy should be the enemy of other people too, according to age-old practice.

After all this preamble, he mentioned his business. 'You remember our temple elephant I spoke to you about, though you couldn't see him that day? He had gone into the jungle for grazing? He's sick; and we want your help to see a doctor!'

Our doctor, Dr Rao of Town Medical Stores, how would he react to the presence of an elephant in his clinic? I said doubtfully, 'I don't know if our doctor knows enough about elephant-sickness.'

'Oh, no,' he said. 'We have heard of a Government hospital for animals recently opened. We want your help to get our Kumar treated there.'

I remained speechless – a new set of circumstances seemed to be approaching me in an enveloping movement. This was the first time I had heard of an animal hospital. I could have just said, 'I don't know anything about it,' and ended the matter there, but my nature would not permit it. I always had to get into complications. So I said, 'All right, let us see what we can do for poor Kumar. What is the matter with him?'

'He is not taking his food at all, nowadays. He shuns it.'

The enormity of the problem oppressed me. This was not

something I could evade by suggesting that they looked over the Heidelberg. At the same time I felt flattered. That someone should think of me to tackle such a problem was itself an honour. I felt too proud to say that I knew nothing about elephant doctors; after all the man who had come all this way expected me to do something about it. Suppressing my astonishment at being involved, I asked, 'Is there any hurry? I mean, can't the elephant wait?'

He looked doubtful. 'I came to you because, more than others, I knew you would be able to do something for me. You were kind enough to say I could ask you for any help. Poor Kumar, he used to be so lively, playing with all the children and now, for the last ten days, he is suffering, he accepts no food; I don't know, something is wrong with him. There is a fellow there in Top Slip, an elephant trainer, who looks after some of the elephants working in the timber yards, but he says that he cannot really judge what is the matter.'

'All right. I'll do my best. Now what are his symptoms? At least tell me that.'

'Oh.' He thought it over for a moment and said, 'He seems to get cramps – he lies down on his belly and howls. Have you ever seen an elephant lie down? I have never seen it; he has to be coaxed and cajoled to accept a ball of cooked rice.'

I felt genuinely concerned about poor Kumar now. I said, 'I'll go and meet this doctor you mentioned, and we will see what we can do. How shall I communicate with you?'

'Please drop a card, or send a note with any of the Mempi bus drivers, and I'll be here immediately.'

I noted down various details officiously. Before leaving he said, 'Nothing is more important to me than this, sir.'

I had to overlook the responsibilities on hand. Kumar's welfare became an all-important issue. The visiting cards that I was printing could wait, but not Kumar.

Later in the day I asked Sastri, 'Where is the animal hospital that was recently opened?'

'No idea,' he said. 'Lost interest in animals five years ago; after the death of my cow I vowed never to have another. I'm the first person in our whole family to buy milk from street vendors! My relations laugh at me for it.'

I inquired here and there. Two days were gone. I had the feeling of being a defaulter. As each hour and day passed I grew nervous and finally on the flash of an idea sought my friend Sen, who lived all alone in a converted garage in the compound of a house in Lawley Extension. I had to hire a cycle for this expedition. Sen was pleased to see me in his shed. He had surrounded himself with books and stacks of newspapers, which were all over the floor. He sat on a rush mat and worked by a small kerosene light.

I burst in on him at about seven in the evening. He had a sloping board on which was fixed a sheet of paper for writing. It had been a warm day, and he sat bare-bodied. He was delighted to see me. I sat on his mat.

'I can't give you coffee or anything, but, if you like, let us go to a restaurant. There is one not too far off.' He was visibly overwhelmed by my visit. He was used to visiting, but this was one of the rare occasions when he was receiving.

I said, 'I don't need coffee, thank you. I have come for some information; as a newspaper man, you'll be able to help me.' He liked to be called a newspaper man, and I hoped sincerely that some day he would see his views in print. He was always saying that he was about to secure the finances for a paper, he was on the verge of it, but something always happened, and he sat back, wrote his editorials and waited for the next financier. He was equipping himself for the task all the time. Part of his equipment was knowing what was going on in the town. I asked him about the animal hospital.

'Oh, yes, I remember something about it . . .' He frowned for a moment at all the accumulation of the past, got up, pulled down some stacks of old papers, turned them over, blowing the dust in my face. He thrust an old newspaper under my nose and tapped his finger on a news item. It gave a description of how a Deputy Minister had laid the foundation for a veterinary college and animal welfare hospital on the other bank of the Sarayu, for which ten acres of land had been gifted by the municipality; some foundation had given dollars and equipment for a start, and the Government had promised to take the hospital under its wing during the third Five-Year Plan and so on and so forth. A lengthy speech was reported in which the Deputy Minister dwelt on the importance of *ahimsa* and of animals in human economy, after which he was garlanded and made to tread the red carpet. I wondered how I had missed it.

'Do you know how you missed it?' Sen said. 'They mismanaged the whole thing. The printed invitations went out late and reached most people a day too late.'

'I wonder where they got them printed,' I said to ward off any suspicion that I might be responsible for the mess.

'The result was that no one turned up at the function except the organizers and the Deputy Minister – and he was furious. They had a platform, decorations, and an elaborate tea, but only a handful of audience; the Deputy Minister made his speech all the same. It looks dignified and impressive in print anyway,' he said fondly, looking at the printed column. 'However, the doctor is already on the scene, although little else is ready.'

Next afternoon I went in search of the animal doctor, crossing Nallappa's Grove on my cycle. It was about one o'clock and the sands were hot. A few bullock carts were crunching their wheels along the sand. The mango-trees cast a soft shade and the air was thick with the scent of mango blooms. The river flowed on with a soft swish. It was so restful that I could have set my bicycle against the trunk of a tree and gone to sleep on the mud under the shade of a tree. But duty impelled me on. I cycled up the other bank across a foot-track, and suddenly came upon a bare field enclosed within barbed wire. The gate was barricaded with a couple of bamboo poles. A tablet on a bit of masonry commemorated the laying of the foundation. The south side of the barbed wire enclosure was bounded by one wall of the cremation ground, where a couple of funeral parties were busy around smoky pyres. A howling wind blew across the fields. There was a single palmyra-tree standing up in the middle of this desert, although across the road, tops of green corn rippled in the air.

A signboard stood over the entrance. I left my bicycle at the gate and walked around to read, 'Department of Animal Welfare, World Q.R.L. (World Quadruped Relief League, Calif.).' I saw the roof of a hut shining in the sky and sent a shout in that direction, 'Hi! Who is there?' I was enjoying the hunt. I shouted without any hope, expecting the Mempi hills shimmering on the horizon to echo back my call without an interruption. But 'Who is there?' a voice called back from the hut.

'I have come for the doctor,' I said.

It seemed absurd to be calling for a doctor out of empty space, but it worked. A man appeared at the door of the hut and gesticulated. He cried, 'Come along!'

'The gate is barred,' I cried.

'Come through the fence,' he called. I slipped through the fence, the barbed wire slightly gashing my forearm and tearing my dhoti.

I swore at it, but it gave me a feeling of shedding my blood for a worthy cause.

The man stretched his hand. 'I'm Dr Joshi.'

'My name is Nataraj,' I said, as the wind howled about my ears.

Dr Joshi wore a shirt over white pants; he was a short man, with a small face and a brow knit in thought. 'Come in,' he said, and took me into the hut. A tin roof arched overhead; he had a bamboo table and a couple of folding chairs, a charpoy with a pillow, a few books in a small wooden rack, a kerosene lamp and a stove and pots and pans in a corner. Here definitely was a man with a mission. He seated me in a chair and drew the other close to me and said, 'Yes, Mr Nataraj? What can I do for you, Mr Nataraj?'

I looked around; there was very little of the hospital or dispensary or college about it. I told him about the elephant. He listened to me with the characteristic patience of a doctor and said, 'H'm, I would like to have it under observation and then I'll see what we can do.'

I had not visualized this prospect. I had thought that he would come over and examine the elephant. I suggested it. He said, 'It's impossible. The equipment for tests is here.'

'He is sick and keeps throwing himself down. How can we bring him so far?'

The problem looked frightening, but he had an absolutely simpli-fied view. He brushed aside all my doubts and said, 'He has his mahout, hasn't he? Tell him that he must come here and prod him and prick him and make him walk. Animals, once they realize the pleasure of sitting, will always sit down,' he added. 'It doesn't mean anything. It'll be our business to prod him and keep him on his feet. Unless I have him here, I shall have no means of handling him or testing him. You see there . . .' He walked over to a chest and threw it open – it was crammed with all kinds of shining instruments, tubes, bottles, and a microscope. 'This is the standard equipment that our League ships to every centre; it contains everything that a veterinarian can need, but you see, we are doing very little with it now.'

'Why so?' I asked.

'Our League provides equipment and a basic grant for a doctor like me, but the local organizations also have to do their bit. For instance the college and the hospital must be built before we can do anything.'

'When do you expect it all to be ready?'

'How can we say? The question is full of politics. People do not want it here, but somewhere else. Our Deputy Minister has no interest in the project and so it goes on at its own pace. The Public Works should give us the building and the sheds for the animals, but they are still in the stage of estimates and sanctions. I really cannot imagine when we shall start or what we can do. I alone am ready, because I'm being maintained by the League and there's a lot of equipment to guard. As matters stand, I'm just a watchman. I'm sticking on because I feel that if I leave even this will be gone. I have a hope that things will be O.K. some time. I'm not allowing things to rust, you know. All the time I'm bombarding the headquarters with letters and so forth . . . I'm happy that you have heard about us and want our service.'

'It was in the papers,' I said knowledgeably.

'Bring your elephant over. I'll do what I can for the poor creature. I have always wanted to try my hand at an elephant.'

'What could be wrong with him?'

'Well, anything. Colic, or an intestinal twist, or he might have swallowed a sugar cane without chewing it and that sometimes causes trouble.'

'Do you know all about all animals?'

'Oh, yes, about most of them. Our League headquarters in California has one of the biggest collections of animals in the world and I went through a four-year course. Although our main job will be to treat the cattle of our country, we like to do our best for any creature. Most animals and men are alike, only the dosage of a medicine differs,' he said. He was a man completely serious, living in a world of animals and their ailments and diseases.

At Mempi the affair caused a sensation. The village elders gathered together in front of the tea-shop and a great debate started over the question of the elephant. Muthu was all for bringing the elephant over. After carrying on their discussion in front of the tea-shop, everybody trooped to the little temple. Lorries and cars passed by. I marched with them to the little shrine at the cross-roads; the four-armed Goddess watched our proceedings serenely from her inner sanctum. Within the yard of the temple the elephant was tied by his hind leg to a peg under a very large tree. He had flopped himself down like a dog, with his legs stretched out. His trunk lay limp on the ground; his small eyes looked at us without interest; his tail lay in the dust; his tusks seemed without lustre. Muthu patted his head and said, 'He has been like this for three days now.' He looked unhappy. A few boys stood outside the ring of elders and watched the elephant, and commented among themselves in whispers.

Everyone looked at me sourly as a man who had come to abduct their elephant and make things worse for them. I said, 'If you do not send the elephant along, what is the alternative?'

'Bring the doctor here,' said the tailor, who kept his machine next to the tea-shop and who was one of the trustees of the temple. There was a schoolmaster in their gathering who was not sure what he wanted to say but kept interrupting everyone with his reminiscences. 'There was once,' he began, 'an elephant,' and he narrated a story which was considered rather inauspicious as by the end of it the elephant had become incurably ill. 'Oh, master!' appealed Muthu. 'Should I teach a wise one like you what to speak and when, and what not to speak?' He looked sadly at the teacher.

I began afresh to outline the whole proposition by stages. 'Our main business will now be to see that the elephant Kumar gets well.' This was the only part of my statement which received universal and immediate accord. 'And so,' I began, 'what is most important is that we should see that he gets on to his feet and moves freely.' It was the same sentiment in another form; they hesitated for a moment, examined it critically, and accepted it also as one without a trap. Now I mentioned something really dangerous. 'And so he should be made to get up and move in the direction of the doctor.'

'No,' said the obstinate tailor. 'The doctor must come here. Have you no pity? How can a sick animal tramp fifty miles? It'd be cruel.' For a moment, everyone made noises of sympathy for the tailor. This brought the question back to its starting point. The tailor had won his point; he looked triumphantly obstinate, and moved away.

I felt desperate among an immobile elephant, an equally immobile doctor and a mentally immobile committee; there seemed little to do except pray for the elephant. I realized that in a committee there was likely to be no progress, and so I didn't press the point. I knew that the tailor would not go on standing there for ever; sooner or later someone would come to his shop and demand his clothes back. So Muthu and I spent the time morosely watching the recumbent elephant, suppressing the suggestions which occurred to our minds, but which we knew would be thrown out in no time. The ring of children grew smaller as they had grown bored with watching the gloomy elders and had exhausted themselves in suppressed giggles (for fear of the elders who were constantly turning to them and ordering them to shut up). There were really five on the committee of the temple, but except Muthu and the tailor the rest were men of no consequence. All they did was to simper and evade any commitment.

I had not too much time to waste today; I had come by the first bus in the morning and the last bus was leaving at six. At four o'clock there was still no sign of an agreement. I was still hoping that the tailor would be called off; and as if some customer of his had been hit by a thought-wave from me, an errand boy from the shop came up panting with the statement, 'The trouble-maker is back, and won't go until he can talk to you.'

The tailor lost his head at the mention of the trouble-maker, whoever that beneficent soul may have been. 'Has he no other business than bothering me for those miserable jackets of his wife's? This is the fifth time he has visited me!'

'Perhaps his wife has barred the house to him until he brings home the jacket,' I commented under my breath.

'Throw his pieces out. Fling his pieces in his face,' cried the irate tailor.

'But you have locked them up,' said his errand boy seriously.

'That settles it. I'll be back soon,' the tailor said and rushed out in a rage. I felt relieved, lighter in my chest. This was my chance. Now I had the committee in my pocket. I told Muthu hurriedly, 'Before my bus leaves, I must see this elephant on his feet. We will discuss the other things later.'

'But how to get him up? Kumar,' he appealed, 'please, please stand up!'

One of the stragglers, a young urchin who had been watching us with a thumb in his mouth, took out his thumb and said suddenly, 'I know how to make an elephant get up.'

'How? How? Come on, do it!' I said eagerly, pulling his hand from his mouth and propelling him forward.

He grinned, showing a toothless gum, and said: 'If you get me a frog, I can make him get up.'

'What! How will you do it?'

'When a frog is put under an elephant, it'll jump, and the elephant will jump with it,' he said.

I was even prepared to dig a crowbar under Kumar and lever him up if necessary, but a mahout arrived at the crucial moment. He was attached to the timber yard five miles up in a mountain jungle. They had sent a desperate summons to him four days ago by a lorry-driver who passed that way, and only today had the man found time to turn up. He arrived just when we were hesitating between applying a jumping frog or a crowbar, wanting to do something before the tailor should return. The mahout wore a knitted vest and over it a red sweater and a white dhoti coming down to his knees, a combination calculated to strike terror into the heart of any recalcitrant elephant. He pushed his way through the ring of watching loungers, and looked us all up and down questioningly. 'Why is he lying down?' he asked.

'That is what we would like to know,' said Muthu. 'He has been like this for four days.' The mahout looked at Kumar questioningly, put his face close to the elephant's and asked, 'What is your secret?' in a soft murmur. He told us, 'Keep away. He doesn't like a big audience for his speech, you understand? Move off, and he will tell me.' We moved away. He put his face close to the large trunk of the elephant, murmuring something, and after a while we turned to look as we heard a swish proceeding from a very thin green switch in his hand, which lashed the underside of the elephant within his reach. He repeated it at intervals of a second and the elephant was on his feet. He flourished the green switch (it looked no different from any trailer of a plant), and said, 'This is . . . ,' he gave us the name of some obscure plant grown in mountain thickets. 'This is more serviceable than one's own brothers emanating from the same womb,' he explained. 'I have still to see an animal that does not respect this stick.' As he flourished it the elephant blinked and gave a loud trumpet. I only hoped that it would not bring the tailor scrambling in. The trumpeting was loud and prolonged.

The mahout leaned on the side of the elephant as if posing for a photograph and smiled at the gathering. He seemed to fall into a mystic trance as he drew the switch across his nose. 'Now get me a broken coconut and a little jaggery and a piece of sugar cane.'

We sent a youngster running to fetch these. While waiting for his return, the mahout leaned on the elephant and regaled us with his memoirs; he recounted the tales of all the elephants that he had coaxed and taken to the various zoos in the country and he spoke of a chance that he once had of taking an elephant to Tokyo or New York, which was frustrated by his brothers who did not like the girl he had married and wanted to punish him for not marrying according to their own arrangements. From Kerala, far-off Kerala, this mahout had brought a girl to marry, but his brothers advised him to pay off the woman and raised among themselves two hundred rupees. The mahout went up to her with the money and asked her to go back to Kerala. She quietly said, 'Keep your money, only tell me if there is any deep well or tank near by where I can drown myself. I want you to know that I have come to you not for your money. If I can't be worthy of being your wife, I shall be quite happy to be dead at your feet, rather than go back to my village with two hundred rupees.' He explained, 'Two hundred rupees, not just two rupees, and she did not want it. I immediately told my brothers that I did not care for them, told them to do their worst and married the girl. You think that I married her on the money from them? Not me. I returned it to them. I actually threw it out of the door and told them to pick it up, and borrowed a hundred rupees on which I am still paying interest of five rupees a month, and married her. Such a wonderful woman. She won't eat her food unless I am back home, even if it is midnight. What can I do? Sometimes I have to be out for days and days, and what does she do? She starves, that is all,' he said, and added, 'A dutiful wife.'

He never finished his narrative to tell us how it prevented his going to Tokyo or New York, for at this moment the elephant coiled his trunk around his back, and he patted it and said, 'Now we are friends, he wants me to sit on his back.' He tapped the elephant's knee, and took hold of its ear, and pulled himself up even as he was talking. By this time the youngster had brought the coconut and jaggery. The mahout stooped down to take them, and held them out to the elephant, saying something. The elephant just picked up the bamboo tray, raised it and sent it flying across the field. Muthu was crestfallen, 'See, that's what he does to food!'

'Never mind,' said the mahout. 'He is not hungry, that is all. I would myself fling the dinner plate at my wife's face if I did not feel hungry and she persisted. Now I am ready, where is he to go?'

'Ride him to the town,' I said promptly. 'I will meet you at the toll-gate outside the city.' And before we knew what was happening, he had flourished his green switch and was off, all of us trooping along behind. All the children let out a shout of joy and ran behind the elephant. I was not very happy about the amount of public notice the whole business was receiving. It might stir the tailor up once again. Muthu walked with a look of triumph beside the elephant. I felt triumphant too in a measure.

To put our ideas in proper perspective the mahout leaned down to say, 'Because he is trotting don't imagine he is not ill. He is very sick. I have my own medicine for his sickness, but you want to see an

English doctor; try him and come back to me. I never stand in anybody's way of doing something, although I know what English doctors can do. They will sooner or later call me . . .'

This made Muthu once again thoughtful. He suddenly remembered that he had come out without thanking the goddess. He ran back to the temple, lit a piece of camphor before the Goddess and rejoined the procession. At the Market Road, when the procession passed in front of the tea-shop, he invited the mahout to stop for a moment, and ran into his shop.

The mahout said, 'If you can, reach me a glass of tea here, otherwise I can't get down. If I get down, Kumar will also sit down immediately, that is his nature.' Kumar seemed to understand this, I could detect a twinkle in his small red eyes, and he swayed his head in appreciation. Muthu brought out a tray covered with buns and a tumbler of tea, and held it to the mahout. The flies that swarmed in his shop sought a diversion by settling in a mass on the back of the elephant for a ride. The mahout sat comfortably in his seat, set the tray before him and started to drink his tea. And now the tailor came flouncing out of his shop, demanding, 'Everyone get out of the way and tell me what is happening.'

The mahout thought the remark beneath his notice and looked down from his eminence with indifference. This irritated the tailor. He repeated, 'This is our elephant. Where are you taking him?' The tailor's sense of ownership was comical, and everyone laughed. Muthu, who had gone back to his seat at the counter, now said, 'He knows how to handle the elephant, don't worry. He is taking it out for its own good.'

'What? To the city? I will never have it, never, never . . .' He stamped his feet like a petulant child.

The mahout was confused. He looked puzzled and asked, tying a towel around his head as a turban, 'What does it mean? Am I stealing an elephant?'

Muthu came out of his shop, put his arm around the tailor, and said, 'Come and have tea,' and managed to say at the same time to the mahout, 'Yes, yes, you go, it is getting late, remember where you will be met . . . We will look to other things.'

The mahout flourished his green switch ever so gently and the elephant was on the move again, with the trail of children behind it. Soon his green turban vanished from the landscape around a bend.

The tailor was disconsolate until Muthu poured oblatory tea into him, unwashed glass after unwashed glass. 'At this rate,' I said to myself, 'Muthu will be a bankrupt, if he has to treat all his elephant associates to tea. He will close down his business, and then who will pay for the elephant doctor at the other end?'

I sat on the plank bridging two empty kerosene tins in front of Muthu's shop, watching the scene with detachment. Now that the elephant was gone, a big worry was off my mind. I didn't care what the tailor thought or said. Refreshed by tea and buns, he came out of the shop, wiping his mouth with the sleeve of his shirt, and passed me without a word. But his look, the brief one that he cast in my direction, was enough to indicate what he thought of me – an abductor of elephants. He was soon out of view in his own shop four doors off. I could hear him say to someone, 'Take away those pieces if you cannot wait. I promised you the jackets only at the end of this week.'

I could not hear the rest of his sentence as the dreaded jeep drew up in front of me on the road. Vasu had come down the hill. He looked at me from his seat and said, 'Coming along? I am going back to the town.'

I hesitated for a moment. The bus had been due any time the last ninety minutes. Still there was no sign of it. But how could I go with this man? We were facing each other for the first time after months. I didn't like to tell him about myself or my mission here. I would be at his mercy if I climbed into his jeep. I said, 'I am not coming back yet.'

'Why not?' he asked persistently. 'What do you want here? You want to spend the night here?'

He was blocking the road; a lorry was trying to pass, the driver sounding his horn impatiently. Vasu merely waved his arm, 'You have enough clearance, get along.'

'There is a ditch.'

'All right, get into the ditch. Don't disturb me now. Don't you see that I am talking to a gentleman?'

The lorry-driver edged close to the drain and passed. Vasu said to me, 'I will take you back home.'

'You may go,' I said.

He indicated the back seat. 'I have nothing there today. I knew that you would swoon at the sight of a dead creature. That is why I came without any today.'

How did he know my movements? Perhaps he had been watching me all the time. In any case I did not like to talk to him about it. I merely said, 'I have another conveyance. You may go, thank you.'

'What other conveyance?' he persisted. 'Your bus has broken down at the tenth mile up, axle gone. Men, women and children are sitting by the roadside. They will have to be there until . . . I don't know. If anyone has a gun there he may shoot a tiger or a rogue elephant that may prowl around tonight. If you are keen on catching the bus, I will take you there and leave you with that crowd.'

I wondered for a moment if there might be truth in his report. As I hesitated he commanded, 'What are you waiting for? If you want to spend the night with that tea-shop crowd, go ahead, please yourself. I have things to do, if you don't mind,' he said cynically.

He had irritated me at first, but I suddenly realized that this was a good chance to establish contact with him again. He spurned me and picked me up again as it suited his fancy: this was a galling thought no doubt, but it was better than being continuously ignored. So I climbed into the jeep without a word. He drove off. We remained without speaking for some time; he drove at his usual reckless speed, swearing at bullock carts, threatening to smash them up and calling insults at passers-by. He was disappointed when they accepted his bullying unprotestingly, but when one or other of the cartmen turned round with a frown or a swear-word, he was delighted, and he nudged me and confided, 'That is how I like to see my countrymen. They must show better spirit; they are spineless; no wonder our country has been a prey to every invader who passed this way.'

I could not accept his view, and so I asked, 'Do you want everyone to be a blustering bully in this country?'

'Yes,' he said simply. He was in an extraordinarily good humour. I wished he would continue thus. It was becoming dark and the lights were on in the homesteads on the way. He said, 'How busy are you nowadays?'

'Well, the usual quantity of work.'

'And the usual quantity of gossip-mongering?'

'What do you mean?' I asked rather sharply.

'No offence, no offence,' he said with mock humility. 'Just my fun, that is all. I meant those chair fixtures in your press.'

'Why can't you leave them alone?' I asked. 'They hardly ever think of you; why should you bother about them?'

'No offence meant, no offence meant,' he said with a great display of humility. 'I just wanted to know. I am their wellwisher, and I just wanted to know how they are faring, that is all.'

'Look here, Vasu,' I said, with a sudden access of foolhardiness, 'you should leave others alone; it will make for happiness all round.'

'I can't agree with you,' he said. 'We are not lone dwellers in the Sahara to live self-centred lives. We are members of a society, and there is no point in living like a recluse, shutting oneself away from all the people around.'

There was no use arguing with him. I once again became aware of my mounting irritation and wanted to guard against it. I said, moderating my tone, 'After all the poet has done a remarkable performance with his life of Krishna. He is completing *Radha Kalyan*, that is the marriage of Krishna with Radha, and his book will be out soon.'

'H'm,' Vasu said with a half-interest, 'and what about the other?' He was referring to his favourite target, the journalist.

'Well,' I said, with considerable pride, 'his plans are almost ready for starting a small news-sheet in this town; he is already issuing printed manifestoes.'

He remained thoughtful for a moment and said, 'I like people to do something, whatever it may be.'

So the journalist and poet had secured this man's approval, I reflected. I wanted to tell him, but could not, that it was impertinence on his part to think that the world waited for his approval. He was pleased to think that humanity could move only after securing a clearance certificate from him. There was no use arguing with him as he was one of those strong men who had no doubt at all about their own conclusions. He asked suddenly, 'I want to know if you are willing to print a book I am writing. I have been busy with it for some weeks now.'

'Aha!' I cried unable to restrain myself. It was unthinkable that he could be busy with a literary composition. He brightened up on hearing my interest and said, 'It is a monograph on wild life. Every day our papers are full of speeches and meetings on the problem of preserving wild life, and most people don't know what they are talking about. I have some very important points to make on the subject. What has happened in this country is that amateurs have invaded every field. People just talk their heads off. I have made many important points in my book, and I want it to be ready for the conference on wild life at the end of this year.'

'But that conference will be for the preservation of wild life?' I asked.

'What if it is? My book is also about better methods of preserving wild life. This cannot be achieved by refusing game licences to honest folk, or by running behind animals with cries of sympathy.'

I restrained my interest. I did not want to get involved in his affairs again. I dreaded the prospect of having him again in my parlour, sharpening his wits against the poet and my other visitors. I maintained my reserve and silence for the rest of the journey as the jeep sped along the dark highway.

Chapter Eight

The poet was in a grand exalted mood. He had completed the portion of his poem where Krishna meets his future wife Radha, and their marriage is to be celebrated. He had written several hundred lines of crystal-clear monosyllables; he had evolved his own prosody and had succeeded. His manuscript was ready, several little exercise books stitched by himself and wrapped in brown paper, closely filled with writing in green ink. He had written till late on the previous night. His eyes were red with sleeplessness, but his face glowed with triumph. With the marriage, the book would make about ninety-six pages. Sastri had printed the book at the rate of four pages a month over a space of countless months and it had now assumed the shape of a volume. Sastri himself was excited at the completion of the volume with the marriage episode. He brought in the proofs of some pages, and hesitated for a moment. When Sastri stood thus I always knew he had something to say, and I hoped that if I did not turn round and meet his eyes he would be gone. As I bent over my paper, I was aware of his shadow behind me. 'What is it, Sastri?' I asked sharply. He looked at the poet and both of them smiled. So I knew it was a good piece of news, and felt relieved. 'When a poet has arrived at the stage of the marriage of a god, it would be auspicious to celebrate the occasion.' He went on to explain how the celebration was to be conducted. I was fond of the poet and anything that was going to give him a place in our society was welcome to me.

Enormous preparations began. Once again, my normal work of composing and printing was pushed to the background. The fruit-juice man had prospered more than ever and wanted four thousand more of the three-colour labels, but I was not prepared to give him his labels yet. I had only time to print the first basic grey. I put it away to dry and said so every time the messenger came from Fruit Juice. Let him try and print it elsewhere and I should not object. But where would he get the magenta, that thirst-creating shade which drew people in a rush to wherever his bottles were displayed? The sixth time when I turned back the boy, K.J. himself came thundering in, and shouted at Sastri beyond the curtain. He did not know I was also there, helping Sastri to compose an appeal for our celebrations, for which we needed funds. We were also in conference with an astrologer in the composing room. We did not want to be disturbed. There now hung a thickly-woven bamboo mat which screened us off from whatever might be on the other side of the grille. Vasu might have all the dead animals in creation on the other side, but it was not going to affect us. All the prostitutes in the town might be marching up and down the steps, but that was not going to distract either me or Sastri. We could hear footsteps moving, but that didn't distract our attention. We went on with our jobs, although if I felt too curious I could always peer through a pin-hole in the bamboo curtain and get a lovely circular vision of a hyena's snout or the legs of some woman or the hefty feet of Vasu himself stumping upstairs. But it was a luxury I permitted myself only under very special or extraordinary conditions, never when Sastri was around, as I did not want him to get into the habit. I don't think he even knew of the existence of the peep-hole.

The astrologer was sitting on the floor beside the treadle. He had a page of an almanac open before him, held far away at arm's length for better focus, and was explaining, 'On the full moon, the moon is in the sixth house, which is the best place we can have for the moon, and the presiding star that day is . . . , which means –,' he shrunk his eyes to catch the figure in the column and muttered, 'I've left my glasses at home,' whereupon Sastri took his own glasses off his nose and handed them to him. He put them on and said, 'You see this here . . . What's the number?' It was now Sastri's turn to snatch the almanac from the other man's hand and hold it at arm's length. Still not being able to see, he held his hand out for the glasses, which the other removed from his nose and handed back. Now Sastri saw the number and said something, and the other, wanting to verify it, held his hand out and thus they bandied Sastri's silver-rimmed glasses back and forth. The conference proceeded on these lines – I'd not much to do, a veritable ignoramus among the stars. The idea was to fix a day suitable to the poet, also coinciding with the spring festival at the Krishna temple.

A loud voice called through the curtain, 'Sastri!' I was offended by the commanding tone. I signalled to Sastri to find out who it was, but before Sastri could take a step forward the voice continued, 'Are you delivering the labels or not? If you can't, say so, instead of making our boy run to you a dozen times.' Now I knew who it was. He went on in a big way cataloguing his grievances, our lapses, and threatening us with dire consequences. Sastri and the astrologer looked intimidated. I could notice on Sastri's face a slight satisfaction too at the realization that I had not heeded his warning.

It was time for me to show myself. I said, 'Who is it? Is it K.J.?'

There was a pause and the man said from the other side of the curtain, 'Mr Nataraj, you are letting me down. How can you expect us to deliver our bottles when . . .'

I could have spoken for him. I knew all his points. So I cut him short with, 'Why don't you take a seat, my friend? I'll be with you in a minute.' I had hesitated for a moment whether I should tell him to come through the curtain as a special gesture, but abandoned the idea for fear it might create a bad precedent. People respected the curtain, and it was better so. Vasu alone had pierced its privacy and this had turned out to be a nuisance in every way. I did not want it to happen again, and so I said to the angry fruit-juice seller, 'Sit down comfortably in that big chair, and I'll join you in a moment.'

He made no reply. A silence ensued and I heard the movement of a chair and guessed he must have acted on my advice in a mood of sullen compliance. I allowed him to wait, giving him time to cool off. We resumed our conference with the astrologer, who sat carrying on his investigation among the planets, unruffled by the happenings round him. After half an hour's silent calculations, with Sastri's spectacles perched over his nose, the man lifted his head slightly but would not yet speak. He behaved like one still in a trance. I knew that the man in the other room was impatient. He was kicking the floor and clearing his throat in order to attract my attention. I felt satisfied that I had cowed him. The astrologer sat beside the treadle and still said nothing. Sastri stood respectfully looking down at him. I asked, 'What are we waiting for?' The astrologer merely looked up. The visitor in the other room again cleared his throat. Sastri said, 'He may take another fifteen minutes.' I thought it would be best to dispose of the visitor. I passed through the curtain.

The drink-seller sat cross-legged in the Queen Anne chair, his sandals abandoned on the floor under the chair. He was an old-type orthodox, who wore a red caste-mark on his forehead. It was clear that he was there to see this thing through and to have it out with me. Initiative was half the victory in a battle, and so before he could open his mouth I remarked, wearing a look of grievance, 'What's the use of my friends losing their temper here? I never delay anyone's business without a reason.'

'What's it this time?' K.J. asked cynically, and added, 'Blocks not ready? Ink not available? That's why I made sure of sending with my order that can of ink which I got from Madras.'

'And your can of ink is perfectly safe here,' I said, producing it out of my drawer. I turned the can in my hand, scrutinized the label and gave it to him. 'This is unsuitable. If I had used it, people would have run away from your bottles. Do you know what it looks like when it dries? It assumes the pink of an old paper kite picked out of a gutter.'

'I got it from Madras, the same brand as you suggested.'

'But I use only the imported variety. This is canned in Delhi, did you know that?'

This was good, as it made K.J. look so ignorant, wrong, and presumptuous that he remained dumb. I said, 'I wouldn't use stuff like this on your work even if you forced me at the point of a gun. I have my responsibility.'

He asked like a child, 'So what shall we do about it now?'

'Well, I won't let you down, an old valued customer. If you have trust in me, I'll never let you down,' I said as if I were a god speaking to a sinner. 'Sastri!' I shouted. 'Please bring that magenta ink.' Turning to K.J. I said, 'You can see the difference for yourself . . .'

There was some vague movement of response inside the curtain. I knew Sastri would not pay any attention to my call unless I called him again. K.J. grew interested and asked, 'Is Sastri in?'

'Why?' I asked.

'He never answered, although I called him.'

'He is a very busy man,' I said. 'He carries a hundred things in his head.'

'Except my work, I suppose,' K.J. said with a sort of grim humour.

'Don't blame him. He has a hundred different things to do.'

'May I know the nature of his hundred activities?'

I could easily have snubbed him, but I said quietly, 'A poet is going to be launched on the world soon, and he is busy with the arrangements connected with it.' I realized that in the last resort truth was more convincing and effective than any fabricated excuse.

K.J. looked stunned on hearing it, and asked, 'Does it mean that nothing has been done about our labels?'

'Yes,' I said, 'the main reason being that we could not use your ink and had to wait for our usual brand. The other reason was that this poet's business came up suddenly. We are in search of a good day for the function; as soon as the date is settled, we'll approach you. It's a good cause for which everyone should do his best.'

'How? How? What do you expect me to do? Give money?'

'Yes, that'd be best, but we leave it to you. The only thing is that a good man like you must share the honour with us in doing this noble task; in what way, we leave it to you.'

He was afraid to ask further questions for fear of involvement, but still he was curious to know. 'How am I concerned? What do you want me to do?' he asked.

I could see that he was scared. He was not one who gave a donation cheerfully, or mustered the courage to say no straightaway. He was an in-between type. So I said, 'Some people give a hundred rupees, some have promised to give more. How can anyone set a limit on these things?'

He mumbled faintly, 'A hundred rupees! I'm not so big, sir . . .'

'What is a hundred rupees to you?' I asked. 'You make it every hour. Don't I know how you sell?'

He looked forlorn. He felt sorry that he had walked into this trap, and wished that he hadn't ventured out of his orbit. He looked as if he were facing the Income Tax Commissioner.

'No compulsion, no compulsion,' I said. 'Whatever is given must be given out of free will, otherwise the money will be worth nothing. Another thing, even in accepting donations we are selective. We don't care to take money from all and sundry. Money is not our main consideration. I mentioned the matter to you because your name is first in our list, and you came just when we were discussing you.'

He began to fidget in his seat: he was eager to get up and get out of sight. I was unwilling to let him go. I practically held him down and enjoyed it immensely. I said, 'What do you propose to do for us? It's always easy to adjust these things, and I'd hate to trouble you unnecessarily. What exactly would you like to do for us?'

'I'm very busy just now. I am going round organizing our sales in the surrounding country, where we are facing a certain amount of competition. A host of imitators have come into the field . . .'

'It's perfectly all right. We are not suggesting that you should disturb yourself. All we want is encouragement from people like you. After all you are an important citizen of this town, and we feel honoured when people like you are associated with us.' I laid it on thicker and thicker till he became panic-stricken. He got up suddenly and dashed out, muttering that he would see me again.

After he was gone the astrologer and Sastri emerged from their seclusion. The astrologer clutched a sheet of paper and the open page of his almanac in his right hand, and in his left dangled Sastri's silver spectacles. 'I have a date for you . . . No, actually I have three dates: good, not so good, and half-good,' he said. 'You may make your choice according to your convenience. Each man should choose what is convenient.'

The good date was five months hence; the poet would never survive such a delay. I knew him. He was impatient to launch his work within the next twenty-four hours. We rejected the half-good date, so there remained only the not so good day, which was four weeks hence, when the full moon came up a second time over the municipal tower and, more important, coincided with the festival at the temple. The astrologer said, 'This is as good a date as the best one, but do you know why it's classed not so good? You see, there is a slight aspecting of Jupiter, and the poet's ruling star is ——, and it might not prove so beneficial after all. Jupiter's aspects remain for four and a half hours; that will be until 5.25, and it may mean a slight setback in one's efforts, that's all.'

'What sort of a setback?' I asked, rather worried.

'Well, it's hard to describe. It may be nothing more serious than a stubbed toe. Or the milk kept for coffee may turn sour. Are you going to give coffee for all the guests that day?'

'Certainly not,' I said.

He was wondering how he should describe the impending setback. 'Or the water in the tap might suddenly stop flowing.'

'Or flow into K.J.'s bottles a little too much,' I said. 'K.J. was here and he may probably offer to serve drinks to all the visitors and fill up his bottles with just water and nothing more.'

'Oh, that's possible,' the astrologer echoed. 'Or anything else in a general way.'

Sastri now interpreted, 'You see in astrology anything is a setback. If a fly settles on your nose at a crucial moment and annoys you, you may treat it as one astrological setback worked off.' He laughed, and the astrologer laughed, and both of them said more or less simultaneously, 'When it comes, it comes; when it goes, it goes; but it is useful to know ahead approximately.' 'Or the ink in the pen may not flow,' added the astrologer. 'Or it may be . . .' They were now at the game of drawing up a list of minor annoyances. The list grew. Jupiter's aspecting seemed to bring about a set of minor worries. The astrologer probably felt that he was belittling the planet too much, and suddenly drew himself up to explain, 'He could be very vicious, left to himself – bring enough harm to a man's life itself or to his limbs; but when the presiding planet is Saturn, he yields place to him. You understand me? Saturn has more powers, although Saturn will not actually interfere with Jupiter's activities.'

I had to send people to be served by Heidelberg, as neither myself nor Sastri had any leisure to attend to our profession. I sent my printing customers in a steady stream next door. Sastri and I had a hundred things to do, morning till night. I kept walking in and out of my office. I saw very little of my wife and child. I went home for dinner late every night. We printed appeals for donations in the form of a letter, setting forth our cultural heritage and so forth. We had to gear up our press to compose the final forms in readiness for the great day. I went out to meet the townfolk and get their subscriptions for our function, by no means an easy job as everyone of our citizens had the same temperament as K.J. – affluent, afraid to reject an appeal, but unwilling to open the purse. We needed a lot of money. We were planning an elaborate ritual, a procession, and a feast for a thousand. A few of the people we approached asked point-blank why we wanted to do anything at all if we had no money in hand – a reasonable question, but we did not contemplate a retreat. We had to keep going on, and the city was flooded with my notice. Sen was good enough to compose it for me. He wrote a few hundred words, beginning with the origin of the world; then he went on to the writer's duty to society, the greatness of the tale of Krishna and our cultural traditions, the merits of monosyllabic verse, concluding with some spicy remarks on the Nehru government's attitude to creative writing. These were totally erased by Sastri himself before he set up type. 'Let Sen write a separate book on Nehru, if he chooses. Why should he try to display his wisdom at our cost?'

Our appeals were scattered far and wide and its effect was to draw Vasu into our fold again. He caught me late one evening as I was opening the door of my press in order to pass through to the back door. His jeep stopped at my door and he followed me in. I hadn't even switched on the lights. I was for passing straight in. He followed, asking, 'Are you in a hurry?'

'Yes . . . I'm . . .'

'Then slow up. Such frenzy will do your heart no good. Slow down, or slow up. Why stand in the dark and talk? Switch on the light. Where is the switch?' He fumbled along the wall and found the switch. He sat in his usual chair and ordered me to be seated too.

I said, 'I'm hungry, I've to go in and have my dinner.'

'I too am hungry,' he said. 'You are not the only man who eats, are you?'

I sat down reluctantly on the edge of my table. 'Well, what is it?' I asked.

'Look, Nataraj, I'm trying to be good to you. Don't be naughty. I don't like anyone to talk to me in that tone.'

'Can't we meet some time tomorrow? I am very tired, that's all,' I said.

'What has tired you? Being a busybody? Do you think I don't know what's going on?'

'What do you know?'

He produced one of our notices from his pocket and flourished it. 'I'm as good a citizen as any, and even if you don't send me one I can always get one. You print it right under my floor' (I winced at his expression 'my floor') 'and yet no one has the courtesy to send me a copy! Strange world!'

I had no answer. While we had posted several hundred envelopes, I had deliberately avoided sending him one. Though our cold relationship was slightly improved, I could not bring myself to send him an invitation. There was an uneasy thought at the back of my mind that something might go wrong if this gunman was called in. But he was not the kind who would wait to be called. I merely said, 'I knew you would get it, and so I did not think it was particularly . . .'

'Important?' he said while I was fumbling for an expression. 'Why? Did you think I'd not be good enough to give you money, that I have no money?' This was really crushing. Why was he trying to have a fight with me?

'Do you want to find a reason for a fight with me?' I asked.

He said, 'I'm not going to fight with anyone. If I had to fight, there'd be no half measures and it would not be at all good for the man who asked for it. You want to fight?' he asked solicitously as if he were asking 'Would you like to wash or take a cup of coffee?'

I adopted diplomacy and said, 'I thought of coming to you late, because I knew you would be here.'

'That's better,' he said. 'Now you sound better. H'm. I had no notion that the poet had gone so far. A hard-working fellow!' he added with a sort of appreciation. He took out his purse and held out to me a ten-rupee note, holding it carelessly at the tips of his fingers. 'Well, this is my contribution, although you wouldn't ask for it.'

I stared at the note uncomprehendingly for a while and then said, 'Is this all? I was going to ask you for a hundred.'

'A hundred! H'm, that's interesting. If my business were as good as it used to be ... Those bastards are trying to lock away the animals, very unhelpful,' he said, thinking of the big army of forest guards. 'Still, they can't put me down, you know. It only makes my business a little complicated, that is all. Who are they to tell me how to shoot or when!'

'You are right in a way,' I said in order to sound agreeable, without bothering to think what I meant – without thinking of the river of animal blood which would have flowed if he had had his way.

He looked at me for a moment. 'Nataraj! You really think so? I don't really need anybody's support or encouragement. I can get on very well by myself.' The ten-rupee note still fluttered at his fingers' ends. 'Well, do you want this or not?' he asked with sudden aggressiveness.

My mood began to match his. 'I said I want a hundred from you, not less.'

'Okay,' he said and put the money back into his pocket. 'Now you can tell me how much you have collected in one hundred rupees.'

It was a challenge and I said, 'So far I have got fifty donors of the hundred-rupee class.' That made him thoughtful.

'So! Five thousand rupees! How much of it is in your hands?'

That was a point. I said, 'I don't want to take it yet. Nearer the time of the function. Why should we burden ourselves with the custody of so much cash?'

He made a sound of deprecation with his tongue and said, 'Such a lot of cash! After all it's five thousand rupees, not five lakhs!'

'It is big enough from our point of view,' I said, 'Someone else's money is always a burden to carry.'

'That's an unphilosophical way of looking at things. Money is only a medium of exchange and has no value by itself, and there can be no such thing as your money and my money. It's like the air, common to mankind.'

'Then why not let me take your purse?'

'Why not indeed!' He took it out of his pocket and dropped it on my lap, rose, strode away to his jeep, and drove off. I sat transfixed. It was a large, well-stuffed purse, the size of a lady's handbag. I sat for a while wondering what to do with it. I couldn't guess where he was gone. I had never expected that I would be charged with the custody of the man's purse. Its flap was buttoned with an old-type metal head which could be pressed in. If you applied your thumb in the gap under the flap and lifted your finger, the flap snapped open. It had several compartments. It was stuffed with letters and currency. There was a photograph, plastic-covered, of a brawny young man with wavy hair standing up like a halo ear to ear, and bushy eyebrows. If you scrutinized it for a few minutes, you could easily recognize the face – Vasu at eighteen or twenty; you could recognize him by his bull-neck. There was a larger side-flap into which were stuffed currency, some letters, bills to be paid, and one letter in a blue envelope. The colour blue always arouses my curiosity. I pulled it out, toyed with the idea of going through it, but put it back. I lacked the courage to read it. If he came back suddenly and caught me reading, he might perhaps break my spine or hold me upside down and rattle my teeth out of my skull. I also wanted to know urgently how much money he had in his purse and what were the unpaid bills standing in his name, but I lacked the courage to undertake the research now. I folded back the purse, pressed down the metal buttons, and put it carefully in my drawer and locked it. I shut the front door and went in for the night.

Three days later Vasu came to claim his purse. He peeped into my roll-top desk when I was looking through a list of persons who had promised us funds, snatched the list from my hand, glanced through it, and asked, 'How much money do you expect to collect?' I opened a green folder in which all the papers relating to accounts, receipts and cash already collected were kept. I examined the account and mentioned a figure. 'Give it here,' he said, snatching away the green folder too. 'I will double it for you. You mind the other things.'

I stammered, 'But . . . but . . . ,' and stretched my hand for the folder. He pushed away my hand. 'Leave this to me, and attend to other matters.' I tried to argue with him, but he didn't stop to hear me. He walked briskly to his jeep and drove away.

A week later he came into my office with a triumphant look. He flourished the green folder and asked, 'Can you guess how much I have managed to get out of all the tight-fists in your town?' I mentioned a figure. He said, 'You are wrong. Try again,' and went away.

After that, during my round of visits I met people who remarked, 'What a money-gatherer you have engaged! One will have to sell the vessels in the kitchen and find the money, only to be rid of him!

What a specimen!' There could be no doubt that he was extremely active.

I had to know exactly what he was up to. I waited patiently. When he came in one afternoon I asked him straightaway, 'Where is the green folder?'

'It is locked up in an iron safe,' he replied.

I ceremoniously showed him the Queen Anne seat, and began, 'We are all grateful to you for your help. You know a poet is . . .'

'Oh, no!' he cried. 'I can't stand all this thanksgiving rigmarole.'

'You are doing so much,' I said ignoring the insult. 'Part of the collections will be utilized for expenses connected with the festival, and then whatever is left over . . .'

'Why do you tell me all this?' he snapped.

I said, 'We need funds now for making a few advance payments.'

He thundered, 'So what?' He cooled suddenly and asked, 'How much do you want anyway?'

'At least five hundred rupees,' I said.

'All right, you shall have it.' He made no movement to fulfil his promise.

I asked, 'When? When shall we . . . ?' He was trying to swat flies with a piece of cardboard.

He said, 'Why do you let these flies swarm here? Have you stored sweets in your desk for your favourite poet?'

'It is important we should know how much you have been able to collect and from whom,' I said firmly.

'All in proper time,' he said. 'Meanwhile, observe proper manners, keep your expenses down. Don't imagine you are millionaires!' He rose abruptly, glared at me for a moment, and was off.

Chapter Nine

We were a grim and silent trio that night. I had never worked harder as a printer. Details connected with the celebration had kept us so busy that I had had to neglect the most important item – the book to be dedicated on the day of the spring festival at the temple. I had to have at least one copy of the first volume ready in a special binding of hand-woven cloth. We still had a thousand lines of verse to be printed to bring it up to the end of the marriage of God Krishna with Radha. The poet had given us the last instalment of the manuscript weeks before, but it had lain in storage. I found no time even to open the cover. The poet was patient. He could not hustle me as this was practically a free service I was doing. He had always said that if the whole of it could not be got ready, they could always make use of the manuscript for the ceremony. But it was a matter of prestige for me as a printer to get through it and have at least one bound copy ready.

So we were working on this desperately tonight – myself, Sastri, and the poet: Sastri to compose each page, the poet to pass the proof, and I to print off the page as it came through. We had between us a large flask of coffee. We were weary and tired. All speech between us had ceased. During the earlier part of the night we had discussed the various aspects of the function and cracked a few jokes, but an hour before midnight we were irritated by each other's presence. My legs ached, my eyes smarted and I longed for bed. There were moments when I wondered why I had involved myself in all this, when I could have spent the time profitably printing K.J.'s fruit-juice labels. The poet sat in the Queen Anne chair and nodded; the sight of him provoked wild thoughts; I felt like flinging a tumbler of cold water over his head; I felt furious at seeing him nod, as I sat in the chair opposite him. 'We are doing all this for your sake. How dare you sleep?' was my thought. And I took a pleasure in shouting in his ear, 'Here, should it be — or — ?' a doubt, a query, any excuse to pull him out of sleep. Looking at his mild face one would never imagine that he was a fanatic, but he was an implacable foe of all disyllables, and this drove him to attack and pulverize polysyllables so that they might fit into his scheme. A new syntax had grown from this, which caused Sastri endless headaches. Every few minutes Sastri called out to me from the composing room to clear his doubts and I in my turn prodded the poet to give me an answer. Strange problems faced us. The poet had used too many K's and R's in his composition, and the available poundage of K and R in our type-board was consumed within the first twenty lines; I had to ask him whether he could not use some other letters in order to facilitate our work. Sometimes he was obliging and sometimes he refused point-blank. At these moments we managed to put in a star in place of K or R and continue. Whenever he saw a star, the poet went mad and asked, 'What does it mean?' I answered pugnaciously, 'Don't worry, we will take care of it while printing. Otherwise we may add a footnote to readers to say that whenever they see a star . . .' All this upset the poet very much, and kept him awake.

When I threw on the poet's lap a particular complicated, star-filled galley, I watched him from my chair with calm satisfaction for a while. I always told him, every time, monotonously repeating myself, 'Proof-correcting is like child-bearing. It is to be performed by you and you alone; no one else can step in and help you,' and I sat down and rested my neck on the high back of the Queen Anne chair and watched him. He was a man of few words, probably because most expressions are polysyllabic, and he just glanced at me and got absorbed in proof-correcting. He held between his fingers a very small, white-handled pencil, and often nibbled its tip and brushed it against his cheek. The sight somehow annoyed me and made me say, 'Is your cheek a pencil-sharpener?'
'I do that whenever I think.'
'Stop thinking when you correct a proof. Let only your eye watch the word, letter, punctuation. If you start thinking, we shall have to go on with corrections and proofs till eternity.' I suddenly felt that I sounded like Vasu, and added softly, 'If we had had more time I would not have minded anything, you know.'
'That's why I said . . . ,' he began and I cut him short with, 'Let's not waste the midnight hour. Go on, go on with the proof. Only when you have passed it, can I print it.' Watching him working under the twenty-five-watt bulb, my eyes swam. I ceased to notice anything. A radiant light gathered around him and isolated him as if he were within an illuminated capsule or cocoon. His frayed jibba and dhoti, and the silly jute bag on his lap in which he carried his papers, were no longer there; they became smudgy and vague. I could see only his face – unshaven (he was saving up a blade for the

great day); the light fell on his nose-tip and the rest receded in shadow.

The policeman's whistle sounded far off somewhere, and everything conduced to a dopy state of mind. I felt light and floated and sank into sleep, forgetting everything for the moment – Sastri, the temple, the poet, the celebrations, and the funds locked up with Vasu, the pipe and drum, the feeding arrangements and garlands. Like a dagger-jab, I heard the words 'Shall I stop with this line on this page?' Sastri stood over me and bellowed his question, and all the fine fabric of my oblivion was completely torn and messed up. Evidently Sastri got jealous when he saw me asleep and invented a doubt in order to pull me out of it.

Then it was Sastri's turn to seek a corner chair. He arranged it perfectly; after turning a chair to face the wall, he curled up in it. His deliberate preparations to sleep upset me, but I could do nothing about it, as he had an unchallenged right to doze. It was my turn to work, for until I printed off the formes he had no types left to compose; for the poet's work had swallowed up all the contents of the type-case and left them blank. Until I released the types there was nothing for Sastri to do but sleep, and of course the poet was entitled to sleep because until Sastri gave him a galley . . . I wished I could make them do something instead of letting them sleep, but my devilish brain was too dead at this hour to devise anything, and so I stuck the types on the treadle, adjusted, and operated the pedal. I could hear them snore in the other room beyond the curtain, but there was nothing I could do about it. Perhaps I might have splashed a bucket of water over them, had I felt able even to contemplate the lifting of a loaded bucket. The sound of the treadle parts came in a series, *chug, gluck, pat* and *tap*. I was trying to classify their sounds. I poured out a little coffee in the thermos lid, and paused ever so slightly to sip it.

Now over the *chug, gluck, pat* and *tap* I heard a new sound: a repeated tap on the grille that separated me from Vasu's staircase. I hoped that the stuffed hyena had not come to life. I tried to ignore it and go on with my printing. *Tap, tap*, on the steel mesh. I applied my eye to the private pin-hole and saw a vague outline stirring. 'Oh, the ghost of the hyena has come back!' I cried. A thrill of fear lifted the hair on my scalp and forearm. I wondered if I should wake up the other two – it was a perfect excuse – and make them share my fright.

'Sir, sir,' whispered the animated hyena, 'this is urgent – listen.'

I lifted the edge of the bamboo curtain. The light from the treadle fell on the other side and illuminated the face of Rangi. My hair stood on end. Rangi! The woman to avoid.

My first reaction was one of thankfulness that Sastri was on the other side of the curtain, facing the wall. It was impossible – that woman whom I saw going down the steps every morning with the flowers crushed in her hair, the awful fleshy creature whom Sastri considered it a sin to look at! Was it possible that I was a prey to hallucinations? Perhaps overwork and the strain of the last few weeks had done their trick. I turned away to my treadle, smiling indulgently at the pranks my mind was playing. But the phantom sounded husky as it called again, 'Listen to me.' Was the woman trying to seduce me at this hour? I looked around. If my wife happened to come in, it would be the end of my domestic career. Although Rangi was black as cinders and looked rugged, there was an irresistible physical attraction about her, and I was afraid that I might succumb to her charms. But there was the safety of the grille between us. I asked, with needless sternness in my voice, 'Why do you disturb me at this hour of the night? Have you no . . .?'

'Sh! Sh!' she said, gesturing with her fingers to cover her mouth. 'You will wake him up if you talk so loudly. Listen to me, sir,' she said. 'I have very urgent news for you.'

'What is it? Couldn't you have spoken to me earlier in the day?'

When I saw her nearer, she wasn't so rugged. The light touched her high cheek-bones, and I found myself saying to myself, 'Not bad, not bad. Her breasts are billowy, like those one sees in temple sculptures. Her hips are also classical.' I resented the attraction she exuded from a personality so rough. She wore a thin reddish sari. She interrupted my midnight dreaming with, 'I must get back before he awakes. Listen: he is talking of shooting your Kumar tomorrow. Be careful.'

I took a little time to grasp the sense of her information. The name Kumar stirred up in me all the necessary memories, from the first day when we had made him get up on his legs, through all our effort to restore him to health, to this day, when he was peacefully swaying and crunching all the sugar cane that the children of the neighbourhood brought him.

During his convalescence Kumar had become our own temple elephant and was living in the compound. He was to be a main feature of our festival, and afterwards he would be returned to Muthu.

'I am also a woman of the temple and I love that elephant. It must not be shot. Sir, you must somehow see that he doesn't do it. Please save the elephant.'

'How? How can I shield the elephant? What sort of an armour can we provide for him?' I asked. And then on a sudden doubt I whispered, 'Are you in your senses? Or have you been taking opium or something of that kind?'

She glared at me angrily, 'Sir, I am only a public woman, following what is my *dharma*. I may be a sinner to you, but I do nothing worse than what some of the so-called family women are doing. I observe our rules. Whatever I may do, I don't take opium.'

I felt apologetic for uttering so outrageous a remark and said, 'What you say is so unbelievable.'

She looked nervously up the stairs, as there was a slight stirring noticeable above. 'If he wakes up . . . .,' she whispered. 'Wait here, don't go away,' and she ran up the steps. My blood tingled with an unholy thrill. I let my mind slide into a wild fantasy of seduction and passion. I was no longer a married man with a child and home, I was an adolescent lost in dreams over a nude photograph. I knew that I was completely sealed against any seductive invitation she might hold out for me, but, but, I hoped I would not weaken . . . My mind speculated on how I was to neutralize the grille between us if it came to that; the grille had a lock, and the key was in the drawer of my table in the other room. I stepped up to the curtain, parted the edge of it, and was relieved to see Sastri continuing his sleep, his position unchanged. The poet slept equally soundly, but he had drawn up his legs and curled himself in the Queen Anne. If I approached the desk for the key, it was bound to disturb the sleepers. Anyway, I left the problem alone, resolved to tackle it somehow at the right moment.

When I tiptoed back to my place beside the grille, there she was, ready as it seemed to swallow me up wholesale, to dissolve within the embrace of her mighty arms all the monogamous chastity I had practised a whole lifetime.

I found her irresistible. She stood on the last step, a goddess carved out of cinder. The shadows cast by the low-powered lamp were tricky and created a halo around her. I pressed my hands on the grille and put my face close, and, adopting the appropriate tone of a man about to succumb to seduction, I said, 'Oh, you are back!' I tried to put into the sentence all the pleasure I was anticipating.

She looked at me indifferently and said, 'I only went up to see if he was sleeping; he was just rolling over, he won't get up till five, I know him.' She sat down on the last step, took out of the folds at her waist a pouch and from it a betel-nut and leaf and two inches of tobacco, put them into her mouth and started chewing. She looked completely relaxed. In my fevered state I wanted to ask her if she was aware that the grille was locked and the key was where Sastri was sleeping.

She asked, 'Are you going to save that elephant or not?'

'Why do you ask? Tell me all about it.'

'He will kill me if he knows I have been talking. But I don't care. He has been telling me his plans. Tomorrow night, what time does your procession pass this way?'

'You should know, you are in it.'

She was to perform her original function of a dedicated woman, and dance in front of the God during the procession, although her dance would consist only of a few formal flourishes of her arms. She was perhaps the most indifferent dancer in India, but no one expected anything else of her. People were used to seeing her before the God and no one cared how she performed. Her place would be right between the decorated chariot and the group of pipers and drummers.

'He doesn't want me to go in the procession tomorrow,' she said, 'because he says it'll not be safe for me.' She giggled slightly, and threw the end of her sari over her face, feeling shy at the thought of Vasu's considerateness.

I asked in a panic, 'Aren't you joining the procession?'

'Yes, I'll be there. It will be my duty.'

'But, but, what about Vasu?'

'Oh, let him say what he pleases; no man so far has stopped my doing what I like,' she said proudly.

'Why doesn't he want you there?'

'He doesn't want me there when it happens.'

'What happens?'

'When he shoots the elephant from his window.'

'I never thought Vasu cared for anyone so much.'

'He cares for me very much, although sometimes he is completely mad and picks up all kinds of women and expects me to quarrel with them – but not me. Let any man do what he fancies. I don't care what anyone does, so long as he doesn't dictate to me what I should do.' She chewed her tobacco contentedly. 'He wants to take me with him to Bombay – that's why he doesn't want me to get lost in the crowd.'

'What will you do in Bombay?' I asked, my curiosity roused.

'Cook for him. He likes the *pulav* I make, so he wants to take me along with him. I want to see new places too when the time comes. In a year or two who will care to have me?'

'Oh, you will have your charms,' I wanted to say in my impassioned state, but I restrained myself. She treated me with much respect, always addressing me as 'sir', and she would have been shocked if I had spoken to her like a lover. Even at that mad hour, I am glad to think, I kept my head and tongue. 'Good man,' I said, 'he cares for you so much!'

'He is tired of his restaurant food, he says, and he doesn't want me to risk my life in the crowd when he shoots the elephant from his window.'

'Why shoot the poor thing?' I persisted. 'Does he think I will let him do it?' I asked heroically. 'I will tell the police.'

'Oh, sir,' she begged, 'don't do that. How will it help? The police themselves may ask him to shoot it. They may want someone able to shoot.' And then she explained, 'When the elephant is passing here, it may go mad and charge into the crowd.'

'Oh, God. Why?'

'Well, elephants are easily excited; and then he will take aim from his window and shoot it. He is certain that he can finish it. His aim is always accurate, you know,' she said.

I said, angrily, 'If he is such a good shot, the place for him to demonstrate it is elsewhere, not here.'

'Master,' she implored, 'don't be angry. Think calmly what you should do, and act before it's too late.'

'Anyway, why does he want to shoot the elephant?' I asked.

'He says it's more useful dead. He may kill me for speaking, but I don't care. I want to save poor Kumar.'

'Neither you nor Kumar need have any fear. The time has come for me to hand him over to the police, the devil!' I said with a lot of passion but little idea of what I could do about it.

I finished printing the formes, woke up Sastri to do more, woke up the poet to proof-read, printed four more pages, and it was nine o'clock in the morning when I saw the last page off the machine and one set of formes was assembled ready for the binder. The sacred copy was to be bound in Benares silk and kept in the temple. I said to the poet, 'It's all right, go home and wash and be here in time. We have to be at the temple before three.'

He yawned, scratched the back of his head and went down the road muttering, 'I'll be back soon. Tell me if there is anything more I can do.'

I sent Sastri with two copies to the binder. Sastri hesitated for a second. 'Can't I go home for half an hour – for a wash?'

I was irritated. 'Why not me? I also would like to go home and sleep and wash and relax.' As I was talking my little son came running down the road. 'Father, Mother says . . .' Even before he finished his sentence, I said, 'Tell your mother not to call me for the rest of the day. Tell your mother that even Sastri is not going home today. We are all very busy.' I handed him a bunch of coloured notices. 'Give one of them to your mother and the rest to your friends or anyone you like – let them all turn up at Krishna's temple. We'll all meet there. Tell Mother I'll come home, but I don't know when.' Even as I spoke I remembered Rangi, and for a moment I wondered whether to ask my son and wife to keep out of the crowd. 'Damn it!' I said to myself. 'Nothing shall happen. I shall have Rangi and that paramour of hers in the police lock-up.' This thought gave me strength although I had no notion how I was going to achieve it practically. The police would not listen to my orders if I said, 'Lock up that man.' Why should they?

Every hour of that day was like a tenth of a second to me, it was so compressed and so fleeting. After sending everyone away I sat down to take stock of all I had to do between now and the grand function. I found my head in a whirl. I didn't know where to make a start in drawing a schedule. Every item appeared to be important and clamoured for immediate attention. I could now understand why Government officials liked to stack up on their desks trays marked Immediate, Urgent, and Top Priority. Everything today was on the top-priority level.

Although we had been working madly for weeks, everything seemed to be crowded into the last minute. First I must remind the flower-dealer to get us the first supplies for decorating the chariot by eleven. We had engaged two specialists, brothers from Talapur, who were in demand all over South India. Given the foliage and the quantity of chrysanthemums they demanded, their decoration of a chariot was a masterpiece, but they needed a clear eight hours to arrange the flowers. The chariot must be ready for the procession at eight in the evening, and they would have to begin their work at eleven in the morning. I had paid a visit to them at Talapur ten days before. They accepted the engagement only because the police inspector with whom I had influence interceded; otherwise they had a much bigger job to do at Madras. I gave them an advance of fifty rupees and noted down their indent: seven thousand yellow chrysanthemums, four thousand of a certain green plant, two thousand red oleanders, two hundred thin bamboos splintered according to their specification, which they'd loop around the pedestal of the God, working the flowers into them, and seventeen bundles of banana fibres thinly torn off for binding the flowers. In addition to these basic requirements they had asked for a thousand roses, twenty measures of jasmine buds, and bouquets and garlands ready-made to be strung according to their specifications. These latter items could arrive after six, but the first supply of chrysanthemums must be there before eleven. The brothers were arriving by the bus at ten o'clock behind the market depot, and they were stars who expected to be received on arrival. I was the only one who had seen them, and it meant that I would have to wait for them at the market stand. Also I had to visit the florist who had his shop at the farthest corner of Market Road, a man amenable only to my influence. He waited in his turn on the suppliers from the surrounding gardens. We were taking all the flower supplies coming into town that day, and the price of flowers for common folk shot up.

I had also to make sure that our piper and the drummer, who lived not too far away, would arrive in time. Our chief piper blew through a silver-covered pipe, and the drummer had gold beads around his neck and beat his drum with ivory-tipped fingers; they were stars in their own line, and so expected personal attention from the organizers as represented by me. They were in demand all over South India for marriage and temple festivals, but they had condescended to accept a local engagement because it was the first of its kind in our town. They lived right on the edge of the town, the last house in Ellaman's Street, but, since they were cousins of our barber whose house abutted Kabir Street, we were able to exert pressure on them through him and set him to bring them to the temple at three in the afternoon.

We had an enormous programme of feeding the public too. We had planned to offer the God rice cooked with jaggery and spiced with cardamom and coconut and distribute it to the crowd following the procession. One of the rice merchants had donated us all the rice that would be needed together with the coconut and jaggery. All that he wanted in return was that, in any public speech, his shop should be mentioned. We had a kitchen in the temple, and an enormous cauldron was fetched and mounted over a fireplace with half a ton of chopped wood burning under it. Four professional cooks were engaged, and several thousand little receptacles made of banana bark would be filled with sweetened rice and distributed. And then there were the Kitson lights and petrol lamps for the illumination of the temple and the procession, in addition to torches soaked in oil. And above all fireworks.

The whole town was at it. The Chairman of our Municipal Council had agreed to preside over the function, the advantage in that being that the municipal services were easily secured for us! When it was known that the Municipal Chairman would be there, the roads were swept and watered, and the licence for a procession was immediately given. Along the corridor of our Krishna temple we had erected a *pandal* and a dais, on which the Mayor (he liked to be called Mayor) would stand and harangue the gathering before the dedication.

All the public relations and the general arrangements at the temple were undertaken by Sen, who never left the temple precincts for seven days, working at it night and day. He had managed to get a band of young volunteers from Albert Mission College and High School to assist him and run small errands; he had managed to erect a *pandal* with coconut thatch and bamboo; he saw to the decorations, and kept a hold on the Municipal Chairman by writing his speech for him. He had also arranged to keep in readiness hand-outs and photographs for newspapers. K.J., our aerated-water specialist, had set up a booth at the temple gate and had offered to open a thousand bottles free of cost and thereafter charge only half-rate to the public gathered at the temple. There were three donors who had offered five hundred rupees each, and they expected me to fetch them by car, although one had to be brought from New Extension, the other from Gandhi Park and a third from Lawley Road. I had fortunately the assistance of Gaffur, who ran his 1927 Chevrolet as a taxi. It was always available around the fountain. 'Any time, anywhere, this car is yours,' he had declared. I had only to fill the petrol tank, ask him to drive and give him ten rupees at the end of the day.

'First things first, and I have to be at the temple at three,' I told myself. There was Dr Joshi, the elephant doctor beyond Nallappa's Grove, who wanted a car to be sent for him. 'I must remember to take with me six bottles of rose water and the sandalwood paste, and then . . .' Items kept coming to mind, like the waves beating on a shore. 'Oh, when Muthu and his party arrive, I must leave a guide at the bus-stand to take them to the temple.' Everything was important and clamoured for first attention.

I dropped what I was doing, dashed through the press, opened the back door and stepped across to my house. I'd have no time to visit the river today. I went straight into the bathing-room, saw that there was cold water ready in a brass cauldron, undressed and poured the cold water over my head, shouting through the door to my wife, 'Bring me my towel and a change of clothes.' She thrust the towel through the half-open door, and I cried, 'I forgot to shave; bring me my safety razor and mirror. I'll shave here.' She ran back to fetch these, and presently my son entered, bearing them in his hand. I shouted, 'You should not handle razor blades.'

'Mother asked me to carry them.'

I called his mother urgently and told her, 'After this never let the young fellow handle razor blades.'

'He insisted upon fetching them himself.'

'That's no excuse,' I said, 'You must watch him.'

'What else do you think I am doing?' she asked. 'But now I have your breakfast on the fire, and I know how you will dance for it and make us dance who serve you, the moment you come out of the bathroom.'

'No time for arguments today.'

Within fifteen minutes I was leaving home again, completely refreshed by my bath and food. I took leave of my wife. 'Try and manage to come to the temple at five with Babu. I'll give you a good place for watching the show, then you can go back home and come again before the procession. The decoration will be the finest. Come with some of our neighbours.' I was off.

Across the street, back at my press, I was troubled with a secret uneasiness that perhaps I should have asked her to stay at home in view of Rangi's warnings. 'First things first . . .' If I devoted four minutes to each task, I could get through everything and reach the temple in time before the Chairman arrived. But, but, I had to get this affair of Vasu straightened out; I braced myself to face him. I did not want to give myself any time. If I began to think it over, I'd find an excuse to go ahead with all the other tasks, while the lives of thousands of men and women might hang by a thread depending on my interview with Vasu, not to speak of the survival of poor Kumar who had proved such a delight to our neighbourhood!

I dashed home for a minute to ask my wife to pack up and give me some eatables that she had prepared, and then turned to go to Vasu. I went around to the yard. Until I turned the corner I had a hope that the jeep might not be there. But there it was. My steps halted for a second at the bottom of Vasu's staircase, where I noticed the plaster on the walls peeling off. 'I must attend to this,' I said to myself, and immediately felt a pang at the thought of how little I had to do with this part of my property. At the foot of the stairs the hyena was still there. 'There seems to be no demand for stuffed hyena nowadays,' I said to myself. The python was gone, but a monitor lizard, a crocodile, and a number of other creatures, looking all alike in death, cluttered the staircase. I went up to the landing, making as much sound as I could. It was about eleven and I knew Rangi would not be there. I stood on the landing and called, 'Vasu, may I come in?' I didn't knock on the door as I felt it might upset him. 'How can I find time today for this?' I thought. 'I hope they'll remember the rose-water bottles.' I stood brooding, waiting for Vasu. The door opened.

'What an honour!' he cried ironically. I passed in, took my seat on his iron chair, and settled myself for a talk with him, although one part of my mind went on repeating, 'Where is the time? Rose-water, sandal-paste, New Extension, Gandhi Park . . .' We had avoided each other since the day I asked for my accounts and thus entered a second phase of our quarrel. Last time it was he who had come with peace overtures; this time I was initiating them. My heart swelled with pride; I was performing a mighty sacrifice on behalf of God and country. By approaching him and humbling myself I would be saving humanity from destruction . . .

I said, 'Vasu, I have no time today for anything, as you know, but I've come to invite you personally to our function this evening.' He received my words coldly, without even thanks, and made no reply. I looked around; the room was once again cluttered with hides and stuffed creatures and packing-sheets and materials. I noticed a small tiger cub in a corner. I tried to win him by saying, 'A pretty cub that!'

He picked it up and brought it closer, 'Someone picked it up right in the centre of a road while coming from . . .'

'Its mother?'

'Will miss her, of course. I was busy with other things, and could start on it only last week.'

'You could have kept it alive and brought it up,' I said, trying to discover ways of pleasing him.

'Me? No. I've spent a lifetime trying to make you see the difference between a zoo-keeper and a taxidermist,' he said with weariness as if I'd been trying to place him among an inferior caste of men. 'Anyway it's easier to rear a dead animal. For one thing it saves complications with a landlord.'

I felt proud that he still recognized me as the lord of this attic. Vasu without a live tiger was quite problem enough, and I had made the suggestion only to please him. In the hope of pleasing him further I added, 'Of course, a baby anything is a beauty. I'd have loved to have him around.'

'It was a she,' he corrected.

'What is the safe age?'

'What do you mean?'

'Up to what age can a tiger be kept as a pet?'

'Until it starts licking the skin off the back of your hand,' he said, 'Anyway, how should I know? I am not a zoo-keeper.'

I tried to find something nasty to say about zoo-keepers, that odious tribe of men whom he loathed, but failed. I merely said, 'Most peculiar profession. I would not be a zoo-keeper for all the wealth in the world.'

He set the tiger cub before me on a stool. I shivered slightly at the thought of anyone taking so young a life. 'Doesn't she look cute? I have had more trouble shaping this than a full-grown one. Guess what I am charging for it?'

This was really a problem for me. If I undervalued it, I might antagonize him. If I mentioned a fantastic figure, he might despise me, seeing through the trick. While my mind was working fast, I stole a glance through the little window over the street. Yes, the fountain would be within his range. From the fountain, down the road, branching off to Lawley Road – he could aim anywhere within the perimeter.

'What are you watching?' he asked suddenly.

'Nothing. I always look at far-off things when I have to do a calculation. I've been thinking over your question. If you charge five thousand rupees, as you told me once . . .'

'Oh, the question is unimportant, leave it alone,' he said. He carried the cub off and put it back, covering it over with a piece of cloth.

I was not to be quenched so easily. I said, 'About two thousand? The labour of shaping it must have been equally great.'

'You are right. It's slightly less. I never charge a round sum. My bill for it would be eighteen hundred and twenty-five, packing extra.'

I gave appropriate cries of admiration for his cleverness, and after talking a little more on the same line we came to business. 'Why don't you come along with me at three o'clock?'

'To your wonderful function? I have had enough of this tomfoolery.'

'Well, you were enthusiastic about it once!'

'That's why I want to keep away. Let me alone, enjoy it yourself.'

He had still to render us an account, but this was not the time to tackle him about it. There was enough time ahead – after tonight, after the elephant was safely returned to Muthu. I wanted to assure him now that I had not come about the accounts. I said, 'Everyone is bound to ask why you are not there. You have done so much for us already.'

'I have had to spend over two thousand rupees out of my pocket. You have no idea how much of my business I have had to set aside. Time is money. I can't be like some of your friends.'

'Let us not talk of all that,' I said.

'Who are you to ask me to shut up!' he cried.

We were coming dangerously near another clash. I did not want to lose my head and lose the chance of keeping him with us and saving the elephant. This was the only tactic I could think of. He spurned me again and again as I repeated my invitation, and finally said, 'Your whole crowd sickens me! You are a fellow without any sense. Why you are so enthusiastic about a poetaster obsessed with monosyllables I don't know. And then that local Nehru. Who does he think he is? All of you joining to waste everyone's time and money! If I had any authority I'd prohibit celebrations of this kind as a waste of national energy.'

I did not want to say that he could keep out if it didn't suit him. I wanted to stretch my capacity for patience to the utmost in the cause of God and country. He was abusive and angry. I wanted to assure him that I was not going to mention accounts for a considerable time to come. So I said, 'Vasu, I have come to you as a friend. I thought it would be fun to have you around. We could see things together and laugh at things together. Perhaps you are worried we might ask about those collections . . .'

'Who? Me, worried!' He laughed devilishly. 'A hundred of you will have to worry before you can catch me worried.'

I laughed pretending that he was joking. I looked at the time. I had wasted nearly three-quarters of an hour in the *tête-à-tête*, and still I had not come to the point. How was I to ask him for an assurance that he would not shoot the elephant?

I now took the rice cake and sweets out of my bag, and placed the packet before him. 'Ah, I forgot about this,' I said. 'I have brought you something to eat. I found it at home and I thought you might like it.'

'What is it?' he asked. He opened the packet and raised his brow. 'You want to practise kindness on me! All right. This is my first experience of it from you. All right, all right, while it lasts.' He put a piece in his mouth, chewed it with critical seriousness and said, 'Not bad, but tell the person who made it to fry the pepper a little more before putting it in. Anyway better than nothing.' He trans-ferred the whole of it, and swallowed it at one gulp, accepting it as something rightfully due to him. I was a little upset to see him take it so casually and critically, and was especially hurt to think that he couldn't pay a compliment to my wife even for courtesy's sake. He merely said, 'If you want to find this stuff at its best, you must taste it at . . . ,' and he mentioned some exclusive place of his own.

'This was prepared by my wife,' I said, trying to forestall any nasty statement he might make. But he merely said, 'Modern women are no good at this. Modern women are no good at anything when you come to think of it.' I did not want him to elaborate the subject as I feared he might say something nasty about my wife, so I desperately changed the subject to the real issue. I said, 'Vasu, I have come to appeal to you not to harm our elephant tonight.'

'How can anyone harm an elephant, of all things? Don't you know that even if you drive a bodkin into its skin, it will only break the point? Anyway, what are you trying to tell me?'

This was challenging. He had risen from the cot, which showed that he was agitated by my question. He tried to look calm, but I found that he was roused. 'Who has been gossiping, I wonder.' He paced up and down, then stood for a moment looking out of the window – as I guessed, at the market fountain. 'Has that bitch been talking to you?'

'Which bitch?' I asked.

'That woman Rangi,' he said with heat.

'Who is Rangi?' I asked.

'You pretend you don't know her!' he cried. 'Why all this show? I'll wring her neck if I find . . .' He didn't finish the sentence. He asked suddenly, 'Well, suppose I decide to shoot that elephant, what can you do about it?'

I had no answer. I only asked, 'What has the poor elephant done to you?'

'Has it occurred to you how much more an elephant is worth dead? You don't have to feed it in the first place. I can make ten thousand out of the parts of this elephant – the tusks, if my calculation is right, must weigh forty pounds, that's eight hundred rupees. I have already an order for the legs, mounted as umbrella stands, and each hair on its tail can be sold for twelve annas for rings and bangles; most women fancy them and it's not for us to question their taste. My first business will be to take out the hairs and keep them apart, while the blood is still hot; trunk, legs, even the nails – it's a perfect animal in that way. Every bit of it is valuable. I've already several inquiries from France and Germany and from Hong Kong. What more can a man want? I could retire for a year on the proceeds of one elephant.'

'Why don't you go and shoot one in the forest?'

'Forest! I want to show them that I can shoot anywhere. I want to teach those forest men a lesson.'

A strange way of teaching a lesson to foresters. I said weakly, 'Shoot a wild one, and no one will blame you.'

'This will be wild enough, don't worry.'

'What do you mean?'

'You watch out,' he said. 'You will thank me for my services. That Kumar is mad already; none of you have noticed it. Have you ever observed his eyes? See the red streak in his little eyes; that means at the slightest provocation he will fly off. . . .'

'What sort of provocation?' I asked.

'How can I say? Elephants are really crazy animals. Anything, any slight . . .' He did not explain.

I felt worried. What was he planning? How was he going to excite it? 'Have you plans to excite it?' I asked point-blank.

He laughed diabolically. 'You want to know everything, my boy. Wait, and you will know. Whatever you have to know will be known one day,' he said in a biblical manner.

I said, 'Whatever horrible plans you may have, remember there will be thousands of people around – men, women, and children dragging the chariot.'

'Let them go home like good citizens before midnight. They can have all the fun they want until midnight.'

'Who are you to say when they should go or come?'

'Now, now, don't try to be nasty. Let them stay or go, that's their business. If the elephant runs wild . . .' He ruminated.

'A few will be trampled and choked in a stampede,' I said.

'You are saying things I don't say. You have a morbid mind.' He said a moment later, 'The elephant has been promised me when it's dead. I have it in writing here.'

'Who has promised?'

'Why should I tell you everything? As far as I'm concerned, you have no business with me at all. How are you concerned with the elephant? It's not yours. I'm not bound to tell you anything. I'm an independent man. You keep it locked away, if you like; that's not going to bother me. Why come and talk to me? Get out of here and mind your morning's work.'

I trembled with excitement and helplessness. I dared not say anything more, lest he should hit me. I pleaded, 'Vasu, you are a human being with feelings like any of us. I am sure you are only pretending to be so wild.' He laughed. He seemed delighted at the way he had brought me down.

'All right, keep your own view of me. I don't mind. You are . . . Shall I tell you what's the matter with you? You are sentimental. I feel sickened when I see a man talking sentimentally like an old widow. I admire people with a scientific outlook.'

'What's scientific about the terrible plans you have?'

'Ah, you see! You use the word "terrible" and are carried away by it. You allow your mind to be carried away by your own phrases. There's nothing terrible in shooting. You pull your trigger and out goes the bullet, and at the other end there is an object waiting to receive it. It is just give and take. At one time I was squeamish like you. It was Hussein who broadened my outlook. He used to tell me the way to be broad-minded is to begin to like a thing you don't like. It makes for a very scientific outlook.'

'It may be science, but the object at the other end does not deserve to be brought down. Has that occurred to you?'

'How can you say? What do you do with an animal which goes on a rampage? Should the public not be protected?'

'This is not that kind of animal,' I said weakly. It was idiotic to try to change his mind, but I wanted to try to the last.

'Unscientific! Unscientific!' he cried. 'What's the premiss for your conclusion? Normal behaviour is one thing and the abnormal behaviour of a beast is another. Exactly when a beast will cross the frontier is a matter that's known only to those who have studied the subject. If you had printed my book on wild life, you'd have found it profitable. I've devoted two chapters to animal behaviour. But you chose to busy yourself with monosyllables.'

I said placatingly, 'I'll take it tomorrow and finish it,' carefully avoiding a mention of the original Heidelberg which was rising to my lips.

'I don't believe your promise,' he said. 'Did you think I'd wait on your pleasure indefinitely? It's already being printed.'

I felt jealous. 'Here, in this town? Who could do it?'

He laughed at my question and said, 'Now I've given you all the time I can. You'll have to leave me. This is my busy day.'

I shuddered at the implication.

The interview knocked out all the joy I had felt in the festival. I had looked forward to it for weeks, and now I felt like a man working towards a disastrous end and carrying a vast crowd with him. I'd have willingly stopped the entire celebration if it had been practicable. But we had started rolling downhill and there was no way of checking our momentum.

It was four o'clock when I managed to reach the temple at Vinayak Street. Men, women, and children thronged the street and the courtyard of the temple. Sen had put up a few bamboo barriers here and there to allow some space for the Mayor and his entourage. He had dressed himself in a dhoti at his waist and had wrapped a red silk upper cloth around his shoulder and his forehead was blazoned with sacred ash, sandal-paste, and vermilion. He was nearly unrecognizable in his holy make-up. The poet had donned a pink bush-coat for the ceremony, and it hurt my eyes. It reminded me of the labels for K.J.'s drinks. K.J. had spread out his coloured water on a wooden platform, and was doing brisk business. Since he had not specified when the free drinks would be supplied, he was freely plying his trade. The babble of voices was deafening. A few shops had sprung up – paper toys, fried nuts, and figurines in red and green sugar, on little trays at the temple gate. The back of the temple was filled with smoke rising from the enormous cooking. Some of the temple priests were busy in the inner sanctum, decorating the God and lighting oil lamps.

Kumar was chained to a peg at the end of the temple corridor, under a tree. A crowd of children watched him; and he was briskly reducing to fibre lengths of sugar cane held out to him by the children. The mahout from Top Slip was perched on his back, painting his forehead in white, red and green floral patterns, to the huge delight of the children, to whom he was appealing, 'Don't make so much noise, give us a chance, give us a chance. Kumar can't hear me if you keep making so much noise.' He had scrubbed and cleaned Kumar's tusks so that the ivory gleamed in the sun. He had decorated the tusks with bronze bands and rings; he was very happy because someone had promised him the loan of gold head-ornaments and brocades. The elephant seemed to enjoy it all immensely and was in a fine mood. My heart sank at the sight of the happy animal.

I found Dr Joshi standing near him, stroking his trunk. In all the rush of work, my promise to fetch him had gone out of my head, but he had somehow arrived. I approached him, pushing my way through the crowd of sightseers. I wanted to apologize for my lapse. But the moment he saw me, he said, 'Sorry I couldn't wait for you. I had to come to the town on business and have stayed on.'

'Oh, that's all right, Doctor, I'm happy to see you. How do you find Kumar?'

He said, 'He is in good shape, I think.'

'Will he stand all the crowd and excitement?'

'Surely. What else do you think he is good for? You will find him at his best in such surroundings.'

'I was wondering whether he would tolerate the fireworks and the band?'

'Why not? But don't let sparks fall on him from the torches or the fireworks. Some elephants get a fright when a flare is held too close. Keep an eye on the torch-bearers, and that should be enough.'

'Do you think he'll go wild if something happens?'

'Why do you ask?' asked the doctor.

'I've heard some people say that an animal can suddenly charge into a crowd.'

He laughed at my fear. 'Don't talk about such ideas. People might get into a panic and that would be really bad in a crowd like this.' We surveyed the jam of humanity. Any rumour might ruin the occasion, and create a stampede. The distribution of the offerings was planned for the end of the procession, when we returned to the temple. That meant that most of the crowd would wait for it. One way of reducing the crowd would be to distribute the sweet rice as soon as possible. I sought out the chief priest of the temple to ask if it could be managed. He said immediately, 'No. The offering is for the eleven o'clock service. How could we distribute anything before that?'

I was obsessed with plans to save the lives of the people who had come out for enjoyment: little girls had dressed themselves in bright skirts, women wore their jewellery and flowers in their hair, and men had donned their best shirts and bush-coats and dhotis and silks. My wife and son were somewhere in that crowd. I had no way of reaching them either. The air was charged with the scent of the jasmine and roses which decorated the chariot.

The Mayor's speech was drowned in the babble in spite of a microphone and loud-speaker. This was the journalist's domain, and I kept away from the dais. I saw from far off the pink bush-coat of the poet rising. He was respectfully presenting the silk-bound copy of the book to the priest. The crowd demonstrated unmistakably that they hadn't assembled there to listen to a speech. The piper and the drummer were providing a thunderous performance. The priest was busy placing offerings at the feet of Krishna and Radha, and Rangi was dancing and gesticulating before the golden images. She had draped herself in a faded brocade and wore a lot of tinsel ornaments on her head and around her neck. I wanted to speak to her – it was urgent – but it would be improper to be seen engaged in a talk with the woman, and the enormous crowd might boo me. I toyed with the idea of sending an emissary to her, any young urchin, but if the fellow was bent on mischief he could expose me and make me the laughing-stock of the crowd. The crowd was in a mood to enjoy anything at anybody's expense.

What did I want to see her for? I wasn't very clear. It seemed vulgar to share a secret with her. If Sastri came to know of it, he would denounce me and leave my service. All the same I wanted to attract her attention, why I couldn't say. I could glimpse her only over several heads and through gaps between shoulders. She was agitating herself in such a way as to make it impossible for anyone to catch her eye. All the same I edged closer, pushing my way through the crowd. The incense smoke and camphor, the babble of the priest's recitations over, the babble of the crowd suddenly proved too oppressive. All night I had sat up working on the formes, and after all this trouble the whole business seemed to be unimportant. I found it strangely irritating to think of the pink-coated poet and all the trouble he had caused me.

The God was beautifully decorated. He wore a rose garland, and a diamond pendant sparkled on his chest. He had been draped in silk and gold lace, and he held a flute in his hand; and his little bride, a golden image draped in blue silk and sparkling with diamonds, was at his side, the shy bride. The piper was blowing his cheeks out, filling the air with 'Kalyani Raga', a lovely melody at this hour. The temple was nearly a century old, built by public subscription in the days when my grandfather and a few others had come here as pioneers. Beyond the temple had been a forest extending to the river; today all the forest was gone; in its place were only a number of ill-built houses, with tiles disarranged by time and wind, straggling houses, mainly occupied by weavers who spread out their weaving frames all along the street. But the temple, with its tower and golden crest and carved pillars, continued to receive support.

The story of Krishna and Radha was now being recited in song-form by a group of men, incoherently and cacophonously, while they acted as vocal accompanists for Rangi's dance, as she swayed and gesticulated. With all the imperfections, the effect of the incense and the chants made me drowsy and elated, and I forgot for a moment all my problems. Vasu was like an irrelevant thought. He should have no place in my scheme of things. People I had never seen in my life acted as a padding to my right and left and fore and aft. I had lived a circumscribed life and had never thought that our town contained such a variety of humanity – bearded, clean-shaven, untidy, tidy; women elegant, ravishing, tub-shaped and coarse; and the children, thousands of them, dressed, undressed, matted-haired, chasing each other between the legs of adults, screaming with joy and trying to press forward and grab the fruit offerings kept for the Gods. Half a dozen adults had set themselves the task of chasing the children away and compelling them to keep out of the main hall of the temple, but when they overflowed into the corridor and the veranda, half a dozen other people set themselves a similar task of keeping them out of the assembly listening to the Chairman's perorations. They chased them back into the hall with equal vigour, and the gang of children came screaming in, enjoying immensely the pendulum swing back and forth.

Through all this babble, the music went on. But I had withdrawn from everything and found a temporary peace of mind. The sight of the God, the sound of music, the rhythm of cymbals and the scent of jasmine and incense induced in me a temporary indifference to everything. Elephant? Who could kill an elephant? There came to my mind the tale of the elephant Gajendra, the elephant of mythology who stepped into a lake and had his leg caught in the jaws of a mighty crocodile; and the elephant trumpeted helplessly, struggled, and in the end desperately called on Vishnu, who immediately appeared and gave him the strength to come ashore out of the jaws of the crocodile. 'In this story,' I told myself, 'our ancestors have shown us that an elephant has a protected life and no one can harm it.' I felt lighter at heart. When the time came the elephant would find the needed strength. The priest was circling the camphor light before the golden images, and the reflections on the faces made them vibrate with a living quality. God Krishna was really an incarnation of Vishnu, who had saved Gajendra; he would again come to the rescue of the same animal on whose behalf I was . . .

Unknowingly I let out a terrific cry which drowned the noise of children, music, everything. 'Oh, Vishnu!' I howled. 'Save our elephant, and save all the innocent men and women who are going to pull the chariot. You must come to our rescue now.' Unknown to myself, I had let out such a shout that the entire crowd inside and outside the hall stood stunned, and all activity stopped. The Chairman's speech was interrupted as my voice overwhelmed the loud-speaker. Rangi stopped dead in her dance. I was soon surrounded by a vast crowd of sympathizers. I felt faint and choked by the congestion.

'Did you shout like that? The Chairman's speech . . .' It was Sen speaking, to whom the only thing that mattered was the Chairman's speech. He was angry and agitated. I heard someone remark, 'This man is possessed, listen to him.' My shout had brought round me all the friends I had been looking for in the crowd. Muthu, the tea-stall keeper, was very tender. He said, 'Are you feeling well?' I felt not unwell but foolish to have brought on myself so much attention. 'Where have you been all along? I've been looking for you.' I had now lost the initiative in my affairs. A number of busybodies carried me out to the veranda under the sky and fanned my face. The veterinary doctor felt my pulse and injected a drug into the veins of my arm. The poet had my head on his lap. 'Doctor, don't give me an elephant dose of anything. I have never seen you curing human ills.' The crowd that stood over me was enormous. Faces everywhere, to my right, left, above and aside. A glut of breathing, sighing, noisy humanity, packing every inch of space. The journalist suddenly lost his head and charged madly into the crowd crying, 'If you don't leave him alone, he'll die of lack of air,' and people made way. The incomplete speech of the Chairman seemed to have given an edge to his temper.

The Chairman sailed in with a lot of dignity. He stooped over to ask, 'Are you feeling better?'

'I'm absolutely well, nothing is the matter with me. Please go and continue your speech. Don't stop it on any account.'

The Chairman looked pleased at the importance given to his speech. He cackled like a shy adolescent. The Chairman of the Municipal Council was actually a man who owned a sweetmeat shop and had risen to his present position through sheer hard work. He was supposed to have started life as a servant and ultimately became the owner of the sweetmeat shop. He always wore (even in his sleep, so people said) a white Gandhi cap as an unwavering member of the Congress Party; a chubby, rosy-cheeked man, who evidently consumed a great deal of his own sweets. Seeing his face so close to mine, I felt reassured. Here was a man who could save the elephant. I said, 'You must protect the elephant.'

'Which elephant?' he asked, rather startled.

I explained. I took my head off the lap of the pink coat and said to the poet, 'Take him to where the elephant is kept.' The poet demurred, the Mayor dodged the suggestion, but I was adamant. The Mayor was being watched by a big circle of the crowd; he did not want to be embroiled in a scene with me and so left. The poet was glad to be out of the spotlight too. I could now sit up. I realized that I had an odd commanding position. People were prepared to do anything I suggested. I felt better. At this moment my wife entered the scene, accompanied by my little son. Both of them rushed to me with agonized cries. I didn't like such a dramatic show, so I told my wife, 'Why are you behaving like this? I only felt a little choked in there and so came out to sit here.'

'You were lying flat on Uncle's lap,' said my boy.

'Only because they would not let me rise to my feet.' My wife burst into tears and remained sobbing. 'Now, now, don't be ridiculous; people will laugh at us for creating a scene and spoiling their day for them. Now, now, go and enjoy yourselves.'

I was on my feet again, and went out of view of the crowd, so that they might carry on normally. I felt rather foolish to have drawn so much attention to myself. I left the temple swiftly by a back door and went home through the lanes. My wife and son accompanied me. I felt bad about depriving them of the pleasure they had come to enjoy at the temple. My son was openly critical. 'Why should we go home so soon? I want to stay and watch the fun.' On our way we saw the schoolmaster going towards the temple, and I handed over the boy to him with 'Please don't let him join the procession, he must come home for supper.'

'I'll bring him back,' said the teacher.

We were not gone long before we heard the piper resume his music, and the loud-speaker's mumbo-jumbo over the babble of the crowd, and that made me happy. Life had become normal again at the temple.

Chapter Ten

At home my wife unrolled a mat, spread a soft pillow and insisted upon my lying down to rest, turning a deaf ear to all my pleading that I was in a perfectly normal condition. She went in to make coffee and nourishment for me. She grumbled, 'Not eating properly, not sleeping, not resting. God knows why you wear yourself out in this way?' How could I tell her about Rangi? It would be awkward and impossible. But if I tried to explain it would be impossible to talk of the matter, leaving out Rangi. And if my wife should ask, 'When and where did Rangi meet you?' I would be unable to reply. I thought it best to accept the situation and rest my weary body on the mat and consume whatever was placed before me. Anyway no one was going to miss me, and nothing in the programme was going to be altered because I wasn't there. The whole programme was so well organized that nothing could be halted. That was the chief trouble now; neither Vasu nor the temple authorities seemed prepared to relax their plans ever so slightly. Each was moving in a fixed orbit as if nothing else mattered or existed.

After the refreshment she had provided me, I fell into a drowse. What had really been the matter with me was lack of food and sleep; now I was having both and benefiting by them. I enjoyed the luxury of floating off through the air on drifting cotton-wool immediately I shut my eyelids. My wife sat at my side, fanning me. She was very anxious about me. I don't know what she had heard. I myself had no notion what my state had been before I let out the shout about the elephant. My wife had dressed herself in her heliotrope silk sari, which she reserved for special occasions; it showed that she considered the temple function a most important one, and it depressed me to see her forgo it. I had implored her, 'Please go and enjoy yourself at the temple. I can look after myself quite well. Don't worry about me.'

She ignored my advice and replied light-heartedly, 'I went there only because you were there,' which pleased me. She added, 'Not that I care for these crowds. Babu was crazy about it, and has taken out all the savings in his money box for sweets and toys.'

'Oh, I should be with him. I could give him such a nice time,' I said remorsefully.

'You will do us all a favour if you keep away from the crowd,' she said, and added, 'Now sleep a little.'

'Why am I being treated like a baby?' I protested. She did not answer and I fell asleep, until I heard soft hammer-strokes on the walls of cotton-wool which had encased me. When the hammer-strokes ceased, I heard voices, and then my wife stood over me. A ray of evening sun thickened with iridescent specks of dust came in through the ventilator of our dining-hall. It used to have a red glass pane when we were young, and made me sick when the evening sun threw a blood-red patch on the wall. Luckily the red pane had been smashed by a stone thrown by a street urchin one mango season, who had actually aimed at the fruits ripening on the trees in our garden, and the pane was never replaced.

My wife said, 'Someone to see you.' She did not like any visitor to disturb me. Her tone was hostile. She added, 'His name is Muthu. Seems to be from a village.'

Immediately I was on my feet. 'Ah, Muthu! Muthu! Come in, please.'

He had his umbrella hooked as usual to his forearm. 'I wanted to see you and so came. I told the mistress of the house that I would wait until you were awake. Why did you disturb yourself? Go back and rest. I will wait.'

I resisted his suggestion, but he was so firm and insistent that I had no alternative but to go back to my mat. He followed me and sat down on the edge of the mat, carefully laying his umbrella on the floor beside his feet. He looked round appreciatively and cried, 'What a big house you have! Do you live in the whole of it or have you rented out a portion?'

I lay back on my pillow, and hotly repudiated the idea. 'I never want to be or ever wanted to be a rent-collector. We have always entertained guests rather than tenants.' I put into my sentence all the venom I wanted to inject into the memory of Vasu.

'It all depends,' Muthu said. 'There is no harm in making a little money out of the space you really do not need.'

'It depends,' I echoed. 'My wife would never permit me, even if I wanted to.'

'Then you can do nothing about it,' he said. 'It's best to listen to the advice of one's wife – because sooner or later that's what everyone does, even the worst bully. Take my own uncle, such a bully for forty years, but at sixty he became a complete slave to his wife. If people are not slaves before sixty, they become slaves after sixty,' he said. He was trying to amuse me – a sick man. It was obvious that he was trying to steer away from the topic of the procession and the temple ceremony. 'He waits for her command every moment, and even stands and sits according to her direction,' he said and laughed. It really amused me, this picture of the bully fawning on his wife at sixty, and I cried to my wife, 'Coffee for my friend!' at which he shouted, 'Good lady, no, don't trouble yourself, no coffee for me.'

'Don't listen to him, but bring the coffee or make it if you haven't got it ready,' I cried. He called in turn, 'Good lady, if you must be troubled, let it be just cold water, a glass of water.'

'Is it impossible for me to offer you anything?' I cried.

'Yes, yes, I never need anything. I have told you I never take anything outside my home.'

'And yet you want everyone to come and ask for tea in the village!' I said complainingly.

'I never force it on anyone,' he said.

There was another knock on the door, and presently my wife ran across to open it and came back, followed by Sen. 'Another cup of coffee,' I cried as she went back to the kitchen. Sen cried, 'So good to see you again in this state; the speech went off very well in spite of the interruption. You really gave a shout which could have gone to heaven, you know.'

'Why talk of all that now?' said Muthu.

'Why not?' cried the journalist aggressively. 'He is all right. And he was all right. Why shouldn't a man let out a shout if it pleases him? This is a free country in spite of all the silly rules and regulations that our Government is weaving around us.'

By the time my wife was ready with two cups of coffee, there was a third knock on the door, followed by another one a moment after: the pink-coated poet, followed by the veterinary doctor. So there was a full assembly on the mat at my house. My wife had to prepare coffee again and again. She accepted the situation cheerfully; the important thing was to keep me in good humour at home. The veterinary doctor felt my pulse and cried, 'You are in perfect gear, you must have had some temporary fatigue or something of the kind, a sudden attack of nerves.'

'I have never felt better,' I said, although the thought kept troubling me that the veterinarian was trespassing unwarrantedly into human fields.

'Haven't you noticed a dog let out a sudden howl, or an elephant trumpet out for no known cause? It's the same mechanism in all creatures. In our institute we spend a course of six months on comparative anatomy and psychology. Only the stimuli and medicinal doses differ between human beings and animals.'

As we were talking the beam of light on the wall had disappeared and a dull twilight was visible above the central court-yard. It seemed absurd that after the preparation of weeks we should all of us be gathered tamely on the mat in my hall instead of bustling about in the temple. What a difference between the picture of the situation as I had visualized it and as it turned out to be! I said with a sigh, 'All of us should be there at the temple.'

'There is nothing very much to do at the moment,' said the journalist. 'This is a sort of intermission. The main worship is over – the poems have been read and dedicated.'

'I missed it,' I said ruefully.

The poet said, 'You didn't miss much. I felt too nervous, and I don't think anyone understood anything.'

'It was quite good,' said Sen encouragingly. 'Some people came round to ask where they could get copies.'

'Probably they expect free copies.'

'Free or otherwise, the world will have to wait until I am ready to print,' I said.

Muthu said, 'Please give me also a copy.'

I said, 'Yes,' although I was not sure if he read anything.

The poet was by nature silent and retiring, and beyond sniggering a little he said nothing. The journalist had him in complete charge. 'Oh, I am sending review copies to thirty newspapers first thing tomorrow, and a special copy to Sahitya Akademi at Delhi. They are wasting funds giving an award to every Tom, Dick and Harry. This is the first time they have had a chance to recognize real literature. Our Government has no lack of funds, but they don't know how to spend properly, that's what is the matter with them. I am going to show them a way to redeem themselves. I put this into the Chairman's speech, pretty strongly, and he just recited it as I wrote it, although he is a Congressman.' He laughed at the memory of his trick.

Night fell. Lights were switched on. My wife began her work in the kitchen. I could hear the clinking of vessels. I said, all my responsibilities coming back into my mind one by one, 'Did the flower supplies, did the . . .' I fretted until they assured me that everything was going well. And then one by one they came round to asking what really had upset me. I had to tell them about Vasu's plans. They were incensed.

'Who is this upstart to come and disturb us? We will get the police to seize his gun.' 'We'll throw him out of the town.' 'I'll knock him down with a hammer, if it comes to that.'

I suggested, 'Why not change the route of the procession?'

'Why should we? We will change nothing for the sake of this man! We will twist his neck so that he faces the other way.'

'It's not possible. The route has been fixed and the licence taken for it. It's impossible to change anything.'

'Why not drop the procession altogether?'

'Thousands of persons to be frustrated because of this fool, is that it?' 'No – never. We'll deal with him. We have been too tolerant.'

'Or why not leave the elephant out?'

'Impossible. What's a procession without an elephant. You know how much we've spent on the elephant.'

'I'll be with Kumar myself, and let's see what happens. He is more sound in mind than any human being in this town.'

'No, no, let's change nothing,' Sen said. He swore, and the others agreed, 'We'll route the procession as arranged. Nothing shall be changed. Let us see what happens.'

Muthu became extremely nervous about his elephant. He lowered his voice and said, 'I knew something had been going on. It started long ago. Do you remember that tailor? He is a friend of Vasu, fancies himself a part owner of the elephant. And I heard he has already received money from Vasu and has given him a document transferring to him his share of the elephant. I heard also a rumour that it was Vasu who tried to poison Kumar.'

'Aha,' said the doctor. 'I suspected something like it.'

They sallied out in a great rage, determined to tackle Vasu in a body. I could not stop them.

They were a determined lot. In their numbers they felt strong. First, led by the journalist, they started out to find the District Superintendent of Police at his home in Lawley Extension, for which purpose they hired Gaffur's taxi at the fountain. They found that he had just returned from a long journey, had put up a reclining chair and was resting on the terrace with a paper in his hand. Sen was his friend. He went straight to the terrace and spoke to him.

He listened to their complaint and said, 'How do you know that he is going to create a disturbance? How do you know that he will employ his gun in the manner you suggest? He has an arms licence, hasn't he?'

'So any man with an arms licence can shoot at anything, is that it? A wonderful law!'

The D.S.P. was annoyed at the contemptuous reference to the law, and retorted, 'That depends; we cannot simply snatch away a licensed weapon because someone thinks it will be fired.'

'So you want to wait until the damage is done?'

'We cannot take action unless there is concrete evidence or a consequence.'

'Can't you do something to prevent possible damage to life and property?'

'That only a magistrate can do, but even he cannot bind anyone over without a proper cause.'

The Superintendent was a police officer, seasoned in jargon and technicalities. He refused to accompany them to Vasu's room, but telephoned to the Town Inspector, 'Have you made proper arrangements for this evening's procession? Have enough men to handle the crowd along the route. There must be no trouble or complaints anywhere. I've some people here who apprehend a breach of the peace. I want you to go with them and tackle a man who is threatening to create a disturbance. Meet them at the market fountain in five minutes.'

At the fountain, a police officer in uniform was there to receive them. They jumped out of the taxi, and surrounded the officer and gave an account of the impending trouble. He was a tall, lean man, with a lot of belts and cross-belts, a very serious-looking man with lines on his forehead. One look at him, and they were satisfied that here was a man who would stand no nonsense from anyone, a grim, determined man.

He simply repeated the doubts that the Superintendent himself had mentioned. 'If the man possesses a licence, he can keep his weapon wherever he likes. Who can question him?'

'But can he shoot from the window?'

'Why should he do that? What's your basis for saying it?' They had no answer to give and he said, 'All right, we'll see what we can do.'

The Inspector stayed downstairs. Led by Sen, supported by the veterinary doctor, the pink-coated poet bringing up the rear, they boldly went up the staircase and knocked on Vasu's door. They were considerably emboldened by the fact that a real live Inspector of Police was down below, waiting to appear at the lightest summons. The door opened, and Vasu's head appeared with its dark halo of hair, set off by the light from his room. 'You people want to see me now?'

'Yes,' said the journalist. 'Rather urgently.'

Vasu raised his brow. 'Urgent! All of you to see me?' And then he counted, 'One, two, three, four people to call on me! I don't want to see anyone now. So try again tomorrow.' With that he turned back and tried to shut the door in the face of his visitors. Since the door opened outwards, the journalist seized the knob and held it back. Vasu looked amused. 'Do you know, I could easily pick up all four of you and toss you downstairs? When I plainly say I don't care to talk, how can you persist? All right. I will give you each a minute. Be brief. What is it?' He was not disposed to admit them. He blocked the doorway, and they were ranged on the landing.

The journalist stated point-blank, 'We have a report that there is likely to be a disturbance while the procession passes down this road.'

'If you know that, why don't you take the procession around somewhere else?'

'That's not your concern. We will not tolerate any disturbance.'

'Oh, iron-willed men! Very good. I agree with you. Don't tolerate any disturbance.'

'That elephant belongs to no one but the Goddess on the hill road. If anyone tries to harm it . . .,' began Muthu and Vasu cut in, 'Why don't you mind your tea-shop and keep off the flies, and leave these issues to others? Don't try to speak for any elephant.'

'We know what you have been trying to do, and we aren't going to stand any nonsense,' the veterinary doctor said. 'I have examined Kumar and know him inside out. He is in perfect health, more sober than any human being here.'

'So what?' asked Vasu.

'If anyone wishes to drive him crazy, he'll not succeed, that's what I wish to say.'

'Doctor, you may have an American degree, but you know nothing about animals. Do they have elephants in America? Try to get into a government department, count your thirty days and draw your sinecure's allowance. Why do you bother about these matters? Poet, say something in your monosyllables. Why are you silent?

Don't be smug and let others fight your cause. Sell me a copy of your poem as soon as it is read. That's all? Now be off, all of you.'

The journalist warned him, 'We are not bothered about you. We'll leave you alone. You leave our procession alone. This is a sacred function. People are out there to be with their God. . . .'

'If God is everywhere, why follow Him only in a procession?'

The journalist ignored this remark and said, 'Hundreds of men and women and children with the chariot . . .'

'What's this special point about women and children? You are all practising chivalry, are you? If men are to be caught in a stampede, why not women and children also? What's the point in saving women and children alone? What will they do after their men are stamped out? If you are a real philosopher and believe in reincarnation, you should not really mind what happens. If one is destroyed now, one will be reborn within a moment, with a brand-new body. Anyway, do you know why we have so many *melas* in our country? So that the population may be kept within manageable limits. Have you not observed it? At *Kumb Mela*, thousands and thousands gather; less than the original number go back home – cholera, or smallpox, or they just get trampled. How many temple chariots have run over the onlookers at every festival gathering? Have you ever paused to think why it's arranged thus?'

Vasu's philosophical discourse could not proceed further as the Police Inspector showed himself at this moment. He pushed the others aside and accosted Vasu.

The Inspector asked, 'You have a gun?'

'I have two,' replied Vasu.

'I want to see your licence.'

Vasu opened a cupboard, produced a brown envelope and tossed it at the Inspector. The Inspector went through it and asked, 'Where are your arms?' Vasu pointed to his rifle on the chair, and his revolver on the table. The Inspector went over, picked them up, and examined them. 'Are they loaded?' he asked.

'Of course they are loaded. They are not toys.'

'Where is your ammunition statement?'

'In that envelope.'

'When did you discharge your last shot?'

'Shut up, Inspector, and get out. I don't have to answer your questions. What's your authority for coming and questioning me?'

'Our D.S.P.'s order.'

'It's my order that you clear out, with this bunch of men who have no business here.'

The journalist protested. Muthu jumped up and down in rage. Vasu said, 'Inspector, you are trespassing in my house. Where is your warrant to enter private premises? Come on, produce a warrant. Otherwise I will complain against you for trespass and these men will be my witnesses. I'll wire to the Inspector-General and the Home Minister. You think you can fool me as you fool all these wretched bullock-cart drivers and cobblers and ragamuffins whom you order about. Whom do you think you are talking to?'

'Be calm, be calm. I came here only as your friend.'

'Nonsense. You my friend! I have never seen you.'

'I came to ask something of you, that's all.'

'What is it? Be brief.'

'I just want to suggest, why not let me hold your weapons for you in our Market Station. You may take them back tomorrow.'

Vasu said, 'I see that you are still toying with that gun of mine. Put it down where you took it from. Come on. Don't play with it.'

'I'll arrest you for disorderly behaviour and lock you up for the night or for any length of time under the Public Safety Act.' He took out his whistle, and was about to blow it and call the men who were patrolling the road below. Before anyone could realize what was happening, Vasu plucked the whistle out of the Inspector's mouth and flung it away. It sailed over the landing and fell with a clatter down below amid the pythons and all the other stuffed creatures. The Inspector was enraged. He raised his arm and tried to slap Vasu's face. Vasu reared his head back, shielding his face with his hand, then gave a sweep with the back of his hand and brought it down with a slicing movement on the Inspector's wrist and dislocated it. The Inspector screamed and recoiled as if he had touched fire. He still held the gun in the other hand.

'I told you to put that gun back where you took it from. Will you do it or not?'

'You are trying to order me,' cried the Inspector. Tears welled up in his eyes through pain. Vasu took him by the shoulder and propelled him to the cot, then pushed him down, saying, 'Take a rest, you poor fish. You should not venture to do things without knowing what's what.' He snatched the gun from his hand and put it away. The police officer wriggled with pain. Vasu looked at him for a while, and said with cynical laughter. 'You have hurt yourself. I did nothing. I never hit anyone. Years ago I made that vow. If I had hit you with my hand – do you want to see what would have happened?' He brought his palm flat down on the iron frame of the cot and cracked it. The Inspector watched him mutely. Sen asked, 'Do you know what the penalty is for assaulting a police officer in uniform?'

'Do you know what the consequences could be for trespass? Anyway my lawyer will deal with it. Now all of you leave me. I do not want to hit anyone, you now know why. Inspector, you should not have hurt yourself like that!' He mocked the man in pain.

The veterinarian approached the Inspector and said, 'Let's get this dressed immediately. Come along, we'll go to the hospital.' They were all for leaving. Sen said, 'If anything happens to the people or the procession . . .' Muthu said, 'We know what you are trying to do with that elephant. If anything happens . . .' which only provoked Vasu's mirth. The Inspector got to his feet, glared at Vasu and said, 'I'll get you for this . . .' The poet alone tried to sneak downstairs without a word. Vasu just held him by the scruff, turned him round and asked, 'Where is your patron saint? Send him up next. He's the one who has sent you all up on this fool's errand, I know.'

While all this was happening (as narrated to me by Sen later), at home my wife was arguing with me to stay put on my mat. I had got a passing notion that I ought to visit the temple and take charge of the procession. My wife was aghast at the idea. She repeated several times, 'The doctor has said you must not . . .'

'What doctor! He is only an animal doctor!' I said. 'We can't pay serious attention to what he says.'

But she was adamant and pleaded with me, 'Can't you stay in at least one day in a year!' She had prepared a feast for me. She knew all my preferences: potato and onion mash, rice patties fried in oil, chutney ground with green chili, sauce with brinjal and grated coconut, cucumber sliced, peppered and salted. She was so full of enthusiasm that I had to prevent her by my rude remarks from exceeding ten courses. Our house was fragrant with the frying in the kitchen. All this felicity was meant to be a compensation to me for missing the magnificent flower decorations, the music, the lights and the crowd. My son came home with his schoolteacher and was full of descriptions of what he had seen. He said, 'The chariot is made of jasmine buds, and they have fitted small electric bulbs all over it. Father, Father, I bought a sugar cane for the elephant. He snatched it from my hand, and you know how quickly he ate it! I bought him another one, and that left me with only six annas. I bought this whistle.' He produced from his pocket a reed whistle and blew shrilly. 'The mahout has promised to give me a ride on the elephant's back. My friend Ramu says that the elephant is borrowed and that it'll go away tomorrow. Is it a fact, Father? Let us have our own elephant for this temple. The mahout has taught him how to take a garland from a basket and present it to the God. He is very intelligent. Father, Father, please let me go and watch the procession.' His mother added from inside, 'If our neighbours are going and if you promise to stay in and rest, I would like to go and see the start of the procession and come back immediately. The child will love it. We can't say when we may have another chance.'

'All right, why not let me take you both?'

'No, no, in that case I don't want to go,' she said. 'It's not so important.' I enjoyed the status of being more important than the procession. To be fussed over like this came only once in a decade when one fell ill or down a ladder; it was a nice change from protecting and guiding others and running the household as its head.

I lay back on the mat, picked up a picture book and read Babu a story, much against his will as he only wanted to talk about the elephant and the procession. But we had exhausted the topic of the procession. He had been talking of nothing else; whom he met, who fell off the steps leading to the tower of the temple, why the drummer suddenly ceased in the middle of an enraptured performance because he found a grasshopper crawling down his spine – Babu knew who had perpetrated the joke because he had assisted him in tracking and trapping the grasshopper; how he and another friend snatched away from under the nose of the chief priest the plantains which had been kept on a plate for offering to the God, and to this minute no one could guess what had happened to the fruit. He looked at me triumphantly in appreciation of his own exploits. He narrated how he and his gang had devised a game of hide and seek between the legs of the devotees assembled in the hall and how, as they all stood in prayer with eyes shut, his friends had crawled between their legs and roused them by tickling their calf-muscles. I realized how he must have multiplied the task of those men who had been busy since morning chasing the urchins out. Then he went on to tell me how one of his friends was waiting for a chance to poke a needle into the elephant's side. At this I remonstrated, 'Never do that. An elephant will always mark such a fellow down and . . .' I thought I might turn his ideas from these dangerous paths and picked up one of his picture books and tried to read him a story. 'Once upon a time . . . ,' I began, but he was not interested. The activities of the temple were so immediate and real that the images of fiction were uninteresting. He got up and ran to the kitchen on the plea that he felt hungry.

Presently my wife called me in to dinner. She had spread out a large plantain leaf and had served my food on it as if I were a rare guest come to the house. She had placed a plank for me to sit on. She watched me with satisfaction as I made preparations to eat with relish. I suggested, 'Why don't you also put a leaf for yourself and let us serve ourselves?' She turned down my suggestion. She had decided to play the hostess and serve me ceremoniously. Nothing I suggested was going to be accepted today.

I enjoyed my dinner, and kept paying her compliments on her excellence as a cook. There was a knock on the door. Babu, who had finished his dinner, ran out to open it. He came back to say, 'A *mami* has come.'

'*Mami!*' cried my wife. She was busy serving me. 'It must be our neighbour come to see if I'm ready for the procession. Tell her to come in and take a seat. I'll see her in a moment.'

The boy said coldly, 'She is not asking for you. She is asking for Father.'

'What! Who is she?' asked my wife with a sudden scowl on her face.

I trembled within myself and muttered with a feeble, feigned surprise, 'Asking for me. Ha! Ha! It must be a mistake!'

My wife set the vessel down and went out of the room, saying under her breath, 'Let me see.'

The boy tried to follow her. I called him back. 'Boy, fetch me that water-jug.' When he came close to me with the jug, I asked in a whisper, 'Who is she? What is she like?'

'I don't know. She was in the temple dancing.'

I knew now. My worst fears were confirmed. All the fine moments of the evening, the taste of exquisite food, everything was turning to gall on my tongue. I knew my wife. Although I had had no occasion to test it, I knew she could be fiercely jealous. Before I had time to decide what to say or how to say it, she stood before me.

She said, 'That woman wants to see you. What's your connection with her?'

'What woman?' I asked with affected innocence. I got up from my dinner, went out to rinse my hand and wipe it on a towel, and came back to the hall. 'Bring the betel leaf and nut.' I put on a deliberate

146

look of unhurrying indifference, though all the time I knew that Rangi was waiting at the door. I chewed the betel leaves and went back to the kitchen. My wife had settled down to her dinner, serving herself. She did not look up. I said, 'Have you any food left, or have I eaten everything up? If there is nothing left, it's your own fault, you should not have excelled yourself in that way!'

She tried to smile; my praise, very sincere of course, had its effect. She was transferring food from the dining leaf to her mouth with her head lowered. Now she looked up to say, 'I have asked her to wait in the passage. I didn't want the neighbours to see her at our door.' She had to lower her voice in order not to be heard by the woman concerned.

I whispered back, 'You did right, you did right,' and then, 'You could have asked her why she had come.'

'Why should I? If it's your business, it's your business, that's all. I am not interested.'

I made a noise of vexation, and said, 'What a nuisance! It must be something connected with the temple. Can't I rest even for a day?' So muttering, I made my way towards the dark passage. There she was standing in the passage. She had taken off her gaudy dance ornaments and costume and was dressed in a plain sari; even in the dark I could see the emphatic curves of her body. I stood away from her, at a safe distance, right by the inner doorway, and asked rather loudly, 'What is the matter?' I did not want to carry on a whispered dialogue with her.

But she replied in a whisper, 'I wanted to know how you were, master?'

I was touched by her solicitude. 'Oh, I'm all right. Nothing was really the matter.'

'I saw everything, but could not come over because I was on duty before the God.'

'Oh,' I said, feeling rather pleased. 'Are your duties finished for the day? What about the procession?'

'It's at nine o'clock. I shall have to get back.'

'Oh,' I said.

'Won't you go with the procession, sir?' she asked.

My son, who had stood around uneasily, feeling rather shy in the presence of a dancing woman, went away and hid himself in the kitchen. Rangi assumed an even softer and hoarser whisper to say, 'He came to my house in the afternoon when I was at the temple, and left orders that I should see him.'

I grew apprehensive. 'Don't go. Get back to the temple. Be with the crowd.'

'He may come to my house again and set fire to it. Only my old mother is there – deaf and blind.'

'Why should he set fire to your house?'

'He is wild with me and wants to talk to me!' she said with a sigh.

'Talk to you! He will probably murder you!' I said. She brooded over my words. I told her, 'Why don't you tell the police?'

She shook her head. 'He won't be afraid of the police. He is afraid of nothing. The police will laugh at me. What can they do? He is not afraid of anything or anybody. That's how he is.'

'Don't go to him,' I implored her.

My wife had finished her dinner and was passing up and down on various minor errands, casting sly, sidelong looks at the two of us in the dark passage. Rangi was sobbing at the prospect before her. 'I don't know what he will do to me! He has summoned me. He confided in me. I betrayed his trust. I had to . . . I hope, hope, you have taken precautions.'

'Oh, surely,' I said with a grand show of confidence and aggressiveness. 'We won't let a fellow like that get away with his ideas.'

'You don't know him well enough. He is afraid of nothing on earth or in heaven or hell.'

'We have our own methods for dealing with such fellows. We are a match for him,' I said.

'He is so strong and obstinate. If he thinks of something, he has to do it; no one on earth can change his mind.'

The woman seemed obsessed with the grandeur and invincibility of the man. I was not going to tolerate it. 'Rangi, don't be carried away by the notions you have of him. He is just an ordinary common bully. We know how to tackle him.'

'Now, what shall I do, sir? I have come to you because I don't know what to do. I thought of going to him to see if I could get him into a good mood to listen to my words. I have cooked his favourite *pulav* and have it here.' She indicated a hamper of food she had brought along.

'But you said yourself that it's impossible to make him change his mind.'

She whispered seductively, 'I'll try. A woman in my position has her ways.'

I didn't know what she meant, but it sounded mysterious. I said,

'He may not let you go back to the procession. Don't go to him. Go home.'

'If I don't obey his summons he may set fire to my house, with my blind mother not knowing what is happening.'

'I'll arrange for people to guard your house. Don't let him blackmail you into visiting him. He'll hold you back. He may even tie you up hand and foot. I'll send the proper people to guard your house.' I spoke grandiosely, without the shred of a notion how I was going to arrange it. She brought her palms together in a salute and left me, and vanished down the moonlit street.

I went back to my wife. I found her tidying herself up in the dark ante-room, before a mirror. I said expansively, 'You know what's the matter with that woman?'

'Why should it interest me?' she asked. I was struck by the cold, indifferent tone in which she spoke. 'I don't know who she is, and I don't care.' She readjusted her sari and called, 'Babu!' In a moment he was at her side. 'Coming to the temple?'

'Yes, of course.' He had already gone ahead, to the outer door.

I asked her, 'Are you going to the temple?'

'Yes,' she said monosyllabically.

'But you said you would not go!' I said.

'Now I say I'm going, that's all there is to it.' I could see even by the dim light that her ears were red.

'I wanted to speak to you. I thought you might rest here and talk over things.'

She turned a deaf ear to what I was saying. I followed her mumbling, 'You wanted me to stay at home, now you are going!' I sounded pathetic.

'Stay or go, it's all the same to me,' she said and was gone down the steps. She went on down the road, with Babu prancing beside her. She had not given me a chance even to pick a quarrel with her.

I didn't like to go in. I sat on the *pyol*, looking in the direction in which she had gone. What was the use? There was a silly little hope that she would repent her brusqueness and come back to make amends. My only other companion for the night was a street-dog curled up in the gutter. All the other living creatures of that area had gone to the temple. Not a soul remained at home – except the asthmatic in the sixth house, whom I could hear cough and expectorate. Sitting there and brooding, I had time to take stock. The trouble with me was that I was not able to say 'no' to anyone and that got me into complications with everyone, from a temple prostitute to a taxidermist. I repeated to myself all the stinging rejoinders I should have hurled at my wife. I should have behaved like one of my ancestors (the story was often told by my great-aunt), who used to bring home his concubine and have her dinner served by his wife. So when my wife asked, 'What is your business with her?' I should have instantly said, 'I want to seduce Rangi or be seduced by her.' If my wife had said, 'Of all women!' I should have replied, 'Yes, of course, you are blinded by jealousy. No doubt she chews tobacco and looks rugged, but she has it, it comes through even when she whispers to you. How can any man resist her? I'm sorry for you. You should take more trouble to keep me in good humour. It's no good losing your temper or sulking or snapping a reply. If I followed the same procedure, you'd not be able to stand it for a second. As a man I have strength no doubt to stand all your nonsense. But you should not strain it too much. That's all now, don't do it again.'

The moon came over the roof-tiles of the opposite row of houses, full and brilliant. I could hear the hubbub of voices from the temple half a mile away. It saddened me to be detached from all this activity. I felt like a man isolated by an infection. I almost formed, as a sort of revenge on my wife, a plan to appear at the temple precincts and take a hand in the conduct of the procession. Without creating a panic, I would gently navigate the chariot into a different route. That is, of course, if I rushed around a bit, met the D.S.P. and changed the permit for another route. There was not a single person in that whole throng who could organize and guide a procession as I could. I swelled with pride. I was the one man who could still achieve results.

But then I remembered I was an outcast. I felt nervous of appearing before the crowd again. I was not certain what I would do. Under the pressure of the crowd, if I let out a cry again, that would be the end of me. It might have the desirable effect of making my wife regret her petulance, but it was also likely to have me bundled off to the Madras Mental Hospital by the next train. I remembered a boy, a brilliant fellow, who had strode up and down Kabir Street singing all Tyagaraja's compositions for three days and nights continuously and had covered most of the compositions of that inspired saint. If he had been left alone for another day, he would have completed the repertory, but they seized and bundled him off by the five o'clock express to Madras. He came back a year later with a shaven head, but sober and quiet in all other respects.

He was a friend of mine in my school-days, and he confessed that he had sung Tyagaraja's compositions only because he was keen on letting the public get an idea of the versatility of that great composer, but now he was afraid even to hum the tunes in his bath. Our Kabir Street citizens had exacting standards of sanity. I didn't want to be seized and put into the Madras train. Even if I didn't create a scene, the crowd would look at me as if I had recovered from a fit of epilepsy. They would not let me go with the procession.

All my old anxieties, which had been falsely lulled, suddenly rose to the surface. I took stock of the situation. What cause had I for smugness? I had done nothing to divert the procession, I had done nothing to disarm or dissuade Vasu; God knew what trick he might have up his sleeve. He might do nothing more than fling a fire-cracker from his window or bribe one of the torch-bearers to hold the torch close to the leg of the elephant. All evening we had done nothing but discuss the various methods of maddening an elephant – a needle stuck into a coconut or banana and given it to swallow, an ant dropped in its ear, or a grain of sand in its eyes; it would be the easiest thing to drive an elephant mad. If people were lucky they might get out of its range or if they weren't a few might be caught and trampled to death, particularly if there was a stampede at that narrow bend in the Market Road, with the broad storm-drain on one side and the small mountain of road-metal heaped on the other (it was meant for the improvement of Market Road, but had remained untouched since 1945). People would thank anyone who shot the elephant at that moment. That poor elephant! He was enjoying all the fun today, decorated, happy, playing with the children, starting the day so well. Somehow he must return to the Goddess on the mountain road and graze in the forests on the blue hills and continue to delight the children in all those villages. Muthu hoped by hiring out the elephant for processions to earn enough money to build a tower for the temple of the Goddess, which would be visible for fifty miles around. It was impossible to conceive of Kumar stuffed and dissected and serving as an umbrella-stand or waste-basket in some fashionable home in the Eastern or Western world.

I had to do something. My wife had gone out, expecting me to act as the watchman of the house. It would be good to abandon the house and let her discover that after all she could not presume on my goodness. A better plan still would be to lock the door and take the key away so that when she came back after midnight she would wonder how to get to her bed. It was nearing ten, and the procession should be starting any minute now. No one could judge when it would arrive at the fountain. While on the road, the piper might start a big *alapama*, and until he attained certain flights and heights in a particular melody and returned to earth the procession would not move, even if it took an hour. So by stages it might take hours to cover the distance between the temple and the fountain.

There was no sign of the music yet. Only the hubbub of voices indicated that the crowd was still waiting for the procession to start. If it had started, I'd have heard the voices and music moving nearer, and above all my wife would have come back home. However temperamental she might be, I knew she would not go with the procession along with that crowd. She had enough sense to return home in time.

I felt angry at being chained to the house. I would go into the outer fringes of the crowd unrecognized and study the situation. I shut the door behind me and stepped down. I walked to the end of the street. Two men were coming in my direction. I stopped them to ask, 'Has the procession started?'

'No they are waiting for ornaments for the elephant. Someone has gone to fetch them from the Talapur temple, head-ornaments of real gold.'

Ten miles up and ten miles down, and perhaps an hour getting the ornaments out of the temple vaults. No chance of the procession starting before two a.m. What madness! Did it mean that my wife was going to stay at the temple till two? With the boy? I was in a measure relieved; every hour's delay seemed to me an hour's reprieve. I went back home; if the procession was starting late, then there was no purpose in my loitering at the temple gate. I went back home and laid myself down on the *pyol*. If I was to be a watchman, I'd better be one thoroughly, not a haphazard one! I didn't want the house to be looted; this was just the chance thieves waited for, when every householder would have gone out to the festival.

Lying on the mat on the *pyol*, as I kept gazing on the moonlit street, I fell asleep. I woke up hours later as I heard drums and pipe music approaching – I knew that the procession was in Market Road, parallel to our house. I grew worried about my wife and son, thinking that they were still out. On second thoughts I went in. I saw her asleep in her bed, with the child also asleep. I must have been soundly asleep indeed not to have known when she arrived. She must have come in long ago and gone to sleep. She ought to have wakened me, but she had preferred to go on practising her coldness towards me. In order to mete out to her the same treatment, I went back to my mat on the *pyol*.

I lay tossing on my mat. Far off the piper's music came from the procession. I followed it, visualizing all the stages of its progress. Now it must be passing the elementary school conducted on the top storey of the Chairman's sweetmart, a rickety terrace which would come down any day, but no one could prevent it being there because it was the Chairman's building and was certified to be safe. Some day when it fell it was going to imperil the lives of a hundred school-children and six or eight teachers. But so far it had lived up to the optimistic estimate of the municipal authorities and most of its ex-pupils were now adults working and earning a living in various walks of life all over India; I preferred to send Babu to another school, however. The drummer made enough noise to shatter the foundations of this precarious building, but it was a matter of courtesy for the procession to stop there, and the piper had saved his breath for his masterpiece – 'Bhairavi'. He was beginning an elaborate, intricate rendering of this melody, and that means the crowd would gather round him, the God would repose in his chariot, the elephant would stand ahead of the procession with the mahout asleep on his back. People would crowd around the piper and behave as if they had no further way to go.

It was much better that the procession halted here than at the fountain. The time was around midnight now, and it would take at least an hour for the procession to approach the market fountain. I had plans to join the procession and mix with the crowd an hour hence, and till then there was no harm in sleeping. 'Bhairavi' could be heard as well here half asleep as anywhere, and so I allowed myself to be lulled by it, my favourite melody in any case. It brought to my mind my childhood, when visiting musicians used to come as our guests; there was a room in our house known as the musician's room, for we always had some musician or other staying with us, as my father was very proud of his familiarity with all the musicians in South India and organized their recitals in our town. (One of the charges levelled against him by the opposing lawyer was that he had squandered the family funds in entertaining musicians.) This room was also used as a storing space for old bottles. The great joke in those days was to answer, when anyone questioned why old bottles were kept so safely, that if my uncles sued for them, they could be given their due share. The room contained too about seventy philosophical works; the entire philosophical library collected by my father or someone before him in Sanskrit and Tamil, along with bronze images used for worship. They had been willed to the third uncle, but they were left in our custody as my uncle was in the railway department and never stayed in the same place for more than three months. He was never known to have opened a book in his life after leaving school, but still he occasionally sent us a postcard to inquire if the volumes of philosophy were safe. Whenever my mother got into an argumentative mood, she would arraign my father for being a custodian of other people's property, and demand to know why he did not throw the articles out and get rid of all the responsibility. But my father was fond of his brothers, whatever they might do, and told her not to peep into that room as there was sufficient space in the rest of the house for her to mind.

I must have fallen asleep. When I woke up 'Bhairavi' was no longer being played but some other tune, and the music was coming from close quarters across the row of buildings on Market Road. If my judgement was right the procession must now be near the silkware house. The next stop would be the fountain. I was seized with anxiety. The procession was nearing the range of Vasu's window. What reason had I for my inactivity? What right had I to presume that Muthu and the rest would have succeeded in restraining Vasu? Suppose they had done nothing, and a torch-bearer scalded the toe of the elephant and drove it mad? My duty now was clear. I must go and divert the procession away from the fountain and turn it into a side-street. But this might itself start a panic, and if Vasu really meant no mischief I should become responsible for a lot of panic and confusion.

There was no use lying here and cogitating while every minute a vast assembly was moving towards its doom. I had to do something about it. I got up briskly. I could hear my wife stirring, awakened by the pipe and band; she would probably come out to watch from the end of Kabir Lane, in which case I did not want to meet her. I walked across the road, opened the back door of my press and shut the door behind me. I was going to make a last-minute attempt to stop Vasu. He was not such a bad fellow after all. He would listen to me. He was considerably mellower than he used to be. I looked up at the attic. There was no light in it. Of course he would put out all lights. He was the prince of darkness, and in darkness his activities were to be conducted.

Suddenly I was inspired by all sorts of wonderful and effective plans. They were not shaped very clearly in my mind yet, but I was positive that all would be well. If you had asked me to see a blueprint, I would perhaps have fumbled, but deep within me the plans were ready, I felt sure. I would first steal up to his room, walk softly to his side; he was sure to be watching the window. Why not stun him from behind and save everyone all the worry and trouble of argument? Not practicable. One might talk of finishing off a cobra with a staff of bamboo, but it was always more likely that the cobra would prove smarter. Vasu might after all not be facing the window, but facing the door. Non-violence would be the safest policy with him. Mahatma Gandhi was right in asking people to carry on their fight with the weapon of non-violence; the chances of getting hurt were much less.

I had to squeeze myself through a little fence between my press and the staircase; the jeep was there all right. He was undoubtedly upstairs. It might be a good idea to set its petrol tank on fire. That would keep him busy until the procession passed. Of course he might make pulp of me if he discovered me doing it, but why not? No one was going to miss me. My wife was separated from me, there was none to bemoan my loss; true, Babu was likely to miss me for a few days, but children adapted themselves to new circumstances with surprising ease. It was pleasing to reflect that my wife would after all learn a lesson, that sulking did not pay. When Rangi spoke to me on an important matter, the thing for a rational being to do was to ask what exactly it was all about and approach things in a scientific frame of mind . . . No wonder Vasu was bitter against the whole world for its lack of scientific approach. If people were scientific-minded they would not jump to conclusions when a man spoke to Rangi in a half-dark passage.

I was at the foot of the staircase. The hyena was still there but pushed away to the side; it must have been a wasted labour for Vasu. It was surrounded by a few other odds and ends of dead creatures, nothing outstanding among them, but a miscellany of small game, such as a wild squirrel, a fox, a jungle dog, a small cheetah, and several reptiles. Vasu seemed to have turned his attention to small things in keeping with our Government's zeal for small industries. The smell of hide and packing-cases overwhelmed me.

I climbed the stairs. I had presumed all along that the door would be open. What if it should be shut? I would knock on it and allow events to develop. I was going to stop him from disturbing the procession; that was certain, but how was a question I still could not answer. I was going to depend upon my intuition. I was prepared to lose my life in the process.

I found the door open. I gave it a gentle push and peeped in. There he was as I had visualized him, beside the window, on a long easy chair. The lights, the Kitson vapour lamps and the torches of the procession were already illuminating the walls of the room, and there were moving shadows on them. The band and the pipe and the shouts of the men pulling the chariot could be heard from below. I could see his silhouette at the window, where he seemed to have made himself comfortable, with a pillow under his head. He had stretched his leg on a stool, he had his timepiece on another small table, and his gun lay on the floor within his reach. I could see so much by the flares flickering along the wall through the narrow window. Other silhouettes, of the small tiger cub and a few animals, stood out in the semi-darkness. He didn't move. That was a good sign. He had probably fallen asleep waiting for the procession to come along. All the drumming (they could at least have had the sense to pass the spot noiselessly, as a precaution) had apparently made no impression on him. He was obviously a sound sleeper, thank God.

My decision was swift; I would make a dash for his gun and seize it. My heart palpitated and my breath came and went like a bellows as I crawled towards the gun. If he woke up before I reached it, that would be the end of me. I started crawling like one of those panthers of the Mempi jungle, the distance between me and the gun being only a dozen feet; I covered half of it, the other half seemed interminable. My knees were sore, but I felt that it was for a good cause that I was skinning them. He was still asleep. As my fingers reached the cold butt of his gun, I could have swooned with excitement. I had never touched a gun before and felt scared. I rose to my feet and covered him with the gun. Below the window the procession was passing rather quickly, as I thought. I wished I could go up and take a look at it, but he was between me and the window, and if he slept through it that would be the best arrangement possible. If he woke up, well, I had the gun with me at point-blank range. I would follow the method they used in films and command him not to stir until the procession passed. If he made the slightest movement, I would pull the trigger. My finger was on it already. Although I had had no practice with guns, I knew if I fiddled with the trigger the shot was bound to go off. I held the muzzle directly at his head, keeping it away, just out of his reach, in case he attempted to snatch it from my hand. I would hold him until the procession passed our road . . . and then how was our encounter to conclude? I couldn't say. I felt rather worried about it, although I was triumphant at my success thus far. I couldn't keep my eyes off him, although I was curious to watch the procession. From my place I could see the flower-decked top of the chariot and the little bulbs sparkling on it, the head of the elephant brilliant with the gold plates from Talapur, and the hunched form of the mahout. While passing he cast a look through our window. I supposed he had been advised to drive fast. In a moment he was out of view, and soon the procession itself was gone. The reflections on the walls vanished and the drums and pipes sounded far away, leaving a faint aroma of jasmine and roses in their wake. Just at this moment I was startled by the alarm bell of the clock going off. I gave a jump, the gun dropped from my hand, and I made a dash for the landing out of Vasu's reach.

Chapter Eleven

Life resumed its normal pace on the Market Road next morning, although the day started late. It was as if our town were waking up from a fantasy full of colour, glitter, crowd, and song. After this, it was difficult to wake to a dull workaday world. The Market Road was covered with litter, banana peels, coconut shells, leaves, and flowers. Municipal sweepers were busy. Sastri came only at nine o'clock and went straight to the type-board; he seemed determined to complete K.J.'s labels today. Muthu and the rest had left by an early bus for their respective homes. I sat at my desk and placed a pad and a pencil in position in order to make a note of payments to be made, cash in hand and cash promised. My head was still very unclear about the practical aspects of everything.

Our postman, Thanappa, whom we had known as children, old enough to have retired twice over but somehow still in service, was my first visitor for the day. I remembered seeing him in the days when postmen were given a red turban and a shining belt, a leather bag and khaki uniform. He had passed from that to the latest stage of donning a forage cap – a portly old man who not only knew the address of every citizen in the town but also the ups and downs of their fortunes. He was a timeless being. At his favourite corners, he spread out his letters and bags and packets and sat down to a full discussion of family and social matters; he served as a live link between several families, carrying information from house to house. All this took time, but nobody could hustle him, and we accepted our letters when they came. He was welcome everywhere. His habit when he came to my press was to stand in the doorway, rest his shoulder on the doorpost, and spend at least half an hour exchanging information with me. Only before leaving would he remember to give me the letter or book-packet. Today he stood on my door-step and looked serious, blinking through his inch-thick glasses. There was a frown on his face, and he breathed hard with excitement. He held up a letter without a word. I said, 'Come in, Thanappa,' and asked, 'How did you like the procession last night?' He mumbled something and moved in as if he were in a trance. He placed the letter on my desk. 'This receipt has to be signed.'

I saw it was addressed to Vasu. 'This is for him, Thanappa. Take it upstairs.'

'I went up, but, but,' he wetted his lips with his tongue, 'he is dead.' He spoke softly, he looked scared. 'I usually take his mail to his bed, though I hate to go to his room. I thought he was sleeping in his chair. I went up with the letter. I almost touched him,' he said with a shudder. The man looked desperate with the disgust he felt at the memory of that icy contact.

I said, 'Thanappa, go and deliver those letters and try to get this thing out of your mind. Don't speak about this to anyone. I will go up and see things for myself and come back.'

Thanappa hesitated for a second and decided to follow my advice. He asked, 'So this registered letter goes back? Has no one else authorization to sign for him?' He picked up his bag and stepped out.

I went down the steps, around the side street and through the yard, and stood for a moment at the foot of the stairs, with the hyena shoved aside and mouldering in a corner, its glassy stare fixing me at the foot of the steps. I hesitated for a moment in the desperate hope that I might hear the stirrings of feet above. But there was the unmistakable silence of death. I reluctantly took myself up.

There he was as I had seen him last night on his canvas chair, with his arm dangling at his side. I went near and peered closer to see if he was really dead. For the moment I was not bothered with the mystery of his death but only with the fact. He had accustomed us so much to a still-life view that he seemed logically to be a part and parcel of his own way of life. The alarm-clock which had screeched in the dark on the previous night was now ticking away modestly. Its pale pink face must have watched the process of Vasu's death. I looked around. The frame of his bed was smashed; that was probably the reason why he could not sleep there but only on the easy chair. Somehow at that moment I took it very casually and felt no bother about how he might have met his end. I folded my arms across my chest, remembering that I had better not touch anything and leave a fingerprint. Anyway, Thanappa's fingerprints were bound to be there, so why add mine to the confusion and complicate the work of the police? My desire to search for Vasu's purse and read the blue letter in it was really great, but I didn't want the police to conclude that I had killed him and taken his purse. I peered closer to see if there was any injury. His black halo of hair was rumpled and dry. His eyes were closed. I could see no trace of injury. 'Where is all your bragging,' I thought, 'now, and all your pushing and pulling and argument? Are you in heaven or hell? Wherever you are, are you still ordering people around?' I noticed on a low stool the jute bag containing food which I had seen in Rangi's hand on the previous night at my house. I wanted to see if he had eaten it, but the lid of the brass vessel was covered tight and I did not like to give it my thumb impression. His clothes lay, as usual, scattered on his cot and on every available space. The lid of his trunk was half open, revealing his familiar clothes, particularly the red check bush-shirt and the field-grey jacket he affected when he went out on his depredations. I stood over his trunk and kept looking in; if I could have rummaged in it without touching anything I would have done so. I wished I had gloves on, but this was not a part of the world where gloves were known. Not all my precautions to leave things alone could keep me from giving a jump when I saw the green folder peeping from within the folds of his clothes. What an amount of trouble he had given us over it! He had said, 'An orang-utan has carried it up a tree and gone back to the jungle. If I see it again, I shall ask it to return it to the rightful owner, namely Mr Nataraj. I know he will oblige us, he is a very reasonable orang . . . .,' and laughed at our desperation. All I had been able to muster was, 'We didn't know orang-utans existed in India.' 'You want to teach me wild life?' he had asked aggressively. That was before our last break, after which he walked out of my office and I never saw him again until I swallowed my pride and went up to the attic to plead with him for the elephant. The green folder peeped out of a linen bush-coat and a striped Singapore *lungi*. I brooded for a moment about how to extract it without disturbing the arrangement. I went out to the terrace to see if I could find some handy stick with which to grasp it and pull it out. I became desperate, as I realized that I must hurry now. The voices of people in the street frightened me. I was afraid that Sastri might suddenly come up and scream for the police. It was essential that I should take charge of the green folder before anyone else saw it here. I fervently hoped that Thanappa had the sense to keep his mouth shut. The alum solution, moulds and various odds and ends and nails were there, but not a cleft stick with which I could pry the green folder out. I thrust my hand under my shirt, worked my fingers through the end of my shirt, and gently tugged the folder from his clothes. A couple of angry mosquitoes buzzed around my ears, but I could not wave them away as my hands were engaged. I now had the folder in my hand. This would solve, more than the mystery of his death, the mystery of the festival accounts. I could give the poet details of the moneys collected on his behalf, though perhaps not the cash. I hurriedly opened the folder and looked in; the papers were intact, the printed appeal and a list of the donors and the receipt book; but cash? Not much to be seen, except a bundle of one-rupee currency notes. I tucked it under my arm and was leaving when I caught sight of the tiger cub on the small table, covered over with a handkerchief. He had valued it at two thousand rupees. I seized it with the covering and quietly went down, leaving the door ajar. I passed into the side street; the cub, his masterpiece, was small enough to be hidden under my arms along with the files. A couple of pedestrians were passing along. I walked bravely with my articles, dreading lest someone should be in my office waiting for me. Luckily there was no one. I quickly opened the roll-top desk, pushed the tiger cub and the file in, and locked it.

My office became an extension of the Town Police Station. The District Superintendent of Police set himself up in the Queen Anne chair. They had found the grille I had put up between the treadle and the staircase irksome, as it made them go round every time by the side street. It was unlocked and the place was thrown open for the entire city to walk about in. All kinds of people were passing in and out, going upstairs and coming downstairs. It became so crowded that I found it impossible to do any work in the press, and Sastri had no space to stand and set his types. The sanctity of the blue curtain was destroyed, gone for ever. Anyone could push it aside and go up; I dared not ask who he was; he might be a plain-clothes police officer, the Coroner's Committee man (there was a body of five to find out and declare the cause of Vasu's death), a newspaper correspondent, a hanger-on, or the thin-legged policemen sent up for sentry duty on the attic landing to watch that no one tampered with evidence. Vasu dead proved a greater nuisance than Vasu alive. Anyone who had had anything to do with him for the past six weeks was summoned to my press by the police. Muthu was there, away from his tea-shop, the poet was there, the journalist was, of course, there, and the elephant doctor and the tailor (who was bewailing all along that he had promised clothes for a wedding and ought to be back at his sewing machine). A police van had gone and brought them all.

Sastri proved to be the shrewdest. The minute he heard of the corpse upstairs he planned his retreat. He hesitated for a moment, smiled to himself and remarked, 'I knew he would come to some such end; these people cannot die normally.' He had been preparing to work on the fruit-juice labels. He just put his work away, wiped his hand on a rag, and took off his apron; I watched him silently. He went through his process of retreat methodically. He said, 'These things happen only in the expected manner. Only I didn't think it would happen so soon and here. What a worry now! Our press has had such an untarnished reputation all through.' He sighed and remained silent as if I had been responsible. Confirming this hint, he said broadly, for the hundredth time within the last few months, 'On the very first day he came here you should have turned him out. You didn't.'

I asked, 'What's your plan now?'

'I am going home and then I am catching the afternoon train for Karaikudi. I have to attend my wife's niece's marriage.'

'You never told me about it!' I said in surprised anger.

'I'm telling you now,' said the imperturbable Sastri. 'You were so busy the whole of yesterday that I couldn't get a word with you.' He pulled out a yellow wedding invitation and showed it to me as evidence.

'When will you be back?' I asked.

'Well, as soon as the marriage is over,' he said and prepared to go. 'Our train leaves at one o'clock.'

'The police may want you here,' I said viciously.

'I have nothing to do with Vasu or the police,' he said with a clarity of logic rare under the stress of the present circumstances. It was true. He had resolutely kept away from contacts with Vasu. While all of us were running around him, Sastri alone had maintained a haughty aloofness. No one could ever associate Vasu with Sastri. I had no authority over Sastri. I could not stop him. He went out by the back door to Kabir Street. At the doorway he paused to say, 'Anyway, what is the use of my staying here? There is no space for doing any work here.' With that he was off.

As I said all my friends were there as if we were assembled for a group photo. Rangi . . . oh, I have forgotten Rangi. After the night's endless gesticulations before the God, she looked jaded in a dull sari, with unkempt hair, and stood in a corner. She would not sit down before so many. The lean man, the Town Inspector, was among those who had to be provided with a seat. The D.S.P. from his seat of honour kept glancing around at us. He had demanded a table and I had to request my neighbour with the Heidelberg to spare me one from his office. He was only too willing to do anything. He looked overawed by the whole business – a murder at such close quarters. He gave me a teak table which the burly D.S.P. heaped with a lot of brown papers and drew up before the Queen Anne chair. To this day I do not understand why he held the inquiry in my office rather than at the police station. Perhaps they wanted to hold us until the body was removed to the mortuary, which was a small tin shed at a corner of the compound of the District Hospital. Under this hot tin roof, there was a long stone table on which Vasu would be laid. I was depressed to think that a man who had twisted iron rods and burst three-inch panel doors with his fist was going to do nothing more than lie still and wait for the doctor to cut him and examine his insides to find out what had caused his death.

At the mortuary, the wise men, five in number, had stood around the stone-topped table, read the report of the pathologist, and declared, 'Mr Vasu of Junagadh died of a concussion received on the right temple on the frontal bone delivered by a blunt instrument. Although there is no visible external injury to the part, the inner skull-covering is severely injured and has resulted in the fatality.' In addition to this they had also taken out his stomach contents and sent them for examination to Madras Institute, there to be examined for poisoning. The wise men reserved their final verdict until they should have the report from Madras. Meanwhile they ordered the burial of the body according to Hindu rites in order to facilitate exhumation at a later stage if necessary. At this one of the five demurred, 'How can we be sure that the deceased would not have preferred to be cremated?' At this they looked at each other, and since there was no way of ascertaining the wishes of the person concerned, they hesitated for a moment until the foreman said, as if on a sudden revelation, 'We shall have no objection to a final disposal of the body in the form of cremation; the present step is only an interim arrangement until we are able to ascertain the causes of the death of aforesaid Vasu with certainty.' Everyone grabbed this sentence as a way out.

Assembled at my press, they desperately tried to discover the origin of the brass food-container found in Vasu's room. They kept looking round and asking, 'Can anyone throw light on who brought this vessel? Can anyone say to whom it belongs?' They turned the vessel round in their hands, closely looking at it for any signature of ownership. They failed. I could see Rangi squirming in her corner, twisting and untwisting the end of her sari around her finger. She kept throwing anxious glances in my direction and fidgeting; if the police officer had not been so hectically busy writing, bent over his papers, he might have easily declared, 'I charge you with being the owner of this brass utensil,' and led her off to the lock-up. When I opened my mouth to say something she almost swooned with suspense. But I merely remarked from my seat on the edge of my desk, 'I often noticed his food coming to him in that vessel.'

'Where was he getting his food from?' An excellent chance to confuse things by making the nearest restaurant busy defending their innocence. I thought over the name of restaurants I might mention. What about the Royal Hindu Restaurant? The owner used to be my customer and had walked out after creating a scene over a slight delay in the delivery of his printed stationery. I dismissed the thought as unworthy, and said, 'I've really no idea. The deceased must have been getting his food from various quarters.' I spoke breezily. The Superintendent looked up coldly as if to say, 'Don't talk more than necessary.' But I was in my own place and no one had the right to ask me to shut up. I added, 'It doesn't seem as if its lid has been opened.' The Superintendent made a note of this also, and handed the vessel around for inspection to the Committee. They all examined it and said, 'Yes, the lid does not seem to have been opened.' The Superintendent made a note of this again, and then asked, 'Shall we open this to see if it has been touched?' 'Yes,' 'Yes,' 'Yes,' 'Yes,' 'Yes.' He took a statement from the five to say that the lid had been opened in their presence. They watched with anxious concentration as the lid was prised off. It was placed on the table. The smell of stale food hit the ceiling. A strong-smelling, overspiced, chicken *pulav*, brown and unattractive, was stuffed up to the lid. Everyone peered in, holding his nose. 'It has not been touched.' The verdict was unanimous. 'Shall a sample be sent to Madras?' 'No.' 'Shall we throw this food away?' 'No.' 'What shall be done with it?' 'Keep it till the report from Madras is received. If there is suspected poisoning, the food can be analysed.'

The Superintendent wrote this down and took their signatures. He passed the container to be sealed in his presence to an orderly, and then the five men appended their initials on the brown paper wrapped around it. The D.S.P. worked like an impersonal machine. He did not want to assume any personal responsibility for any step and he did not want to omit any possible line of investigation, always laying the responsibility on the five wise men chosen for the purpose.

If they had said, 'Put this Nataraj in a sack and seal him up; we may need him in that state for further investigation,' he would have unhesitatingly obeyed. Sealing up was the order of the day. Vasu's room was sealed, the food-container was sealed, and every conceivable article around had been sealed.

The Superintendent's writing went on far into the night; he must have written several thousand words. Each one assembled there had to say when he saw Vasu last, why, and what were that worthy man's last words. While Rangi totally denied having seen him last evening, the others were not in such a lucky position, the whole lot of them having gone there in a body after seeing the Superintendent. They gave a sustained account of what he had said to them. It was computed that he must have died at about eleven at night, and where was I at eleven? – at home sleeping on the *pyol* after seeing my wife off to the temple. My wife was brought in by the back door to corroborate me, my son too. Fortunately no one knew of my last visit to the attic. I bore in mind our adjournment lawyer's dictum, 'Don't say more than you are asked for.'

The only satisfaction I felt was that our Town Inspector was treated as one of us, made to sit in our group and answer questions before the Committee. Normally they would have let him handle the investigation, but the situation was no different; he was also one of us, an aggrieved party. His hand was in a sling and his finger was encased in a plaster cast, having suffered a slight fracture. He had to clear himself first – a most awkward thing. When his turn came to make a statement, he began bombastically, 'I was ordered to supervise the peace and security arrangements on the Market Road on ＿＿ at ＿＿ when I had a call at the control room from our District Superintendent of Police ordering me further to investigate a complaint of threat to the safety of the crowd from one Mr Vasu of Junagadh. When I went up to question the said person and take charge of his licensed weapon, he assumed a threatening attitude and actually assaulted the officer on duty, causing a grave injury.' He held up the bandaged part of himself as an exhibit. And then, according to him, he went away to take all reasonable precautions for the peaceful conduct of the procession. He intended to file a complaint as soon as they were free in the morning, and proceed against the same person officially for assaulting an officer on duty. He failed to mention that he had told Vasu before leaving, 'I will get you for it.'

I and Muthu discussed it later, when the incident was officially

closed. If anyone had breathed a word then, it might have complicated the Inspector's version and placed him definitely on the
defensive. But everyone was considerate. Still, the Inspector had to
prove where he was at the time of Vasu's death, which occurred two
hours after he had been visited by the Inspector. He explained that
he had left the security arrangements in the hands of his assistant
while he had gone in the police car to the District Superintendent's
residence to report to him, and then to the District Headquarters
Hospital to secure medical attention. He could cite both the District
Superintendent of Police and the medical officer on duty at the
casualty section as witnesses. But still Muthu felt, as he confessed
later, 'What prevented the man from sending someone to do the job?
A number of them might have gone and overpowered the man. I
don't say it is wrong, but they might have done it, and hit his skull
with a blunt instrument.'

During the following days the air became thick with suspicion.
Each confided to the other when the third was out of earshot. Sen,
who walked down the road with me for a breath of fresh air after the
police left us, said, 'That tea-shop man Muthu . . . I have my own
doubts. People in rural areas are habitually vindictive and might do
anything. How many murders are committed in those areas! I won't
say in this instance it was wrong. Someone has actually done a public
service. I wouldn't blame anyone.'

'What would be Muthu's interest in murdering Vasu?'

'Don't forget that the elephant was his and that he was anxious to
save its life at any cost. He could have just sneaked up. Where was
he at eleven o'clock?' He cast his mind back to remember if Muthu
had by any chance slipped away from the procession. He gave it up,
as they had been too much engrossed in the procession to note each
other's movements.

The poet came to me three days later all alone. 'I was with Sen
this afternoon in his house in New Extension, and, do you know, I
noticed in a corner of his room, amidst a lot of old paper, a blunt
thing – a long iron bolt which they use on railway sleepers. He looked
embarrassed when I asked why he had it. Easiest thing for him to
have slipped upstairs, gone up from behind . . . I don't blame him.
He had stood enough insults from that man. I knew that Sen would
do something terrible sooner or later . . . I wouldn't blame him.'

I knew that they were all unanimous in suspecting me when I was
not there. I could almost hear what they were saying about me.
'Never knew he could go so far, but, poor fellow, he had stood

enough from him, having made the original blunder of showing him hospitality. Whether he took him in as a tenant or just as a friend, who can say? Who will let his house free of rent to another nowadays? Whatever it may be, it is none of our business why he gave him his attic. But how that man tortured poor Nataraj! Poor man, his patience was strained. Deft work, eh? What do you say? Smashed the vital nerve in his brain without drawing a drop of blood! Never knew Nataraj could employ his hand so effectively! Hee, hee!'

My wife said the same thing to me that night when I went home. Our friendly relations were resumed the moment she heard that there was a dead body in the press and that the police had assembled in my office. Since the Rangi episode, the first words uttered between us had been my urgent invitation to her to come and say where she had seen me at eleven o'clock on the previous night. She hesitated, wrung her hands in fear and despair. 'Oh, why should you have got mixed up in all this affair? Couldn't you have minded your own business like a hundred others?' I was very humbled now, and very pleased that at least over Vasu's dead body we were shaking hands again. I had been gnawed by a secret fear that we might never resume friendly relations and that all was over between us. She rubbed it in now. 'That woman, and all sorts of people – what was your business with them really?'

I had no satisfactory answer for her, and so said, 'I have no time to explain all that now; the D.S.P. is waiting; you will have to come and say where I was last night at eleven o'clock.'

'How could I know?' she asked. 'I will tell him that I didn't see you.'

'Yes, say that and see me hanged, and then you will probably be able to collect a handsome insurance on my life.' She screamed and covered her ears. 'You could also describe how you deserted me on the *pyol* to guard the house and went out. It will do you good to speak the truth. And if you remember your visit to the temple, you will probably also remember having seen Rangi there, so that you will not be tempted to say I had gone out with her.'

'I didn't see her at the temple,' said my wife simply. She had got out of her suspicious mood of yesterday but had not decided to let go of it fully.

I said, 'While we are bantering here, the police . . .'

'Why should they believe what I say? Won't they think you have tutored me?'

'Oh, it is only a formality, they are not analysing evidence of any sort. They will record whatever you say or I say or anyone says, and that is all that they want at this stage, so you had better come along.' She was very nervous at coming before the Superintendent, but she would not hear of the public recording her statement at home. She said, 'After all these years of honest and reputable living, we don't want the police marching in and out. Even in the worst days when the property was partitioned no one dreamt of asking the police to come. We don't want to do that now.' She preferred to walk across the street when the neighbours were not looking and slip into my press by the back door and face the police.

That night I went home at eleven o'clock. Babu had gone to sleep. My wife said, 'Hush, speak gently. Babu wouldn't sleep. He was too excited about everything. I managed to send him to sleep by saying that it is all false and so forth. But he is terribly excited about everything . . . and, and, feels proud that you killed a *rakshasa* single-handed! At least you have Babu to admire you.'

'For God's sake don't let him spread that sort of talk. The noose may be put around my neck.'

She sighed deeply and said, 'A lot of people are saying that. After that rent control case . . .'

'Oh, shut up,' I cried impatiently. 'What nonsense is this!'

'You may close the mouth of an oven, but how can you close the mouth of a town?' she said, quoting a proverb.

I saw myself as others saw me, and was revolted by the picture.

Chapter Twelve

At first I resented the idea of being thought of as a murderer. Gradually it began to look not so improbable. Why not? It had been an evening of strange lapses. I could remember nothing of what I had said or done to cause the fuss around me that evening at the temple hall. Later was it quite impossible that I had battered someone's skull and remembered nothing? Going over my own actions step by step, I remembered I had gone up the staircase stealthily, opened the door on the landing. So far all was clear. The procession was passing in the street below. Vasu lay in a long chair beside the window. I had crawled towards his gun and run out when the alarm-clock screamed. Between my entrance and exit I remembered holding the gun at Vasu's head until the lights of the procession vanished. Perhaps while he slept I had rammed the butt of the gun into his skull. Who could say? But what about the time of his death? The doctor had declared that the man must have died at eleven, long before I had sneaked up the attic stairs. But the doctor might have hazarded a guess; it was one more item in a long list of conjectures!

I had clung to the hope that Rangi had poisoned Vasu and then smashed his head, but the chemical examiner at Madras reported, 'No trace of poisoning.' With that the last trace of hope for myself was also gone. While I sat in my press all alone I caught myself reconstructing again and again that midnight visit to the attic, trying to gain a clear picture of the whole scene, but each time I found it more confounding. When people passed along Market Road and looked at me, I averted my head. I knew what they were saying, 'There he sits. He ought really to be hanged for murder.' My friends of Mempi village never came near me again. They had had enough trouble with the police as the result of knowing me and visiting my press. 'That press! Lord Shiva! An accursed spot! Keep away from it!'

There was not a soul with whom I could discuss the question. Sen avoided me. The poet was not to be seen. He took another route nowadays to the Municipal School. During my morning trip to the river and back no one stopped to have a word with me. The adjournment lawyer and the others hurried on when they saw me in the distance. All the same one morning I accosted the adjournment lawyer at the bend of the street where the barber's house abutted. He pretended not to see me and tried to pass. 'Sir,' I cried, stepping in front of him.

He was flurried, 'Ah, Nataraj! Didn't notice . . . I was thinking of something . . .'

'I want to ask you . . . ,' I began.

'What about? What about?' he asked feverishly. 'You see I am out of touch with criminal practice. You should really consult . . .'

'Consult? For what purpose?' I asked. 'I have no problem.'

'Oh, yes, yes, I know,' he cried, fidgeting uneasily. 'I remember that they left an open verdict, nothing was imputed or proved. After all who can be sure?'

'Oh, forget it,' I said with the casual ease of a seasoned homicide. 'It is not that. I am more worried about the collection of dues from my customers. When did you celebrate your daughter's marriage? Months ago! Why don't you pay my charges for printing those invitation cards? What are you waiting for?'

'Oh, yes, by all means,' he said, edging away.

'I have no one in the press to help me. Even Sastri has left me. You had better send the cash along instead of waiting for me to send someone to collect it.' A touch of aggression was creeping into my speech nowadays. My line of thinking was, 'So be it. If I have rid the world of Vasu, I have achieved something. If people want to be squeamish, they are welcome to be so, but let no one expect me to be apologetic for what I have done.' I hardened myself with such reflections, and suffered at the same time. The press was silent. I kept my office open at the usual hours. Visitors were few. I spent my time attempting to read Tolstoy's *War and Peace* (discovered among the seventy philosophical volumes in the family lumber room) and diverting myself by following the complex fortunes of Russian nobility on the battlefields of ancient Europe.

I caught sight of the poet one morning beyond the fountain. Before he could avoid me and take another route to his school I ran forward and blocked his way. I implored him to come into the press and seated him in the Queen Anne chair.

'What has happened to you all?' I asked.

'They have given me eight more hours of work a week, with so many teachers absent!'

'Ah, innocent poet!' I thought. 'What clumsy guile you have cultivated within these last weeks!' I asked aloud, 'What about Sen?'

'I don't know, he was expecting a call from a Madras Paper.'

'Don't lie!' I cried, suddenly losing my temper. 'Haven't I seen him sneaking in next door to get some work done on the Heidelberg? You people are avoiding me. You think I am a murderer.' He remained silent. I checked myself when I noticed the terror in his eyes. He glanced anxiously over his shoulder at the doorway, interpreting the glint in my eyes as maniacal. I wanted to speak to him about the accounts entombed in the green folder, about the moneys collected on his behalf and spent by Vasu, and to explain to him about the tiger cub I had seized; but all I could produce was a shout of abuse at the world in general. I realized that I was frightening the poet. I modified my tone to a soft whisper, smiled, and patted his back. I said, 'I want to give you a present out of the money collected for your benefit. Something in kind, something salvaged.' I fixed him with a look lest he should try to escape, flicked open the roll-top desk, and brought out the stuffed tiger cub. I pulled off the kerchief covering and held it to him. He looked transfixed.

'A tiger! What for?'

'It is yours, take it,' I said. 'He valued it at two thousand. Something at least . . .'

He gazed back at me as if noticing in my eyes for the first time unplumbed depths of lunacy. He pleaded desperately, 'No, I don't want it. I don't need it. I do not want anything. Thanks.' He suddenly shot out of the Queen Anne chair, dashed out, and was soon lost in the crowd on Market Road.

'Poet! Poet!' I cried feebly. In addition to thinking me a murderer, perhaps he thought I had embezzled his funds and was now playing a prank on him. This was the greatest act of destruction that the Man-eater had performed; he had destroyed my name, my friend-ships, and my world. The thought was too much for me. Hugging the tiger cub, I burst into tears.

While I was in this state Sastri parted the curtain and entered. 'I came by the back door,' he explained briefly.

'Ah, Sastri!' I cried in sheer joy. 'I thought you would never come back.'

He was business-like, and turned a blind eye on my emotional condition. 'After the marriage at Karaikudi, my wife insisted on going on a pilgrimage to Rameshwaram, and to a dozen other places. A couple of children fell ill on the way. I was fretting all along to get back, but you know how our women are! Sickness or not, my wife insisted on visiting every holy place she had heard of in her life. After all, we get a chance to travel only once in a while . . .'

'You could have dropped me a postcard from somewhere.'

'True,' he said, 'but when one is travelling it is impossible to sit down and compose a letter, and the idea gets postponed.' He took out of his pocket a tiny packet containing a pinch of sacred ash and vermilion and held it out to me, saying, 'Offerings from all the temples mixed together.' I daubed the holy dust on my forehead.

He noticed the tiger cub on my lap and exclaimed, 'Ah, what a tiny tiger!' as if humouring a child. His silver-rimmed spectacles wobbled and his face was slightly flushed. I knew he was shuddering at the sight of the stuffed animal, but still he pretended to be interested in it and stretched out his hand as if to touch it. He was trying to please me. He said, 'It must have been a pretty baby in the forest, but what a monster it would have become when it grew up! Did *he* give it to you?' he asked after a pause. I couldn't explain that I had stolen it from the dead man, and so I remained silent.

'I meant to give it to the poet,' I said, 'but he spurned it and went away.' I was on the point of breaking down at the thought. 'He may not come again.'

'It is natural that a poet should feel scared of a tiger. In any case what could he do with it?'

'He may never come this way again.'

'So much the better for us. Anyone who refuses to come here and waste our time must be viewed as a well-wisher. K.J. is our customer, and you may be sure he will always come to us.'

'Naturally. Where else can he get the magenta, even if he wants to leave us?'

'People who have business with us will always come and keep coming.'

'Everyone thinks that this is a murderer's press,' I said gloomily.

He gently laughed at the notion and said, 'They are fools who think so, but sooner or later even they will know the truth.'

'What truth?' I asked.

'Rangi was with him when he died. You know I am on the temple committee,' began Sastri, 'and she came to see me on business last evening. I had a feeling all along that she was hiding some information. I refused to listen to her problem unless she told me the truth. Much against my principles, I called her inside the house, seated her on a mat, gave her coffee and betel leaves to chew, and induced her to speak. My wife understood why I was asking this woman in and treated her handsomely on the whole.'

'What did Rangi say?' I asked impatiently.

'It seems that evening she carried a hamper of food to him. He refused to eat the food, being in a rage over many things. Rangi had perhaps mixed some sleeping drug with the food, and had hoped that he would be in a stupor when the procession passed under his window. That was her ruse for saving the elephant that night. But the man would not touch the food!'

'He might not have felt hungry,' I said, remembering the eatables that I had plied him with earlier that day.

'It may have been so, but it embarrassed the woman because she had duties at the temple that night. She was really bothered as to how she was going to get out of the place. When he understood that the procession might start late, he set the alarm-clock and sat himself in his easy chair. He drew another chair beside his, and commanded the woman to sit down with a fan in hand and keep the mosquitoes off him. He hated mosquitoes, from what the woman tells me. He cursed the police for their intrusion, which had made him break his cot-frame to show off his strength and now compelled him to stretch himself in an easy chair instead of sleeping in his cot protected by a mosquito-net. Armed with the fan, the woman kept away the mosquitoes. He dozed off. After a little time she dozed off too, having had a fatiguing day, as you know, and the fanning must have ceased; during this pause the mosquitoes returned in a battalion for a fresh attack. Rangi was awakened by the man yelling, 'Damn these mosquitoes!' She saw him flourish his arms like a madman, fighting them off as they buzzed about his ears to suck his blood. Next minute she heard a sharp noise like a thunder-clap. The man had evidently trapped a couple of mosquitoes which had settled on his forehead by bringing the flat of his palm with all his might on top of them. The woman switched on the light and saw two mosquitoes plastered on his brow. It was also the end of Vasu,' concluded Sastri, and added, 'That fist was meant to batter thick panels of teak and iron . . .'

'He had one virtue, he never hit anyone with his hand, whatever the provocation,' I said, remembering his voice.

'Because,' said Sastri puckishly, 'he had to conserve all that might for his own destruction. Every demon appears in the world with a special boon of indestructibility. Yet the universe has survived all the *rakshasas* that were ever born. Every demon carries within him, unknown to himself, a tiny seed of self-destruction, and goes up in thin air at the most unexpected moment. Otherwise what is to happen to humanity?' He narrated again for my benefit the story of Bhasmasura the unconquerable, who scorched everything he touched, and finally reduced himself to ashes by placing the tips of his fingers on his own head. Sastri stood brooding for a moment and turned to go. He held an edge of the curtain, but before vanishing behind it he said, 'We must deliver K.J.'s labels this week. I will set up everything. If you will print the first colour . . .'

'When you are gone for lunch it will be drying, and ready for second printing when you return. Yes, Sastri, I am at your service,' I said.

MORE ABOUT PENGUINS, PELICANS
AND PUFFINS

For further information about books available from Penguins please write to Dept EP, Penguin Books Ltd, Harmondsworth, Middlesex UB7 ODA.

In the U.S.A.: For a complete list of books available from Penguins in the United States write to Dept DG, Penguin Books, 299 Murray Hill Parkway, East Rutherford, New Jersey 07073.

In Canada: For a complete list of books available from Penguins in Canada write to Penguin Books Canada Ltd, 2801 John Street, Markham, Ontario L3R 1B4.

In Australia: For a complete list of books available from Penguins in Australia write to the Marketing Department, Penguin Books Australia Ltd, P.O. Box 257, Ringwood, Victoria 3134.

In New Zealand: For a complete list of books available from Penguins in New Zealand write to the Marketing Department, Penguin Books (N.Z.) Ltd, P.O. Box 4019, Auckland 10.

In India: For a complete list of books available from Penguins in India write to Penguin Overseas Ltd, 706 Eros Apartments, 56 Nehru Place, New Delhi 110019.